MW01242685

BACK TO BONAIRE

A Lyle Cooper Story

On Bonaire
Back to Bonaire
My Bonaire (2024)

Back to Bonaire

A Lyle Cooper Story
Book 2

Anne Bennett

CALYPSO HOUSE PUBLISHING

This is a work of fiction. Names, characters, places, and incidents either are the product of the author's imagination or are used fictitiously. Any resemblance to actual persons, living or dead, events, or locales is entirely coincidental.

Cover design: Lynn Andreozzi
Interior design: Danna Steele
Author photo: Amanda Cramp

Copyright © 2023 by Anne Bennett
All rights reserved.

No part of this book may be reproduced or used in any manner without written permission of the copyright owner except for the use of quotations in a book review.

ISBN (paperback) 979-8-9864896-5-0
ISBN (eBook) 979-8-9864896-4-3

"The sea, once it casts its spell, holds one in its net of wonder forever."

~Jacques-Yves Cousteau

PART ONE

Lyle's Tattoo

One

The GPS announced its final direction: "*You have arrived at your destination. On the left.*" It was a two-hour drive from Raleigh to the North Carolina coastal town of Pearl.

"Thank you, Margaret." Lyle Cooper spoke without thinking, using the name she had bestowed upon the unknown voice. With apprehension, she slowed the car to a crawl and read the sign over the door: *Lawson's Tattoo and Piercing*, and underneath it: *Scarification and Branding by T. Hendrix*. A certificate taped in the window assured clients that the establishment was licensed and inspected.

Her boss, Dr. Patel, had offered her his summer home in Pearl for the night. She'd worked for the dentist for seventeen years and knew the beach house well. Though uncertain how long she would be at the shop, she figured her appointment would take most of the day. She'd be in no shape to drive back to Raleigh afterward.

She had placed a bottle of the doctor's favorite brandy and her overnight bag in the trunk of her car, next to her acoustic guitar in its case. She'd been taking lessons for only a few months but would be alone at the house tonight and thought practicing would help pass the time.

Pulling into the parking lot of the single-story building, she squinted, trying to look in through the screen door.

But she was second-guessing her decision to come here.

She had discussed her plan with Victoria, and although her friend wasn't completely on board, she didn't vehemently object either.

She remembered kicking off her shoes and tucking her feet underneath her on Victoria's couch for a rainy Saturday afternoon movie.

Victoria's cat, Professor McGonagall, had looked up at her from the floor. The tabby's aggravated cry meant "Get off my sofa—you're in my spot."

"I'm not moving," she said to the disgruntled feline, patting her thigh. "Come up here and sit with me."

"Any idea what you'd like to watch?" Victoria asked while pointing the remote at the television.

"Angela really liked that documentary about the octopus. I wouldn't mind watching that."

"Great idea. I've been meaning to see that one." She scrolled through the menu.

"Speaking of Angela, her new tattoo is beautiful," said Lyle.

———◆———

The three friends recently had dinner together at Moon Café in downtown Raleigh. After enjoying three courses, the girls were pleasantly full of pasta and tiramisu. They sat finishing their after-dinner coffees.

"Wait until you see what I did!" Angela said, while standing and removing her sandal. She then placed her bare foot on her chair. "What do you think?"

Her new shark tattoo was sleek with great lines and shadowing. Its snout was positioned on the top of her foot, the body continued back past her ankle. Its tail wrapped over her heel as if swimming around it.

"I'm so stoked with how it turned out," Angela said. "I love it."

And so did Lyle.

———◆———

Professor McGonagall jumped onto the sofa, turned in a circle, and found a warm spot in the bend of Lyle's knees. She scratched the tabby behind her ears.

"Are you thinking of getting a tattoo?" Victoria asked.

"Dottie thinks it would be therapeutic for me. I want one, but I need an artist to help me come up with a design."

"Are you sure about this?" asked Victoria. "Ink is more permanent than marriage. And how *exactly* does Dottie see it as being beneficial?"

She cringed at the uncomfortable question. She and Dottie grew up together in the same trailer park in central New York. Dottie understood the scars on Lyle's psyche from her difficult childhood, the damage from being raised by a mother who was an addict. Unwavering, she had stood by Lyle through it all. It wasn't to say Victoria was any less a friend; Lyle simply didn't confide in her the way she did with Dottie. If her best friend thought a tattoo could help her deal with her past, Lyle was willing to try it.

"She thinks it'll help me get over some things," she said, dismissively.

"But how can—" Victoria shifted gears. "Do you mean Rick? Help you get over Rick?"

Two

Victoria had met Rick MacLean while helping at a fundraiser for a children's summer program. This year, she convinced Lyle to volunteer along with her.

At the first organizational meeting, Lyle sat listening to a chairperson explain the logistics of the event. She was having a hard time paying attention. The speaker had a long piece of toilet paper stuck to the heel of his shoe. As he traipsed back and forth in front of his audience, the tissue jumped along behind him like an excited puppy. Others easily ignored the embarrassing issue, but she fought to stifle a giggle. She put her fingers over her mouth and looked away, only to catch the eye of the gentleman sitting next to her.

"Should we tell him, or place bets on how long the hitchhiker holds on?" He whispered to her, himself fighting a grin. He extended his hand. "Rick MacLean."

"Lyle Cooper," she said, quietly. "I'm Victoria's friend. She recruited me to help."

Lyle was immediately taken with him. His crisp pin-striped suit, his charming smile, the confident way he carried himself. He brushed his dark hair straight back but fought the entire night with one strand that insisted on falling onto his forehead. Lyle found the battle endearing.

They next ran into each other while coming out of a bookstore in downtown Raleigh. Purchases in one arm and her purse in the other, Lyle toed the shop's door to try to open it but it only fell closed again. An arm reached over her shoulder, giving it a firm push.

"Thanks for the help." She smiled at the man. "Rick! What a nice surprise."

"I thought that was you." They stopped on the sidewalk out front. He lifted his shoes then glanced at his heels. "Just checking." They laughed.

He invited her to join him for coffee. They walked two blocks to a locally owned bakery and sat at a table at the window. The buzz of conversation surrounding them turned to white noise as they got to know each other.

Victoria gave the relationship a nudge when, the following week, she invited them both to a cookout at her home.

"Did you know," Victoria said, standing at the grill, "that you're both scuba divers? Lyle and I have been diving together for years."

"What are some of your favorite dive locations?" Lyle asked Rick.

"I'm a junkie for the deep-water wrecks. It's the history of the sunken vessels that has me hooked," he said. "Ships that sailed one hundred years ago now at rest on the ocean floor. When I'm swimming through them, it's like visiting the past."

After dinner Rick and Lyle rinsed dishes at the kitchen sink and loaded Victoria's dishwasher.

"I was wondering if you're free next weekend," he said. "I have tickets to the symphony if you'd like to join me."

The next day, she stood in Victoria's bedroom as they searched through her closet.

"I really appreciate this," said Lyle, wearing only her bra and panties. "I don't have anything to wear. I can't remember the last time I attended an event that required more than a pair of jeans."

Victoria pushed her clothes along the rod then removed a garment from its hanger. "Try this one. It falls just above the knee on me, but if you wear heels, it should be perfect on you."

She stepped into the dress and Victoria slid the zipper up. Looking in the mirror, she turned this way and that. The high-necked halter style gown was eye-catching. Victoria insisted she borrow it for her date.

The night of the concert, she had just fixed her hair into a French twist when Lyle heard a knock at her door. She opened it to find Rick looking flawless in a black suit and tie.

She felt ridiculous walking down the chewing gum–covered steps of her apartment building in her elegant outfit. He opened her car door, and she pivoted into the passenger seat of his convertible.

"Let me close the roof. I'd hate to arrive with wind-blown hair," he said, winking at her.

They strolled between soaring white pillars that flanked the front of the Raleigh Memorial Auditorium. Their seats in the massive hall were front and center. Two brilliant crystal chandeliers hung overhead and a heavy magenta curtain shielded the stage.

She perused the playbill. "You donate to the symphony?" she asked, pointing at his name printed among the list of contributors.

He grinned and took her hand. The performance was about to begin.

Three

Their relationship progressed with little effort. One evening, Rick asked about Lyle's family and where she grew up.

"My mother was an addict," she said. "I spent a lot of time alone as a child. I remember times when there was no food in the trailer. She still lives in New York. I hear from her when she needs cash—she has my office number. She usually needs some extra money for buying groceries or paying her lease."

"Have you looked into any agencies that might help? She may be eligible for food or rent assistance."

"You're probably right. I'm afraid I've taken a hands-off approach when it comes to her. The thought of working with that woman to get her signed up for services overwhelms me. The less time and energy I spend on her, the better."

"There must be programs she'd be eligible for," he said. "Let's look into it after we get back from Bonaire. I'd be glad to help. We can try to make things easier on you."

She put all thoughts of her mother out of her mind. Soon they were off for a two-week vacation to Bonaire island. Joined by Victoria and Angela, the friends all enjoyed scuba diving during the day, and world class meals with an ocean view each night.

———◆———

After returning home from Bonaire, true to his word, Rick led the effort to find financial help for Lyle's mother. It took dedicated time to obtain, complete the forms, and gather what was required to enroll her in state and private programs. With paperwork in hand, they only needed her mother's signature and some personal information to complete the applications. All of this could have been done online, but with her lack of understanding the internet, they would need to travel to her.

Rick, Victoria, and Lyle all flew to New York and checked into a hotel near the airport.

The next morning, they dressed then prepared to make the forty-minute drive to Chittenango, the town Lyle grew up in and where her mother still lived.

"I can't go, Rick." She wrung her hands and began pacing the room. "I'm not ready. I can't face her. That woman is horrible, she never wanted me, she hates me."

"Hey, settle down. There's no pressure," he said, tenderly. "Stay here." He picked up the folder of papers. "We'll go meet with your mother. Relax, Lyle." He gave her a gentle kiss. "I'll take care of this."

———◆———

Lyle was in love, she felt certain that Rick was too. She grew wary when his calls became less frequent. She chastised herself for checking her phone for missed messages far too often. When he did call, he sounded anxious and struggled to come up with even simple conversations. What were once easy back and forth discussions, became awkward stop and go exchanges. Lyle waited for the axe to drop, dreading the day she knew was coming. Her heart was crushed when he broke it off with her.

He used that horrible word, the cliché to end all clichés: he told her they should remain friends.

Four

Victoria had found the popular documentary about the octopus and had it queued up to watch. Lyle thought about Angela's new shark tattoo and decided she wanted ink of her own. A drizzle hit the window as she mindlessly scratched Professor McGonagall behind the ears. The cat purred so loudly her body vibrated.

"I'm so sorry about Rick," said Victoria.

"I never should've let him meet my mom. Nothing was ever the same after we came back from New York. He could hardly look at me. I think he saw her and thought I would end up the same way—you know, the apple never falling far from the tree. It scared him off."

"That's nonsense," she said. "You're nothing like your mother. But I do hope you and Rick can be friends. I know he's confident that you and he can make the transition."

"*Friends*. I hate that word." She looked at Victoria. "No offense."

"None taken, friend."

"If I'm going to get this tattoo, I want to be sure it's right for me. I really like Angela's new shark." She picked up her cell. "I'm calling her. I want to get the name of the artist she worked with."

———

Lyle called the shop in Pearl. A woman named Crystal told her the person who created Angela's shark had left the area. She suggested she look at others on the shop's website.

Lyle took it as a sign and tabled the whole thing.

But the idea kept tapping on her shoulder. Weeks later, she gave in to the unrelenting thought. She opened her laptop and found the site. Taking Crystal's advice, she studied each available artist's style.

One clearly favored gothic designs. All their work was created in basic black and blue ink. Lyle studied the skulls, bats and roses drawn with fine lines and intricate detail. Another was a bit of a cartoonist. Brightly colored characters with exaggerated features filled their page like a graphic novel. A third specialized in lettering. Otherwise simple words appeared as beautiful works of art using unique shapes and fonts.

She methodically scrolled through the website until one artist caught her eye. The tattoos they created were a seamless mix of reality and fantasy. Their shading and use of color made the images appear three dimensional—realistic but at the same time fanciful. The work was beautiful with a bit of an edge. A good combination for the tattoo she hoped to get.

Lyle called Crystal back, and several days later, she spoke with the artist himself. Her friend Dottie had suggested getting a spine tattooed down her backbone. Having to describe her vision to him left her doubtful. She explained that she needed strength. She told him she needed a sturdier support. But how could a tattoo make her stronger? Dottie left this fundamental question unanswered. Lyle was putting a bucketload of faith in her dear friend.

As their conversation went on, the artist coaxed her idea out of her. When she described the size of the ink she wanted, he followed up with a bunch of specific questions, making sure he understood her. Once he had enough detail to move forward and create a design, they agreed on a time to meet.

"So, I'll draw this up and, umm…"

"Lyle."

"Lyle. We'll see if you like what I come up with." Then Greyson Locklear hung up the phone.

Five

After the two-hour drive to Pearl, Lyle sat in her car staring at the tattoo shop and questioning her decision to come. It wasn't only Rick ending their relationship that brought her here, but rather years of suffering the nightmares her childhood had carved into her memory. Bad dreams that she felt were getting in her way of happiness.

Three motorcycles were parked in front. Two were nondescript, but one black bike sat low with aerodynamic lines. The words *Harley Davidson* soared in flowing script across the gas tank. It appeared to be flying forward even as it waited on the paved lot.

She stepped out of her car into the blinding sun. If Dottie thought this could help, she was willing to give it a try.

The temperature had already soared into the 80s. The air was thick with humidity, and she chastised herself for her choice of clothes. Having no idea what to wear to a tattoo appointment, she decided on jeans and a blue tank top. She added a brown leather belt to match her high-heeled sandals. Standing in the burning sun, she wished she had worn shorts and flip flops.

The screen door crashed shut, announcing her arrival. Expecting a blast of cool air, she was shocked by the lack of air-conditioning. The building was just as warm, if not warmer, than outside. She hated to think how hot it would feel when the day reached its expected 93 degrees.

She waited for her eyes to adjust to the dimly lit room.

The walls in the shop were covered in flash sheets, premade tattoo designs clients could choose from—mermaids, skulls, brightly colored flowers—everything imaginable. In front of her, a woman sat on a stool behind a counter, talking on the phone. She held a finger up to Lyle and gave her a smile and nod. Assuming she was Crystal, she surveyed the room as she waited.

To her right, three men, one of which was smoking, sat around a table talking. *They must belong to the motorcycles*, she thought. They were all heavily tattooed and carried on like old friends.

The smoker snubbed out his cigarette and stood to leave. He had shaved his head to expose tattoos on his scalp, and Lyle noticed scars on his neck and arms. She thought he might be the T. Hendrix from the sign out front. She tried to imagine the process of placing burns like those. *Why would someone willingly choose to do that to themselves?* Then she realized, people might ask the same question about being tattooed.

The man grabbed his keys and phone from the table. He fist-bumped one guy and side-hugged the other. He walked through the shop with urgency, challenging anyone who stood in his way, lips pressed into a thin line and eyebrows furrowed. As he moved closer to her, she could plainly see demons doing despicable things and innocent victims suffering at their hands—tattoos of violence and hatred on his head. She wondered about the pain when he branded his neck.

He stared at her, daring her to avert her eyes. Frozen by the repulsive images, she could only hold his gaze.

Six

The man bumped Lyle's shoulder then stopped and opened his mouth still refusing to look away. She could only stare back at him. His pierced tongue slithered out, making a licking motion. She smelled thick smoke creeping from his lungs. He shifted his attention to her chest like he had a right to. Kicking the screen door open, he disappeared into the parking lot.

Shaken by the behavior of the scarred man, she considered turning around and getting back into her car. But that was exactly where he had gone.

"Can I help you?" Crystal asked, putting down her phone. "Sorry to keep you waiting. My girlfriend's in crisis mode again."

"What's that guy's problem?" Lyle asked.

"I'm sorry about Hendrix. He can be a little intimidating."

"A *little* intimidating?"

"We call him the Santa Slayer," she said with a grin. "Behind his back, of course. Terry Hendrix is notorious in this town. When he was a kid, he sat on Santa's lap and somehow managed to set jolly old Saint Nick's beard on fire." She giggled. "Santa went on his break and never returned, leaving a line of children in tears. The mall stunk like burnt polyester well into the New Year."

"I bet he got stiffed on the gifts that year. I'm Lyle Cooper. We spoke on the phone. I'm here to see Greyson Locklear."

"Oh yeah, Lyle, welcome to my shop, I'm Crystal. I'm glad you were able to find someone to work with." Crystal wore her blond hair shaved close to her head on one side and let the long locks flow on the other. Her dark eyebrows were in stunning contrast to her pale complexion. She turned to the two men seated across the room and called out: "Grey, she's here for you."

One guy glanced at Lyle and gave her a nod. He finished his conversation and then fist-bumped his friend. As he stood, Lyle envisioned an oak growing from an acorn. Greyson Locklear seemed to unfold, reaching skyward, as he straightened his back and extended his legs.

Lyle recognized *Locklear* to be a common Lumbee Indian surname, but Grey was not what she expected. The artwork on his arms was spectacular: geometric shapes in dark ink, a series of complex but orderly patterns. His sleeveless T-shirt hugged his barrel-shaped chest. When he moved, it was slow and deliberate. His thick dark hair fell freely down his back.

He approached her like a cat sizing up its prey. With each step he took, his black boots echoed off the wooden floor. He stopped directly in front of her. She craned her neck to look up at him.

He jutted his chin toward the door. "I saw your staring match. I hope he didn't scare you." His voice was deep and rumbled. "He can be a little intense. He's actually a pretty nice guy."

She had to fight the urge to move back a few steps. "I'm Lyle Cooper. We spoke on the phone." *Please let him remember our conversation.* She thought she caught him giving her the once-over, but his eyes shot back to hers. "We discussed some ideas for a tattoo on my back? You were going to work on a design?" She ran her hand around her neck. She could feel the sweat starting to accumulate there.

His attention darted from one of her eyes to the other. She knew what he was seeing and beat him to the punch. "I know, they don't match."

"Wild," he whispered.

She had gotten comments about her eyes all her life. The left one was light green, and the right one was a brilliant blue.

"Were you able to come up with an idea? You said you'd sketch something."

"Come with me." He started down a narrow hallway, leaving her behind.

She looked at the screen door. If she left now, she could be back home in time for lunch. But she needed help, and this tattoo was the only idea she had.

He looked back at her. "Are you coming?"

Seven

The stench of burnt coffee hung in the air as she followed Grey into a room at the end of the hall. A massage table had been pushed into a corner. A counter ran the length of one wall with cabinets above and below. The sink held mugs with the remains of yesterday's coffee, now cold and growing rings inside the rims.

Grey slid a wooden chair out from the table in the middle of the room and gestured for Lyle to sit. Then he walked out.

She leaned back and the legs creaked. Looking out the window she could see her car in the lot and a few cars passing on the road beyond. She would stay and see what design he had come up with—she could always express indifference and cancel the appointment.

He returned carrying a leather portfolio. Standing next to her, he put the folder on the table and riffled through it. She admired the tattoos on his biceps, how they strategically fell into the dips and curves of his muscles.

"This is what I came up with after we talked." He removed a folded piece of heavy sketch paper from the binder. "All the elements aren't there yet, but it's a good place to start."

After their initial conversation, it had taken him several days of contemplation before he finally put pencil to drawing pad. He had then spent days on the design knowing she was desperate for him to get it right. She had talked about wanting the new ink to help her with some problem she couldn't get past. It was a ludicrous idea—no tattoo could help a person deal with life—but one that left him drawing and redrawing.

"I think I've nailed it." He smoothed out the paper and hesitantly slid it in front of her.

Having anticipated this very moment since talking with him on her cell, she was finally going to see what she struggled to explain over the phone. She sat up and scooted her chair in closer to the table. She held the sketch by the edges, not lifting it but holding it still. She took her time and studied the details of the design created for her.

He crossed his arms over his chest and watched as she scrutinized his proposal, a child showing his parent the report card. Was this total stranger about to pass judgement on him? He had poured himself into that sketch. She sat silently glaring at his work, looking for any faults, searching for the imperfections. He wiped the sweat from his forehead.

He considered Lyle, who had arrived alone at the shop and was far from a young girl. For the first time in a long time, he couldn't guess if this client would go through with the tattoo or not. It was her first, and it would run from the base of her neck down to her tailbone—a new spine over her real one. But one thing had struck him: She never blinked and never looked away. Lyle Cooper had stared down Hendrix the Santa Slayer.

"This should do it," he heard her whisper. He slumped and exhaled a breath he didn't realize he had been holding.

The bones in the tattoo were somewhere between reality and fantasy. Not genuine bones but fantastical metal pipes. Each was made to look old and worn from the abuse they had endured, but the strength of the material held fast. The shadowing created the illusion of a three-dimensional spine. The drawing was so realistic, one would think they could lift the bones off the paper in front of her.

"What about the gremlins?" she asked, looking up at him.

He stood behind her and placed a hand on the back of her chair, leaning over her shoulder to better show her his plan. His shining thick hair fell freely and swayed with his movements. He placed a finger on the image then traced it down the paper. "I thought a gremlin here." He stopped and pointed to an open area on the spine. "And two more. Here"—he trailed his finger farther down—"and here. I thought if we start with the actual spine, saving room for the gremlins, I can fill them in later. That'll give me time to work out what they'll look like. Once I know you better and understand what you're trying to achieve from the tattoo, the gremlins will become clear to me." He sat on the edge of the table and stretched his long legs out in front of him, crossing his boots at the ankles. "You told me you hoped this new ink would help you with some issues you're having. How did you decide on a spine, and why the gremlins? I know you've put a lot of thought into having this done. I imagine it means something to you."

She searched for the courage to tell him the truth, trusting this stranger wouldn't label her too harshly. She knew her reason was going to sound irrational, but he created the design and would be the one tattooing it onto her back. He, if no one else, deserved an explanation.

"It's actually my friend Dottie's idea."

Eight

"You see, I have…" Lyle fumbled for the words. "I carry a burden—nightmares, from my childhood. Only they aren't nightmares. They haunt me during the day, too." Her face flushed. Grey waited silently, so she continued. "Dottie thinks if my bad dreams are out of sight, I won't think about them anymore. I can shoulder my problems, and at the same time, forget I have them." She shook her head. "I know this sounds crazy."

"It's as good a reason as any other I've heard."

He couldn't fathom her desire to transfer her nightmares into a tattoo. But he was sure it made perfect sense to her. He recognized that this woman was broken, and that she was seeking ways to bring herself peace.

"I once tattooed a rope around a man's stomach," he said. "He claimed it would help keep the bugs inside." They both snickered at the obscurity. "Reasons are as individual as people."

"Thank you for understanding."

"This is a large image. We'll be here most of the day. Tattooing the back isn't always painful but going right down the spine…" He paused for effect. "There isn't a lot of muscle there for padding. This could hurt like shards of glass in your high heels. I just want to be sure you realize that. In my experience it's best to power through it. You don't have to do this, you certainly have a choice. You can decide to leave right now, but if you choose to stay, I need to know you're fully on board." He added, "No quitting."

She sat back in the chair. "If you're done trying to scare me out of this, I think we should get started."

Nine

Grey had asked her to sit facing backward on the chair so her legs straddled the seat. She propped an elbow on the back and held her hair in her left hand. With the right, she clutched her tank top against her bare chest.

He sat directly behind her. "I know it's not the most comfortable position, but this puts you directly in front of me. Like Picasso painting his canvas."

She rolled her eyes as he began the arduous task in front of him. She jumped at the shrill pitch of the electric pen when he turned it on. Jerking from the first few stings of the needle, she fought to steady herself as he tattooed her over the next ten hours.

———◆———

How long have I been sitting here? The room was sweltering. The afternoon sun sliced through the window. The fan oscillating on the counter did little to provide any comfort. Sweat ran off her like a river overspilling its banks. Her hair reacted to the humidity, creating a frizzy halo.

The buzzing of the handpiece was the only sound. Neither of them spoke. She could feel his thighs resting next to her hips. He used an antiseptic-soaked cloth to wipe over the wound he was creating. The odor bit her nose. His free hand rested on her back. He thought nothing of shifting her this way and that. He pushed her to lean more forward. He moved his hand to her ribcage and pulled her back toward him at will. They danced a waltz that Grey was leading.

Push, pause, buzz, wipe, pull, pause, buzz, wipe, pause, buzz, pull. The music played on. His hand was firm as he worked and reassured her she was safe in his care.

He never said a word. His concentration was fully on his craft and the day wore on.

She smelled the man before she heard him. Pungent cigarette smoke snaked through the air as he entered the room. The Santa Slayer had joined them.

"Fierce design, Grey. You gonna finish it today?"

"If Lyle here will let me, that's the plan."

"Listen, I got a beef with my boss. Spot me a few bucks? I'm good for it. You know I always am."

Grey stopped working. He lifted his arms overhead and twisted his back. "Sure Hendrix, but you need to get away from that mob."

"I know, I know," he said, as he left the room.

"Friend of yours?" Lyle asked.

"More of a coworker. He was a few years behind me in school. He may not look it, but he's a very capable artist." He pushed her forward and the buzzing started again. "Back in high school, before he went all goth and turned rebel, the principal asked him to design and paint a mural on the cafeteria wall. The doughnut shop down on Main Street that opened in the early nineteen fifties, the waterfall that only townies know where to find, the old pier, and our school mascot. It was really something. Incredibly visionary. He had a lot of promise but dropped out before he ever graduated." He pulled her back toward him. "After that, his medium became the underpasses and bridges in town. You can still see his graffiti around Pearl. He tagged it with his initials, not caring if he got caught defacing public property."

"It's nice of you to loan him money."

"He's just gotten mixed up in some serious shit and can't find a way out."

They returned to sitting in near silence, the only sound the electric pen in his hand. He forced ink deep into her skin as he pressed it up and down her spine. Relentless bites of the needle buzzed with no end.

How long have I been sitting here?

The room was an oven. The stagnant air hung like an ever-present pain around her. She daydreamed of a glass of ice water, but Grey was so quiet she didn't want to disturb him. Her hair stuck to her head and neck. Beads of sweat dripped down her forehead. She blew a futile puff of air, trying but failing to keep the salty perspiration from rolling into her eyes. She shut them tight and waited while the burning moisture trickled over her eyelids.

As she endured the endless sting of the image being etched, she made a mental note to give Dottie a piece of her mind. She silently cursed her friend and tried distracting herself with thoughts of that conversation.

———◆———

Lyle remembered the day after Rick had broken up with her, she had been distraught. Dottie came to her apartment for support. They sat and talked, Lyle's fist full of tear-drenched tissues.

"There's something wrong with me," she said, sobbing. "I think I'm lacking something on my inside, the parts that would make me whole. My mother never gave me those pieces. I think my nightmares settled into those empty spaces."

Dottie turned her damp face toward her. "Crocodile, nothing is missing in you. You're a fully wonderful person. If anything, you have too heavy a burden to carry, too many memories of your past. None of this is your fault. We can't change your childhood or who your mother is. Quite frankly, I think you've done very well considering what you went through growing up."

"But when will I stop suffering because of her?" she asked, her voice trembling.

"You need to put your difficulties behind you so you won't have to face them anymore. We need to find a way for you to accept your troubles, but at the same time, move them out of sight so you can be free from them."

"But I don't know how to do that." She sniffled.

"I think I might have an idea," said Dottie.

Ten

So here she sat, having her nightmares carved into her back. She was giving her troubles a place to rest, hoping they would find contentment there and leave her in peace.

It was mid-afternoon when Crystal came in holding two bags of fast food and sodas. Lyle inched herself into a standing position and held onto the chair until the cramps in her legs subsided. Crystal offered them both icy cold bottles of water and Lyle held hers to her face. After taking a quick break to eat, stretch, and use the bathroom, they went right back to work.

The sound of the needle's never-ending buzzing a bane in her ear. Sting after sting, up her spine and then down again, the sharp barb bit into her flesh.

The inconsequential fan continued to oscillate as the temperature in the room rose. Sweat ran down her torso and pooled just inside her waistband. The heavy, damp denim of her jeans stuck to her as the air grew thicker.

She stared out the window over-looking the parking lot. A car drove down the street kicking up dirt and dust. She watched as a long-legged dog strolled into her limited view. It sniffed the ground as it trotted forward. The mutt stopped at the shop's sign and after giving it a whiff, lifted his leg and relieved himself. He scratched behind his ear before continuing on his way.

"You're going to have to gather your hair again and hold it up out of my way," said Grey, his voice startling her.

Uncontrolled strings had escaped her grasp and were falling down her back. She scraped her finger over her neck to loosen the wet strands and clutched them in her fist.

The burn of the needle never let up. Her muscles screamed having been trapped against the wooden chair for agonizing hours. The longer she sat, the harder it became to be still.

"You've got to stop squirming," he sighed. "Do you need another break?"

Please give me a break so I can run straight to my car and burn rubber back to Raleigh. Half a tattoo is preferable to sitting for more of this.

The temptation to leave was great, but if Dottie's idea panned out, she could finally be free of her nightmares. The promise of sleeping dream-free, the power to completely let go of the painful memories of her early years, had Lyle defiant. "I'm fine," she snapped.

He returned to his work and the afternoon trudged on.

With each tiny burn of the skin her body heat increased. Her head became soaked and her jeans were now stuck to her legs and hips. *How long have I been sitting here?*

Grey had taken his shirt off early in the process. Out of the corner of her eye she saw him reach for a towel and wipe the sweat from his face and chest. She thought Mr. Locklear without his T-shirt on would have been a nice distraction. Cruelly, he sat directly behind her so she could only imagine it.

Down the hall the screen door opened and slammed shut as people came and went. Crystal spoke quietly with some, with others she laughed and carried on.

Grey's concentration was intense. He remained quiet, lost in the detail of his work. But Lyle reached her breaking point. She could no longer sit on the wooden chair. Frustrated, tears flooded her eyes. "I need a break," she said, whining.

"Just stay with me."

"But Grey, it hurts."

"I told you it would hurt. You told me to stop trying to scare you, remember?"

How long have I been sitting here? She wiped her forehead with the back of her hand in an ill attempt to stop the sweat from rolling down her face. She looked at the tank top she held over her chest and thought, *The hell with it.* She removed the shirt from her breasts and used it to wipe the sweat off her face, around the back of her neck, and behind both ears.

"I need to get in your pants."

"You're not funny, Grey."

"You'll have to get up." He patted her hip, encouraging her to rise.

Moving like the tin man seeking oil, she stood, still straddling the chair. She wobbled, her high-heeled sandals making it difficult to balance on her stiff legs.

He held her waist to steady her, and she hesitantly straightened her rigid body.

She arched her back and took the time to push her arms forward then lift them up. She moved her head left then right and looked up, letting her damp hair fall loose down her back, easing the muscles in her thighs and calves, feeling immediate relief.

Then, like a match being set to kindling, her spine was set ablaze. Salty perspiration ran down over her open wound. Drawing in a shuttering breath, she cringed and gripped the chairback. He snickered behind her.

"Fuck you, Grey!" she yelled. "There's nothing funny about this! You've been carving into me all day in this damned inferno." Holding back tears, she side-eyed him over her shoulder. "Stop laughing at me. Just finish this fucking thing so I can get the hell out of here."

She threw her tank top over the back of the chair and undid her belt. With one knee on the seat to steady herself, she pulled the leather through the loops, making it crack like a whip. She placed it on the table next to his T-shirt then unzipped her jeans and lowered her pants enough for him to continue.

"I knew there was a beast in you," he said. "You hide it well, just below the surface. It moves like a crocodile, slow and steady until it's time to snap."

Eleven

He stood behind her focusing the camera on his latest creation. Its shudder whirled as he took pictures of the spine now permanently drawn on her back. He angled her in different ways, doing his best with the limited light in the room. She stood holding her top over her chest and let out a humph. She'd been drug thru the mill. How dare he ask her to stand for these photos? It was the last straw.

"That's it. I'm done." She walked away.

He put the camera down. "I'm going to put a waterproof adhesive wrap on it so you can shower."

Once the tattoo was covered, he left the room to give her some privacy. The sun had set long ago and had given way to the cool night air that drifted in from the window. Her stomach rumbled. She slipped her sweat-sodden, cold tank top over her head and peered out the door.

Crystal, sitting on her stool and scrolling on her phone, saw Lyle looking at her and pointed to a doorway at the end of the hall.

Seeing her own face in the bathroom mirror, Lyle was shocked by her appearance. Sweat had dried in her hair and the pieces that were still wet clumped on her skin like paste. She tried to push the unruly locks off her forehead, but they were so tangled, she couldn't get her fingers through. She longed for the shampoo and conditioner in the back of her car. Most of her makeup was gone, except for the black mascara smeared under her eyes. She would have thought she looked like a raccoon, but the animal would have better color than she did. Her complexion was perfectly white. She ran the sink. Cupping water into her hands, she drank, but most of it dripped down her front and escaped in the drain.

She returned to the little room and found her belt. Her hands shook, and she couldn't hold it steady enough to thread through the loops. A chill ran over her, goosebumps covered her arms.

"You did really well today." Grey came in the door, shirtless. "I thought I was going to lose you there for a minute. But you stuck with it."

Just as she had thought, the ink she'd seen on his arms extended to his well-defined upper body. Shapes and lines in creative patterns formed eye-catching images and flowed up and over the curvature of his physique.

He took the belt from her and started threading it through her jeans. As he worked the loop at the very back, he reached around her, squishing her up against his chest. He looked down over her head and slid the belt along. Her cheek stuck to him. She could only imagine how bad she smelled and wanted desperately to be in her car driving away. Once it was in place, she fumbled to fasten it.

"I got you." He slipped the leather through the buckle.

When he went to get his shirt that he'd tossed on the table long ago, she was stunned by another of his tattoos. Like the rest of his ink, it was done entirely in the same dark color. Soaring across his back, the eagle's impressive wingspan reached from one shoulder to the other. Its majestic head held a piercing eye and a strong, sharp beak. The detail in each feather was flawless. In its talons, the bird clutched a time-worn leather headband with two feathers hanging from it. Every element of the bird was impeccably drawn. It was the most spectacular tattoo she had ever seen.

"You can remove the bandage tomorrow," he said while putting on his shirt. "Don't be surprised if the area feels warm, that's normal. Do you have any questions?"

Her throat felt like sand paper and her voice cracked: "No, no questions." She was tired, thirsty, and hungry. All she wanted was to walk out that screen door she came in so many hours ago. "What time is it?"

"It's almost ten. Are you going back to Raleigh tonight?"

"No." She pulled her key fob out of her jeans pocket. "My boss is letting me stay at his beach house. I'll head back home in the morning."

There was an awkward silence as she searched for her next words. Not coming up with anything, she turned to leave.

"I'll drive you there."

"No need to do that, I'll be fine." She meant to sound assertive, but she squeaked.

"That ink is too raw for you to sit against the car seat," he said. "Don't chance driving off the road because your back is on fire. Let me take you."

"Fine then." She acquiesced and dropped the keys into his palm.

"Crystal can pick me up at your boss's house. She's got to close up here and run some errands. Let's go give her the address."

"Still working this late?" She asked as they walked down the hallway toward the desk.

"It's not a nine-to-five kind of business."

Lyle handed Crystal her credit card. She ran it through the machine while Lyle scribbled down the house number and street name. She nodded a goodbye and made a beeline for the screen door. She felt euphoric as she heard it slam behind her. She sensed this was how a wrongfully convicted person, made to do hard labor, crawling through the sewer line to freedom would feel. Maybe she was being a little dramatic. "No, that's exactly right, sewage pipe and all."

Grey spoke with Crystal briefly then joined her in the parking lot. He stopped and stretched his arms over his head. It occurred to her that his day had been just as taxing as hers.

He held the car door open as she climbed in. Grey had been right. Just touching her new tattoo against the leather had her back singing a painful song. She sat sideways in the passenger seat, turned the heat on and moved the temperature up.

"You know it's over eighty degrees outside."

She flipped the blower to high. "I can't get warm. I'm shaking I'm so cold." She leaned her cheek against the seat and stuck to it immediately.

He rolled his window down. It was a long and silent drive to the house.

Twelve

"*You have arrived at your destination. On the right,*" Margaret announced.

Grey turned into the driveway. Headlights illuminated the impressive architecture. "What did you say your boss did?"

"Dentist."

Built on a piece of prime property, the house was situated on the intercoastal waterway, allowing Dr. Patel to dock his cutter out back. He was generous in loaning the home out when he and his wife wouldn't be using it. He threw a lavish end of year party for his employees here each December. The home would be decorated with fresh garlands and red bows draped over the entry. Inside, a huge tree with white lights grew from a pile of cheerfully wrapped gifts intended for the office staff.

Grey opened her door and offered her his hand. "You get the front door and I'll grab your bag."

As she walked up the stone steps and put the key in the lock, he asked, "What's this?"

She turned to see him holding her guitar case. "I'm just learning. I've only been playing a few months."

"Oh, I've got to hear this."

They walked in and he put her overnight bag and instrument at the bottom of the staircase. They were drawn to the floor-to-ceiling windows at the back of the house and stood looking out at the property. Lyle then flipped a panel of switches and, one by one, floodlights lit up the outside. Even in the darkness, it was easy to appreciate the beauty of the landscape. The grounds sloped down to the water where they could see the doctor's boat tied to a dock.

"You stay here," she said. "I'm going to shower." As an after-thought: "And don't touch anything."

She grabbed her bag and climbed the stairs. In the bathroom, she peeled off her tank top and tossed it into the corner. Her jeans had dried and now the fabric was so stiff, she had a hard time removing them. Inching the denim down her legs, she was finally free of her pants. She dropped the stiff lump on the floor, followed by her panties.

She held her hand under the water until it ran hot. She stepped in and closed her eyes as the stream ran over her. Dried sweat melted off of her like mud sliding down the side of a hill. Her shivering subsided. After shampooing twice, she then used conditioner until her hair was slick and free of tangles. She worked a bar of soap back and forth, up and down, then around in circles, until her body was covered in a thick, heavenly-scented lather. After a leisurely rinse, she towel-dried and put on her sleep pants and satin top. And as she brushed her hair and teeth, she began to feel like a human again.

Once downstairs, she found Grey sitting on the sofa.

"Care for a beer? I think I'm going to have one," she said.

"That'd be great, thanks." He followed her into the kitchen.

She silently thanked Dr. Patel when she found his stash of beer from her favorite Raleigh brewery. She popped the tops on two and handed one to him.

They clinked bottles and each took a long drink. In this moment, she knew it was the best beer she would ever taste.

"We should've hit a drive-through on the way here," she said. "I'm starving. Let me see what I can find to munch on."

She pulled half a loaf of French bread and some port wine cheese from the refrigerator. She placed them on the kitchen island then rinsed green grapes in the sink. Grey discovered a can of mixed nuts and a bag of chocolate truffles in the cabinet. They sat on stools as they snacked and finished their beers.

"That was great, thank you," he said, as she finished the last piece of candy. "Can I help clean up in here?"

"Thanks, but there's not too much to put away. I'll take care of it."

"If you're sure, then I'm going to check out the view." He left the kitchen, slid open the glass door and walked out onto the deck.

She finished tidying up. Helping herself to a second beer, she joined him outside.

The night was pleasantly quiet, the only sound the gentle rocking of the doctor's boat. Grey sat near the railing, his legs stretching out in front of him. He patted a chair next to his, encouraging her to have a seat. She perched on the edge.

Lights from commercial fishing boats flashed out over the water as they passed. Fisherman's voices floated across the surface and reached them as soft as an echo. She wondered how a day that started out as painful and frightening as this one had, ended so peacefully.

He broke the silence: "I didn't think you were going to do it. I thought when you saw the size of the thing, you'd change your mind."

If she had known how the day was going to go, would she have gone through with it? Would she have left through that slamming door and never looked back? She certainly considered it at the time, but the need to find peace was too great.

"I thought you might end up with a butterfly on your shoulder," he said.

"What? You mean I could've just gotten a butterfly?" She grinned. "Well, damn. A butterfly, really? How long would that've taken—ten minutes?"

"For as much squirming as you did it probably would've taken the entire day."

They both laughed. It was the first time she had seen him smile.

"I saw you stare down Hendrix. I knew then that there was a real possibility you would forge ahead." He drank the last of his beer. "Horrible Hendrix, full back ink—is there anything you're frightened by?"

"I'm afraid of being cold. You know, when you're so cold you shiver uncontrollably and there's nowhere to go to get warm."

This was the second time today she had shared an embarrassing truth with him. Soon Crystal would arrive and Lyle knew she would never see this man again. Her tattoo would remain forever unfinished.

She would certainly not have any gremlins added to it. She would not put herself through the pain she suffered today ever again. He would forget the uncomfortable secrets she shared with him. She imagined that perhaps one day he would wonder whatever happened to the woman who wanted to carry her nightmares in the ink on her back. He'd question why she had never returned to have it completed.

Grey quietly disappeared into the house and returned with two more beers and her guitar case.

She took it from him and removed the instrument. He placed his beer on the deck's railing and leaned back against it. She ran her fingers over the strings. "You asked for this. I told you I'm a beginner."

"Are you kidding? I can already tell it's going to be great. I'm guessing you're a natural."

She found her first chord and began to sing: "*I come from a family of lowlifes.*" She stopped and moved her fingers to the next position. "*We lived underground by and by.*" She looked at Grey to see if he was going to stop her right there, but he nodded his head: *go on.* She looked down and slid her hand into place. "*So I left my poor family of lowlifes.*" She paused, searching for the next chord. "*To see just how high I could climb. I stood—*" She strummed the wrong notes and started over, tapping her foot this time. "*I stood on the shoulders of giants, but the giants were only—*" A pause. "*But the giants were only yea high.*" She smiled at him. "Wait for it," Looking back at the neck of the guitar, she continued. "*So I left the giants behind.*"

Eventually, she finished the first verse and got to the chorus. She yelled: "Everybody sing now!"

Grey sang along: "*I climbed to the top of a mountain.*"

They stopped singing while she moved her hand, then started again. "*But… but the birds were still overhead.*" They continued, stopping then going. "*I grew wings and flew to the sun.*" She again studied the position of her fingers. "*To the sun, but the sun is no place for a lowlife.*" She stopped but kept tapping her foot. "*La la, la, la la la la la…*"

She played and sang all three verses, picking up the pace and gaining confidence, Grey joining in on the chorus each time. She finished the song and held the final note.

"That was really good. I like how you put your own spin on it," he said, clapping his hands.

"Did you really like it?" She beamed. "I love that song. I need to work on it some more." She put the guitar back in its case, snapped it shut, and took it into the house. When she returned, she joined Grey who stood leaning on the railing looking out at the water. They watched a boat as it sailed out of sight.

He moved behind her and put his hands on her hips. He whispered, "I'm sorry I hurt you."

She could feel his breath with every word, his deep voice resonating with each syllable.

"You told me you would."

Thirteen

He slipped his hands under her top and placed them on her waist. They felt newly familiar to Lyle, having had them on her most of the day.

"Let me have a look." He trailed his fingers up her sides, raising her shirt to her shoulders. She lifted her arms, and he took it off.

Maybe it was the two beers, or maybe it was the starry night, but she easily succumbed, having Grey touching her once again.

He held her and kissed her shoulder, his tongue tracing circles on her skin there. She rolled her head, her insides starting to burn.

He brushed his lips up her neck. She relaxed and let out a long sigh, smoldering as he kissed her behind the ear. Although her good sense told her not to do this, she couldn't ask him to stop. She didn't want him to end this perfect seduction, her body tingling under his touch.

He turned her to face him and placed his palm on her breast.

She held his hand as he caressed her. She looked up at his striking face, the sheer size of him shadowing her small frame. She should have felt intimidated, but he moved in such a way that she felt completely at ease with this stranger.

He placed his bristly cheek next to hers, arousing her with the coarseness. His breath felt like feathers as he spoke.

"You feel so soft," he said, mouth touching the corner of hers.

She trembled and melted into him. She might shatter if he didn't kiss her soon. With a slight turn of her head, she found his mouth and he kissed her with an unexpected tenderness. Their lips moved together, and she soon fell into the pulse of his kiss.

A fleeting thought of Rick drifted through her mind. The all-consuming hunger grew and pulled her attention back to the man holding her. His lips devoured her. His body pushed against hers and she willingly fell into him. She grabbed the bottom of his shirt and tugged on it. He pulled it off and tossed it to the ground. She gasped at the artwork covering his upper body and placed the tip of her pinky on his chest. He kept still as she traced her finger over the dark tattoos.

"You're not running away. They're not too much?" he asked.

"No. I like them. They suit you."

She parted her lips and he found them with his. In perfect measure, again and again they kissed. He drove his hands into her loose-fitting sleep pants and pulled her into him.

He pushed her silky pajamas down and they pooled around her ankles. She used her toes to move them out from under her feet.

"Nicely done," he said, grinning.

"It's almost like we've been here before," she said. Having been in such close proximity most of the day, the two moved together effortlessly. The dance they had been practicing all afternoon, now at its best.

He took a handful of her hair and pulled her head back, exposing her neck. He kissed her from her jawline to her collar bone. She closed her eyes as her body burned for him. He lifted her and placed her on the flat wooden rail then took a step back as he unzipped his jeans.

"Grey, please." She placed her palms on the railing. "Come closer." To tempt him further, she tilted her head, offering her neck. He didn't need to be asked twice.

He lifted her and she wrapped her legs around his waist and arms over his shoulders. She again let Grey lead them.

All of the stress and pain she had endured that day, the endless hours under his piercing needle, the sweltering heat, the biting cold, they all faded away as he took her and pushed her on.

"Grey, I—" She panted.

"Hold on to me, I got you."

His words ignited her and the slow burn that had been growing since that first kiss detonated. Her fingernails sank into his shoulders.

"Lyle," he whispered.

———◆———

They both heard it at the same time. Crystal's car was coming up the drive.

"Shit." He glanced at her breasts, ran his hands over them and gave her a gentle kiss. A moment of hesitation and then he picked up her top and pants and helped her back into them. He fastened his jeans then found his shirt and pulled it on over his head. He looked toward the house. "Lyle what if I tell—"

"It would be best if you go," she said.

"If you're sure that's what you want," he said, sullenly.

They went inside and pulled the glass door closed behind them. He put his empty beer bottle on the kitchen counter then met Lyle at the front door. He placed his fingers under her chin and raised her mouth to his. All urgency gone, the kiss was gentle and sweet. A horn sounded and they jumped.

"I think your chauffeur has waited long enough." She grinned.

He opened the front door and she saw Crystal waiting for him in the driveway, motor running.

He took a step outside then turned back to face her. He touched her cheek. "Remember, we still need those gremlins."

Lyle's face went pale and her skin turned cold as Grey walked away.

PART TWO
Dottie

Fourteen

The apartment was quiet except for the voices coming from the tele-vision. Lyle lounged in her most comfortable clothes: jeans and her Greenpeace sweatshirt, old and frayed at the cuffs. She fished popcorn out of the ceramic bowl balanced on her lap, captivated by the award show, although she wasn't interested in the early results; the big winners were yet to come. Broadcast live from Hollywood, the program felt long and drawn out. Nevertheless, she'd been watching since the very begin-ning. Winners took the stage and made long acceptance speeches until music began to play, signaling them to walk off.

Her phone vibrated and her heart raced when she saw his name.

Michael: *u watching?*

Lyle: *Yes, watching now*

Michael: *I'm so nervous my hands are fucking shaking. Wish u were here. Love u*

Lyle: *Fingers crossed 4 u. Love u 2.*

On a recent trip to Bonaire, Lyle had an accidental encounter with film star Michael Miller. At the time she recognized him immediately. Having starred in both television and big-screen productions, his face was known to millions. When they first met, every interaction was a battle. He picked on her, making fun of her age or clumsiness. The annoying celebrity grated on her nerves. Until the day they found themselves together on the *Mi Dushi*. Each arrived on the resort's dive boat alone, but for convenience's sake, dived together.

She wasn't sure if it was the group of diver's excitement, or the anticipation of the day's activity, that somehow brought the two to an understanding that day. They agreed to give friendship a chance. They grew to like each other, and as more time passed, they fell in love. In the end, the tribulations they endured only brought them closer. The once stormy relationship miraculously survived.

As they prepared to leave Bonaire, Michael talked about continuing to build what they had together. But with him filming a movie on the West Coast and her living and working on the East Coast, a long-distance connection was the best he could offer. She feared their love affair would only work to end his career. She worried that Hollywood, and Michael's fans, would judge him unfavorably if they were ever exposed.

It was no secret that part of his appeal was the fact that he was a young, good-looking, available bachelor. His fans dreamed of winning his heart. What would they think if they discovered their fantasy man was dating a woman seventeen years his senior?

Once home from Bonaire, they found it impossible to simply forget the other. Lyle had planned to decline his calls, but when she saw his name on her phone the very first time, she eagerly touched Accept. Soon they were talking every day. She didn't see the harm in it. He was busy making another movie and she was occupied with her job and seeing a therapist. She was trying to overcome some personal challenges that recently had become evident.

Fifteen

Lyle watched from her sofa as Michael Miller sat in the audience of the Academy Awards. He had been nominated for best actor for his portrayal of Lieutenant John Magnum. The movie, a true-life story of an American war hero, was a lucrative hit at the box office and an enormous boost for him. With a win tonight, his career choices would be limitless.

While she waited for his category to be announced, she mindlessly threw kernels of buttery popcorn into her mouth. She liked it extra salty and washed it down with a diet soda.

"Why do you even care about some guy? This show's boring. Let's watch *The Facts of Life* instead." Dottie sat on the sofa next to her. With her little legs outstretched, her feet barely reached the edge of the cushion. The laces of one sneaker had come untied.

"We're waiting to see if Michael wins best actor. And that show hasn't been on in years." She squished her eyes shut and shook her head. She then peeked back at Dottie sitting there. "How'd you get here?"

"I rode my bike."

Her phone vibrated, and she picked up. "Hi, Victoria... Yes, I'm so excited. I'm watching now." Victoria responded. "He just texted me. He's so nervous his hands are shaking." She listened. "Dottie's here with me. We're watching together." She put a handful of popcorn in her mouth while she listened to her friend. "I know, I know." She glanced to her left, where Dottie sat twirling her braids with bows tied at the ends. "She's definitely here. I'm not sure why." She listened to Victoria's advice. "I'll be sure to tell Danesha tomorrow. She'll know what this is all about. See you then. And thanks for going with me.

I really appreciate the support." She smiled at her friend's comment. "I'll get this worked out." She pointed the remote at the television and increased the volume. "I have to go, he's up next."

A close-up of Michael filled the screen as his name was read from a list of nominees. He looked striking in his black tux and slicked-back hair. When he heard his name, the seductive grin Lyle had come to know crossed his face. He was on camera when he kissed the glamorous woman sitting next to him. His date, The Rook.

Ava Rookesby grew up in New Jersey. Her father was once a star football player. After being forced from the game due to a career-ending injury, he earned a substantial living working as a color commentator for a popular sports network. Her mother had authored a series of romance novels with great success. Once Ava was born, she settled into the rewarding job of motherhood and the publishing career faded.

Ava inherited her father's height—at fifteen years old, she stood just under six feet tall. She clearly got her slim build from her mother. Ava's beauty turned heads and at the age of seventeen, she explored the possibility of modeling. With her mother's support, she caught the attention of one of the top agencies in New York City.

She worked in the shadows of the bigger names during her early years. When she landed a contract with Tarente, an international women's cosmetics company, her popularity exploded. Ava was the face for their new line of eye shadow targeting the trendy market.

The first advertisement featured her cuddling a beautiful cat near her cheek. The feline had long snowy fur and stared at the camera with its big blue eyes, which matched Ava's eye shadow. She wore a white faux boa to mimic the feline's luxurious coat. The caption under the photo read, *She found her eyeshadow at Tarente. She found her cat at her local shelter.* The company ran concurrent ads using Ava and a never-ending supply of adorable cats and dogs available for adoption. The combination worked. Tarente's new line of eye shadow was a windfall for the company.

The public loved her and affectionately nicknamed her, The Rook.

"And the winner of this year's best actor in a leading roll goes to…" The announcer paused for dramatic effect. "Michael Miller, in *John Magnum.*"

"Yes!" Lyle threw her hands in the air and popcorn went everywhere. "He got it! I knew he would."

She watched as Michael stood and gave a half salute to the cheering audience. He bent and kissed The Rook then sprang onto the stage to the roar of applause. Gripping the coveted statue in his fist, he approached the microphone.

"Thank you." The applause continued. "Thank you all so much." The audience quieted. "This is a dream come true. I couldn't have done it alone." He thanked a list of directors and costars. He thanked his parents and family for their encouragement. He searched the audience and found his date beaming up at him. "Thank you, Rook." Applause began to grow again. "She's great, isn't she?" Whistles and more applause momentarily stopped his speech as the camera found Ava. The crowd again settled down and music began to play, signaling him to wrap it up. He looked into the camera and said, "I know you're there, Mi Dushi. I love you."

Mi Dushi. My sweetheart.

"Michael, you did it! You won. Oh, Dottie, he's so happy." But Dottie was gone.

Sixteen

Months ago, Lyle's friends became suspicious of her friend Dottie. They had never actually met her, and things Lyle told them about her weren't adding up.

While Rick, Lyle's boyfriend at the time, was in New York helping her mother enroll in programs to pay for food and utilities, he asked her about Dottie. When Lyle's mother explained, it all became clear: there was no Dottie. To Lyle, she was as real as life itself, made of flesh and bone, but in reality, she was a figment of her imagination. Lyle's mind had created her when she was very young, when she needed someone for companionship and guidance.

Rick made the difficult decision to stop dating her. He loved Lyle but felt he could take better care of her as a friend. He thought that by taking a step back, he would be able to see things more clearly. It slayed him to do it, but he chose to break her heart in order to help deal with her mental illness.

He and Victoria sought out help for Lyle. After an arduous search, they found Danesha Clark. Together, they met with the therapist exploring the best way to approach Lyle regarding their suspicions. Danesha cautioned about the possibility of Lyle abandoning them in order to save Dottie. After contemplating the best tactics, they decided the four of them would meet at Victoria's home. Danesha would be introduced to Lyle, and the subject of Rick and Victoria's concern would be broached.

Expecting full-on resistance, they were shocked and relieved when Lyle nodded her head and agreed to therapy. Memories of her friend Dottie weren't all adding up and she couldn't make sense of the discrepancies. She'd explained how her nightmares were affecting her. They tormented her, leaving her tossing and turning most nights. She never once remembered feeling fully rested in the morning. What was worse, her dreams were now clouding her waking hours too. Moments of time were lost to her. If there was any possibility of ending this confusion, she was willing to try. She looked at Danesha sitting across from her and felt full of hope.

"When can we get started?" she had asked.

Seventeen

Danesha Clark's office looked more like a cozy family room than a therapist's workplace. A flat-screen TV hung on the wall across from a plush, rose-colored sofa. Fresh flowers were displayed in a silver vase on a glass coffee table. The scent of homemade brownies hung in the air and had made Lyle's mouth water. Double chocolate with chunks of walnuts. She'd already eaten one and had taken another. The therapist's family portraits hung on the walls. The bookshelf wasn't filled with reference books, but rather, with popular fiction and historical novels. She recognized many of the titles and authors. The classic, Peter Pan, caught her eye. A forever young boy with the ability to fly. No one in the story was concerned about *that* imaginary friend.

Danesha sat behind a pretty antique desk, her laptop closed and pushed to the side. Pen perched in her hand, she jotted notes in a yellow legal pad.

Lyle was impressed with her perfect posture and always sat up a little straighter when in her presence. She reminded her of a swan, lean and tall. Long braids adorned with beads fell to the therapist's waist. A pleasant song tinkled as the tresses moved about.

Lyle sat in a club chair and sipped her coffee, washing down the last of her second brownie. The ceramic mug had been made by Danesha's youngest child. There were small fingerprints fired into the design, and the initials *TC* were etched on the bottom.

The only telltale sign that she was in a professional office were the two diplomas hanging on the wall. Danesha had earned her bachelor's degree in psychology from Shaw University in downtown Raleigh.

She needed only to travel to nearby Chapel Hill to study for her master's degree in social work at the University of North Carolina.

Her parents were hard workers and raised Danesha and her sister, Brittnei, to appreciate the value of a dollar. Her father labored for over twenty years in a manufacturing plant where part of his job description said, *Must be able to lift thirty pounds.* Her mother worked as a cashier. It was hard on her feet, but she never once complained.

The family lived a comfortable life. Although they never allowed elaborate expenditures, Danesha had fond memories of vacationing with extended family in Savannah and visiting the parks in Orlando. Brittnei was two years older than Danesha. The girls shared a love of learning and excelled in their studies.

While in high school, Brittnei detached herself from family and friends. Her mother suggested she "cheer up" and "snap out of it," but Brittnei's unhappiness continued. Her ailment was misunderstood and went undiagnosed. Years of watching her sister ride the highs, and give into the lows, later spurred Danesha's interest in mental health studies.

As an enthusiastic college student, Danesha dreamed of saving the world one person at a time. The reality was, her client list was full of disheartened wives and husbands whose marriages weren't the romantic adventure they had each once imagined. The couples tried counseling as a last resort to somehow try and make their relationships stick. Not the patients she once dreamed of helping, but it paid the bills.

Then, one morning, a new client she had been previously introduced to, sat in Danesha's office. The woman's friends hoped she could address the hallucinations she suffered. She spoke willingly but with great difficultly, sharing her past and stories of her neglected childhood. This patient believed she was imagining a person named Dottie. Danesha knew that all her years of study would finally be put to the test. The person sitting in her office, Lyle Cooper, needed her.

Eighteen

"You've made a lot of progress since we started working together." Danesha said while scribbling notes on a pad. "When's the last time you saw Dottie?"

"She watched the Academy Awards with me last night." Lyle's shoulders dropped. "I haven't seen her in a while, and then bam, there she is. She looked different yesterday. She was a child. She rode her bike to my apartment."

"She's changing, or rather, your perception of her is changing," Danesha said. "That's very positive."

"It's all so confusing. How can she not be real? Dottie's real to me—she's my friend. We don't think, I mean, I don't think she's... It's hard to believe she's truly made-up. I know I saw her last night. We spoke. She was in my home sitting on my couch." She shook her head. "If she's a product of my imagination, how could she be in my apartment last night?"

"You continue to need her. She'll fade eventually, when you no longer rely on her. When you find your inner strength, I think you'll be surprised at how independent you can be, living without her. Once you finally learn to trust yourself and have the conviction to make choices and work through the difficult situations. I believe everything will come together and you'll realize Dottie *is* you."

She ran her finger around the ceramic mug. Danesha always gave her time to think. *Dottie is you.* She'd have to consider that later.

"I'm thinking of having this tattoo finished," she said.

"Okay, tell me why you think that's a good idea." Danesha said with a questioning squint. "We've talked a lot about your tattoo and the reasons you had it done. Remember, it isn't magical. It can't solve your troubles or carry your worries. It holds no power over you. It's just art. It can't help with your past."

"I know, I understand that. I was thinking that if I finish it, it'll be because I want to have it done, not because Dottie thinks I should. I know it can't hold my problems or dissolve my early years. I'd just like to fill in the empty spaces. I don't want it to have holes anymore. It'll be one more thing I can check off my list. Then I can focus on Dottie."

"As long as you know the tattoo can't fix this," said Danesha. "You have to continue working hard. I want you to keep a journal. Set aside time every day to imagine your life without Dottie. How would you feel if she were gone? Who would you turn to in times of need? Write down everything you remember about her. The times you talked, what you did together. Why did Dottie come to see you that particular day? It's a big assignment but I think it'll help you move along with your progress." She waited a moment. "Go ahead and finish your tattoo. I think that's a good idea. You're taking control, and that's wonderful. We'll work on Dottie." She stood and placed the pen on her desk. "Then we need to settle things with your mother."

She left Danesha's office. Victoria, sitting in the reception area, looked up from her Kindle and gave her a smile. "How'd it go?"

"Really well," Lyle said. "We have some concrete plans for moving forward." They walked toward the elevator. "She's given me an assignment and I have an idea of my own."

"You're making headway, really taking the bull by the horns," Victoria said. "I'm proud of you. What's your next task?"

"I need to call Grey Locklear. I'm going back to Pearl to have this tattoo finished."

Nineteen

"*You have arrived at your destination. On the left,*" said Margaret.
"When I left this place last time," Lyle said out loud, "I swore I'd never come back."

She opened the screen door, stepped inside, and waited for her eyes to adjust to the low light. The deep reverberating of a motorcycle engine could be heard pulling into the shop's parking lot. She remembered her uncomfortable encounter with Hendrix, the Santa Slayer, and prayed it wasn't him.

Her hair was cut shorter and no longer shaved on one side, but Lyle knew that face. Approaching the counter, she said, "Crystal."

"Lyle Cooper." A voice rumbled behind her.

"Grey Locklear." She turned.

The hammering of his boots resonated with each step he took. He nodded at Crystal and put his helmet on the counter. "I was beginning to think I'd never see you again. Where've you been with my unfinished tattoo?"

He was just as hot as she remembered yet somehow seemed even taller. His hair was tucked behind one ear and fell to his chest. The dark mane shone even in the dimly lit room. Once again, he was dressed completely in black, and his eyes glowed under his heavy brow.

"Sorry it's been so long."

He leaned back on the counter and crossed his ankles. "What's brought you back now?"

"I want to finish this tattoo."

"The gremlins." He slid his phone from his pocket and glanced at the time. "I've got someone coming in soon. A guy called yesterday, said his wife wants her first ink. Want to hang around? We can talk about finishing what we started."

She watched while he readied his space for the next appointment. She remembered this room well and shuddered thinking about the hours she had spent sitting on one of those wooden chairs.

"If I remember, you hoped the spine tattoo would help you get along in life." He meticulously placed needles, ink, and a gun-shaped pen on the table. "Has it worked?"

"Honestly, I was hoping you'd forgotten about that," she said, blushing. "I know I sounded off the wall, but at the time, I believed it could carry my problems. Now I just want it finished. I have a few things I'm trying to sort out. Stuff that needs to be addressed, including this tattoo."

She heard the screen door slam in the distance, then several footsteps advancing down the hall. She hoped to never run into him again, but there he was. Hendrix, the Santa Slayer, entered the room with a man and his wife following closely behind him. The lady scrutinized the images on Hendrix's scalp. Taking her husband's hand, she dropped her eyes to the floor.

"This is your next client," Hendrix said, motioning to the clearly uncomfortable woman.

Lyle remembered his tattooed skull, covered with gruesome demons performing hideous acts. She shrank into the corner hoping he wouldn't notice her.

"I've got to step out, but I'll be back for my five o'clock," Hendrix said. "I've got a few things I need to pick up before they get here." He shifted his beady eyes up and down the length of Lyle's body.

She crossed her arms over her chest. She was modestly dressed in jeans and a blouse, but his beady rat-like eyes left her feeling exposed.

"No problem, Hendrix. I'll help Crystal if she gets busy," said Grey.

The room felt lighter once Hendrix left and Grey's client appeared to relax. He was asked to tattoo a hummingbird on the woman's bicep.

"This way, when they leave for the winter, I can have a darlin' little birdie with me on my arm."

He asked the woman to slightly recline on the upright massage table. He sat next to her on a chair. "This is my friend, Lyle. I hope you don't mind her joining us. She has a true masterpiece on her back." He winked at her. "We just need to finish it up."

"Ouch! Oooo that stings." The woman looked to her husband for comfort.

"Don't look at me. This here's your idea."

"Any thoughts about your gremlins?" Grey asked. "Surely by now you've come up with something."

"I was kind of hoping you could help me out with that."

He etched vibrant green ink into the woman's arm then wiped the tiny bird with a cloth. He studied his work and then continued.

Lyle thought he hadn't heard her, but he finally answered. "It'll take some time for me to come up with the additions you want. We should talk about what you envision for them. I should be done here in about an hour. Hang out with me and we'll get dinner."

"Ouch! This damned bird. I hope it gets eaten by a cat."

Twenty

"Are you sure this is safe?" Lyle sat behind Grey on his Harley. "Just do what I told you. The bike is going to lean going around turns so don't let that scare you. And remember, after we sit at a red light or stop sign, hold on to me. I don't want to lose you off the back when I accelerate."

The engine rumbled to life and then inched forward. She threw her arms around his waist and held on like a passenger holding her lifejacket while the Titanic sank on the horizon. How much does she trust this guy driving? Is he a risk-taker on the open road? What if they crash? Will his insurance cover her hospital bill? She wished she had offered to drive her car, currently parked just yards away. But Grey said this would be an adventure and her first ride on a motorcycle would leave her feeling invigorated. They left the shop's parking lot and drove through Pearl. The starts and stops had her stomach turning cartwheels. A monster-sized truck pulled up next to them and lurked there, impressing upon Lyle how vulnerable they were on the low-profile two-wheeled vehicle.

Once they had maneuvered through the crowded streets of town, they broke free and he picked up speed on the less traveled rural routes. Her arms were starting to ache, and she wondered if she would have the strength to hold on until they arrived.

He reached behind him and tapped her thigh. "You can let go of me now." He gestured to the open countryside. "It should be smooth sailing from here. Relax and sit back."

She released her strong grasp and placed her hands in her lap, ready to grab ahold again in the event of a catastrophic collision. She sat up straight and finally had a view of more than just Grey's back. As they sped over the pavement, she began to appreciate the wide-open space.

The bike reverberated at a low, constant drum as they cut through the air like a jet plane. The smell of harvested hay fields and wild huckleberry hung in the air. He shifted and the Harley picked up speed. His knee nearly touched the pavement as they snaked around bends in the road. He was happier than a pig wallowing in mud and she felt his aura flowing from him and being absorbed by her. Instantly, her fear evaporated, carried off by the air whipping past them, and she felt thrilled. Her smile grew as they sped over the pavement. Now relaxed and delighted by flying so freely, she had been liberated from her usual stuffy old car.

———

They left the motorcycle in a small parking area designated for hikers. Lyle removed her helmet and tried to fix her disheveled hair with her free hand. The air, now pleasantly warm, smelled of pine needles and wildflowers.

"What did you think of your first ride on a Harley?" Grey asked.

"Absolutely amazing. I knew I'd love it. I never had a doubt." It rolled off her tongue. "Thanks for inviting me along."

He took the helmet from her and fastened both to the Harley. "This is my favorite trail on the greenway. It's off the beaten path and never crowded. It doesn't have any paved walkways for bikes or strollers, so the wildlife is more abundant here. At dinner the other night, I got the impression you like the great outdoors."

His phone buzzed and he looked at the screen. "I'm sorry. It's Hendrix. I should take this." He touched the Accept button. "Hey Hendrix, what's up?" As he listened to a lengthy explanation, he pursed his lips and shook his head. "What did I tell you about that guy? I knew this would happen. No. No I can't help you. I don't have it to give to you." He listened. "Get this straightened out before you end up in prison." He put his cell away. "I'm sorry about that. Hendrix is making bad decisions again."

"More money problems?"

"Years ago, before he got his tattoo license, he was working for some thug, trying to make ends meet," he said. "He always thought he'd get out of it once his client list at the shop grew. Only, the man he's mixed up with is very reluctant to let a good employee go."

He pulled his hair back and fastened it in an elastic band. He then motioned at an opening in the trees and they strolled toward the trailhead. She was glad to see him in a more casual manner. He'd left the black jeans and boots behind and wore a pair of cargo shorts and a T-shirt.

The path meandered through a heavily wooded area and gradually inclined. She easily passed below the tall pine trees, but he had to duck his head under the low hanging branches. They had walked almost an hour when they stopped.

"Stay here," said Grey, approaching a tree a few feet ahead.

He pulled on a sprig and lowered the limb, then untangled a long snake from the vegetation. The animal crawled through his fingers and around his wrist. He handled it gently and showed it to Lyle: orange and yellow scales with black rings. "This is a corn snake." It wiggled in a futile attempt to get away. "Hold on, buddy. I got you." The reptile settled and became docile. She walked toward him and his eyebrows shot up.

"That's a pretty one," she said as she took the scaly critter from him. "We had a lot of them in the woods where I grew up." She grinned at a memory. "I think I may have put one in a shoebox and given it a name. Then, one morning I asked my mom if she knew where ole Hissy was. After that, mama was a hard *no* when it came to allowing my captured pets in the trailer."

"You're not squeamish at all, are you."

"You should see the creatures I scuba dive with. Makes this little guy look like a caterpillar." The snake's tongue darted in and out of its mouth, then it lifted its head and crawled up her arm. Her voice went high: "Hello Hissy, did we disturb you?" She spoke in her baby voice. "Do you want to get back in your tree?"

"I didn't know you were a diver."

"It's my passion. When I'm swimming sixty feet below the surface, in complete silence, surrounded by the most incredible life. I can't explain the feeling I get. I imagine it's similar to you hitting the open road. I have a group of friends that I usually dive with," she said, while handing the squirming serpent back to him. "Do you hike here often?"

"I try to get up here every few weeks." He put the captive back in the tree and it climbed away hastily. "I've been keeping my eye on some of the birds' nests."

They chose their steps carefully as they walked along the stone and branch strewn ground. Once they arrived at the precipice of the trail, he stopped. "Do you hear that?"

She paused. "I can hear a lot of things." She looked at the pine needles at her feet and took another moment to listen. "Birds are chirping, and some bugs are squeaking."

"Come with me." He led her off the path and through a thick line of trees. They stopped at a ridge overlooking a small body of water. Not quite the size of a lake one would find on a map, but too big and clear to be considered a pond. He looked overhead and turned in circles, searching for something. His finger shot into the air, pointing skyward. "There, look there."

An eagle flew directly above them, sailing on an invisible sea. Its massive wingspan easily measured over six feet. The bird soared effortlessly through the air, its brown feathered body and gleaming white head gliding in the pale blue Carolina sky.

"Wow, it's amazing," she said, squinting. "That's a huge bird. How'd you know where to find it?"

"That's the male. He's a little smaller than the female. If you listen, you can hear her calling from the nest."

They kept silent and waited patiently. From up in the trees, where the top branches waved over the forest, a chirping whistle sounded, followed by a shrill, high-pitched peal.

"That's the bald eagle? I thought they'd sound more frightening."

"One of the most powerful raptors in nature and they sound kind of sweet, don't they? Not intimidating at all." They watched as the magnificent bird circled lower. "He's got his eye on something. Let's wait and see what the next meal is going to be." The bird tucked its wings and dived toward the flat water. At the last second, it leveled off, glided over the surface, and took off again with a struggling fish pierced in its talons.

"Nice catch!" said Lyle.

"This pair have been nesting here for several years. There are two offspring in their nest. It looks like the babies are having fish for lunch. What about you, are you hungry too?" He searched the ground and spotted a cluster of daisy-like flowers: thin white petals surrounding a rough green center. He picked the green leaves that encircled the blooms and offered them to her. "Give it a try."

"Are you sure?" She hesitated but then took the handful. He nodded his encouragement and she took a healthy bite and chewed it up. "Tastes like corn on the cob. That's unexpected."

"It's chickweed. Makes a great salad, and if you cook it, the flavor is similar to spinach."

She searched the ground. "Do any of these plants taste like a baked potato with a generous helping of sour cream?"

Twenty-One

"How'd you get interested in all this?" Lyle asked Grey. "The eagles, the plants. These days people are more absorbed in technology and spend all their free time online."

"I grew up with a grandfather who loved the great outdoors. He had a biology degree from State. He always kept a huge vegetable garden in his backyard and the forest was his pharmacy. I remember being in first grade and coming home with chicken pox. He marched me out back where we picked chamomile leaves. He made a salve and spread it over the bumps." He smiled. "I thought he was magic."

"He sounds like a great man. He raised you well."

"Yes, he was a great man. I'm only sorry I couldn't make him prouder of me." They walked back through the trees and strolled down the path hand in hand.

"What makes you think he wasn't proud of you?"

"I think, in the end, I was a disappointment to him." He hesitated. "I had a girlfriend in high school. Elizabeth was so beautiful with her curls and huge smile. I was so awkward then. I was tall and lanky and had ugly acne on my face."

It was hard for Lyle to imagine it.

"A bunch of kids in my class always gave me a hard time. Calling me names, throwing balled up trash at me. To avoid them in the cafeteria, I ate my lunch outside. I sat under a tree near the teachers' parking lot. I couldn't get far enough away from those idiots. A few days after my sophomore year started, I noticed another student eating her lunch outside not far from me." He grinned at the memory. "It was weeks before we acknowledged one another. Eventually, we started to look at each other and nod or give a quick wave. We knew we were each trying to escape the madhouse for a few minutes. One day Elizabeth joined me under my tree. She said I looked like someone who would enjoy a piece of homemade banana bread and sat down next to me. She was so kind. She had just lost her mother and was trying to adjust to life with only her dad."

He stopped and looked at Lyle. "We stayed together all through high school. Our senior year…" He paused. "Our senior year, well, we thought we were being safe. We were kids, really. The truth is we didn't know what careful was. She got pregnant."

He paused and she waited for him to continue.

"I was so afraid to tell my grandfather. I didn't know what to do. But once I got the courage to tell him, he was so understanding. The man talked me down off a ledge. I felt such relief after confiding in him. He was joyful even. He was happy to have a new member of the family on the way. He encouraged me to ask Elizabeth to marry me."

"Did you?"

"Yes, I asked her, and she agreed, but her father wouldn't have it. We always knew he didn't want us dating. We handled it by trying to stay away from him and sneaking around. Looking back, we should've confronted him. Maybe we could've gotten him to accept us, I don't know."

"Why do you think he didn't want the two of you to be together?" asked Lyle.

"The problem is, people have preconceived notions and it's near impossible to change their minds. They don't always know the truth about Native Americans. They have many assumptions about spirituality and think we pray to the wrong God. They say we abuse alcohol. These things are all untrue. My grandfather never drank a drop of alcohol. And as far as the misconceived notions regarding religion goes, he grew up in a Christian home and was spiritually connected to all Creation. The white man had a goal to abolish Native Americans and their way of life. They had a slogan: kill the Indian, save the man."

Lyle cringed.

"After our daughter Cece was born, Elizabeth's father didn't want me to have anything to do with her, or our baby. My grandfather called him and he agreed to allow us a visit." He smiled. "She had a head full of hair and dark eyes like mine. She was so tiny I was afraid to hold her. He picked her up and put her in my arms. It wasn't very long after our visit that Elizabeth's father took them both away from North Carolina."

"I'm so sorry. That must've been terrible for you."

"Harder even on my grandfather," he continued. "He passed away soon after Cece was born. I believe from a broken heart." His face went somber. "I feel guilty sometimes. I'm ashamed that my poor choices cost him his life."

"If your grandfather was disappointed in anyone, it would've been Elizabeth's dad. He was so prejudiced and closed minded, he denied you your own flesh and blood." She motioned toward a clearing in the trees. "Would you like to sit awhile?"

Telling his painful story had taken a toll on him. He sighed as he sat and leaned back against a tree. He patted the dry pine needles next to him. She joined him and took his hand.

"Whatever became of them? Elizabeth and Cece?" she asked.

"Her father kept in touch with me, fed me bits of information to keep me at bay. He brought Cece to see me a couple of times, but he wouldn't let me have any contact with Elizabeth. A year or two passed and he told me she was going to marry. She'd gotten engaged over the holidays. He assured me this guy was a good man with a stable, well-paying career and they were a fine match. For him to be onboard with the wedding, I knew the guy must be top notch. You know, educated and a decent job. He was willing to raise Cece as his own. Elizabeth loved him." He paused. "I was a kid. I couldn't provide a nice home or a comfortable life. I figured this guy would take care of them. After that, the visits stopped."

"He had no right to take your daughter away from you."

"Cece's twelve now and I don't even know her."

"As her father you have some say in this. Elizabeth isn't a kid—she's not beholden to her dad anymore." Voice rising. "You can use your rights and fight for court-mandated visitation. Grey, you could get to know your daughter."

Twenty-Two

The sounds of the forest took the place of their words. As they sat against the tree listening to nature, the sadness that filled Grey while he told his story drained from him. A squirrel stopped near their feet and stood on its hind legs. It seemed to be asking *what are you two doing here?* They giggled as the creature scampered off.

Grey cradled Lyle and ran his fingers down her cheek. He bent to kiss her. Their lips molded together as her tongue stole tiny tastes of him.

She looked up with her mismatched eyes and smiled shyly. "Finally. I didn't think you'd ever kiss me."

"I think I remember doing more than just kissing you when we first met." He patted his thighs. "Come sit here."

She straddled his legs and sat facing him.

He slipped her shirt over her head and tossed it to the ground. She took his hands, placed them on her chest and held them there. He kissed her neck then found her breast with his lips and tongue. She exhaled and watched him as he devoured her. She found the elastic band at the nap of his neck and slid it down his ponytail. She couldn't resist combing her fingers through his wavy mane as he tantalized her. She tugged at his shirt, and he reluctantly let go of her to remove it. Briefly surprised again by his tattoos, she took a moment to admire them.

"Still not running away?"

Looking at him from under her brow she shook her head once. She placed her hands on his chest then ran them down his sides and to the front of his shorts. The snap gave way easily and the zipper slid down like a whisper.

They stood and removed their remaining clothes. He searched the ground and threw some stray sticks and rocks to the side then took her hands and knelt down in front of her.

"Come down here with me," he said.

Kneeling in front of him, his body eclipsed hers. He wrapped his arm around her waist and laid her back. Nature's bed was slightly sharp at first but then softened and molded to her figure. He kissed her neck and soft tufts of dark hair fell over her breasts.

"Grey, please," She was short of breath.

He covered her so completely she could see no forest, only flesh. Dark geometric tattoos on muscled arms and chest moved like a shadow above her.

It was all so natural for them. They progressed like pouring liquid. Two slow, trickling streams coming together, building, falling freely over a cliff then crashing in an explosion of water and mist.

An eagle circled in the sky above, calling out to its mate in the tree top.

Twenty-Three

"How much better do you need to know me before you can de-sign my gremlins?" Lyle stood next to Grey. "I'm pretty sure this is our fifth date." They moved along with the line of people wait-ing to enter the movie theater.

"This could take a while," he teased. "You're hard to read."

"I can't believe you haven't seen this movie yet," she said. "Michael Miller won the Oscar for this film."

Now in front of the movie poster for *John Magnum*, she stared at the familiar face gazing back at her. The perfect mix of determined US military personnel and confident war-time hero. His bright hazel eyes drilled right into her. Michael was dressed in full service uniform with his hair shaved, high and tight. Memories of him transported her back to Bonaire. Suddenly she felt homesick for her lover.

"You must've really liked it the first time. Thanks for seeing it again with me," said Grey.

"We're lucky they re-released it after it's big win. I'm sure it will end up on cable soon, but you really need to see the explosions on the big screen."

She noticed a group of women in the lobby all giggling together. They gawked at Grey and then whispered to each other. She hated that he was the object of their attention. If she were being honest with herself, she'd have to admit she understood why. If she could look up tall, dark and handsome in the dictionary, she was sure Grey's face would be there.

Quit looking at him. She held his hand firmer and moved closer to his side. She stared back at the gaggle until they realized they'd been caught and turned the other way.

Her attention returned to Grey. "I actually know the lead actor. I met him on Bonaire while I was diving there with my friends. He was vacationing with his sister."

"You know Michael Miller?" He was initially impressed but then narrowed his eyes. "How well?"

"Very well?" She wasn't sure why she said it as a question. "I mean, very well."

He raised his chin. She wondered if he was trying to look even bigger than he was. "Was it love at first sight? Or was it more of a one-night only type of thing?"

"Oh, no. We didn't get along at all at first. He was a real pain in the ass and annoying as all hell. He actually reamed me out over destroying his sister's sunhat when I was only trying to help!"

"Really?" He gestured toward the poster of Michael. "This guy right here. Michael Miller yelled at you."

"The hat had blown off her head and was tumbling toward the edge of the dock. I was trying to stop it before it fell into the water but I lost my balance and ended up crushing it with my feet. That was the first time I saw him at the resort. Of course I knew his face from all the movies he's been in. I thought it would be cool talking to a big star, but instead I became the target of his ridicule."

"What did he say to you?"

"Oh, he told me I didn't make enough money to afford a hat as nice as his sister's. Then he said I had clown feet." She giggled at the memory.

"Man, he sounds like a real jerk."

"Yes, but we ended up diving together and put the entire incident behind us. Only then did we realize we actually liked each other. And once we recognized each other as a friend," she squinted and lowered her voice, "we became lovers."

"Jesus, Lyle. You and Michael Miller?"

"Crazy, right? We've kept in touch. We talk or text most days."

"Most days?" The line inched toward the ticket taker. He scrolled through his cell searching for the vouchers. "I'm not sure how I feel about the talking and texting, but I gotta give it to you—you're full of surprises Lyle Cooper."

The employee scanned the tickets and they proceeded into the theater. Her phone vibrated.

Michael: *Talk?*

Lyle: *I'm out. Later?*

Michael: *K. :'(*

Twenty-Four

Back in Raleigh for her next appointment, Lyle told Danesha she had taken a sabbatical from work to concentrate on getting well. She had a modest savings that would cover her bills while she was out. Working her full-time job left little opportunity for self-help. Along with her twice-per-week therapy sessions, Danesha assigned her daily journaling prompts. She encouraged consistent meditation and mantras and recommended regular exercise. She assigned books for Lyle to read that would help her understand what she was going through. All this took time. Danesha explained it was necessary in order to heal.

She was truthful with her boss, Dr. Patel. She explained to him the mental anguish she'd been suffering, including the delusional thoughts.

"The truth is, I'm not sure what's true and what isn't. Some parts of my childhood are so clear to me. How can they be imagined? I need time to work things out. I've been talking with a therapist who I think can help me."

Dr. Patel, who'd been her boss and loyal friend for almost twenty years, didn't hesitate to support her. "If you think you need time away from work you should take it. You've always believed that being close to the ocean and breathing the salty air was cathartic. Let's put that theory to the test. I'm only using the beach house occasionally. If you don't mind me and my wife for company now and again, why don't you move down to Pearl? There's plenty of room. You could take the guest suite on the second floor. It's yours for as long as you want to stay."

"Really? You'd do that for me? I'm not sure how long I'd be there."

"Let's not worry about that. I'll hire a temporary hygienist to cover for you while you're out of the office." He assured her that her job would be available when she was ready to return.

Soon after, she moved into the doctor's home at the coast. She hung her clothes in the closet and filled the refrigerator with her favorite things. She returned to Raleigh twice a week to keep her appointments. Most of her time in the serene surroundings was spent working on her assignments.

As soon as her obligations to Danesha and her therapy were completed for the day, she dashed off to spend time with Grey Locklear.

Twenty-Five

"Who is King Lear?" Lyle spoke confidently.

A gameshow had captured their attention. Each tried to outsmart the other as they snuggled on the couch at Dr. Patel's. Grey, spooning Lyle, had tucked his knees into the back of hers. Absentmindedly, he stroked her arm with a finger as she cuddled in front of him.

"What is carbon monoxide?" she said. The host confirmed her answer. "Yes! I should go on this show."

After hearing the next question, Grey droned, "Benjamin Franklin."

"You have to answer in the form of a question. Everyone knows that." She wiggled her butt into him, teasing him as they waited to hear the next one. When neither of them answered, Lyle asked, "Laura Chinchilla, really? I never would've guessed that." She turned on her back and tilted her chin seeking a kiss. He clicked off the television.

"You give up?" Grey asked. "That makes me the winner." He slid is hand under her nighty and found her breast.

"Oh, I think I'm going to be a big winner here in a minute." She sat up and lifted her nightgown off over her head. The lightweight fabric floated through the air and puddled on the ground. She straddled his hips and leaned down to kiss him. Her breast rested on his chest as she took tiny bites of his ear.

"Grey," she said in a needy breath, "take your clothes off."

He sat up in one fluid motion while removing his shirt. The sheer size of him threw her off balance and she toppled to the floor. She scowled up at him.

"I'm so sorry," he said, trying to suppress his laughter. "I forgot how small you are." He stood and offered her a hand up.

"I'm not that small. You're just ginormous." She took his hand and hopped up, giving him the stink eye. "Maybe we should move this into the bedroom."

She turned down the blankets and climbed onto the crisp cotton sheets.

He dug through his overnight bag. "I got you something. If you're not into it just let me know." He handed her a package, about the size of a carton of eggs, and then removed and tossed his jeans onto the upholstered chair in the corner.

She held the box but her eyes never left him. Just the sight of him standing beside the bed thrilled her—indecent fantasies of what was to come ran on fast-forward in her mind.

He took the item and opened it himself. "You strike me as the adventurous type." He removed a phallic shaped object and began loading it with batteries. He watched her face trying to catch her expression when she realized what the gift was. "I got you a toy. I think you'll like this."

She looked at the thing in his hands. Her eyebrows shot up as he flipped the switch on. A buzzing filled the air. She jumped from the bed. "It sounds like a dozen bees got loose in here. Has anyone checked the amperage on that thing?"

He turned it off and the room went quiet. "This is completely up to you. What do you think? Up for a little fun?"

She took it from him and held it between them. "You had to get the super-sized one?"

He sat on the bed and placed his hands on her hips pulling her to stand between his knees. He cupped her breasts, playing with them until she exhaled, letting out a sweet moan. His large palms rolled over her and she rolled her head back. Her body melted as he slid his hands down her sides and hooked his thumbs in the elastic of her panties. The lacy silk glided down over her hips and thighs. He leaned down to work them from around her ankles.

Standing naked, her body tingled and she grew excited. Now breathless, she said: "I don't think I'm going to need that toy."

Twenty-Six

Lyle held her pen in her teeth and looked out the window at the parking lot. She sat on her sofa with her feet tucked under her and her journal in her lap. She'd returned to her apartment in Raleigh for her appointment with Danesha Clark. She struggled with leaving Grey in Pearl; she felt lost and vulnerable without him. She wasn't sure how long she'd been staring when a knock sounded at her door.

"Dottie! Come in. It's so good to see you." She held the door open for her friend. She came in and took a seat. "What are you doing here? Is something wrong?" Therapy was teaching her a lot about Dottie. "Is something wrong with *me*?"

"You tell me. Is there a problem you need help with?" She patted the sofa next to her and Lyle sat.

"You're not supposed to be here. I think you're visiting because I'm lonely. I left Grey in Pearl and Michael's working in Canada."

"You're being too soft. You're only in Raleigh to see your therapist. Once you're done with Danesha you'll head back to Pearl and be with Grey." She put her hand on Lyle's knee. "You can do this."

"I miss Grey so much. When I'm with him, everything seems to calm down. Life moves slower and is less… complicated. I feel normal when I'm with him. I don't like to be away from him even for a day or two. I start to feel weak, like something's missing."

Her phone vibrated and she looked at the screen. "Dottie, I have to—" But Dottie was gone.

Michael: *RU home?*

Lyle: *Yes! Talk now?*

Lyle's phone lit up and she touched the screen. "Michael!"

"Finally. I've been texting you all week," he snapped. "I'm stuck here in Vancouver and you won't answer my messages? What's taking up all your time?"

"I've been busy," she said, looking at the journal in her lap. "You know, with therapy and everything. Danesha's given me a lot to do. And don't be so dramatic. It's only been three days since we talked, not a week."

"But you're not even working." He shot back. Michael was hot. "Your boss gave you time off so you can get your head on straight. There's no way your appointments are getting in the way of you picking up your phone. Who is he?"

"Michael, you don't want to do this now."

"Who is he?"

She hesitated. "Michael, we—"

"Tell me, Lyle," he demanded.

"Okay, okay. I've met someone. I actually met him a while ago. He's the artist who did my tattoo."

"You never told me about him. For all the conversations we've had about your unfinished ink, you never thought to tell me about the guy who did it?"

"No, I guess I didn't see the need to." She took a breath. "I got in touch with him to have it finished."

"You're adding the gremlins you told me about? The ones to fill the empty spaces."

"That's the plan. He's working on creating a design for them."

Silence lingered. She tapped her pen on her teeth.

"I love you Michael, and I miss you like crazy. Please say something, anything. Say this is all going to be okay."

"I do understand," he said, now calm. "For a lot of different reasons, we can't be together right now. I can't ask you to wait for me, and celibacy would totally suck." They both giggled.

Indeed, it was impossible. His career was taking off. Although they never discussed it, it was no secret he was dating. He and Ava Rookesby were on countless gossip magazine covers. The hottest commodity in Hollywood dating the most stunning model in New York. Lyle was sure he wouldn't deny her a companion of her own.

"Does he treat you well?" he asked, deflated.

"Yes, he does. He's calm and steady. He's what I need right now. He's been a huge support while I work through a lot of my shit. You'd like him. I'm sure of it."

"I'm sorry I can't be the calm and steady one for you," he said. "One thing I can do for you is ease any financial stress you might be feeling. I've gone ahead and paid your rent for the next six months."

"Oh, Michael, thank you. That's a huge relief."

"I had my manager, Catherine, reach out to Danesha Clark's office. Her weekly fee will be taken care of, anonymously."

"Thank you so much for that. I can see how people with psychological problems can end up in the poor house. It's taking a lot of time and all my energy to work through this. I can't imagine having to show up to work day after day pretending everything is fine."

"Anything for you, baby."

"I feel better now that you know I'm seeing someone," she said. "It was weird for me, keeping it from you. We never set any parameters. You have Ava Rookesby—I see you two on those cheap publications every time I check out at the grocery store or watch one of those celebrity news shows."

"I'm sorry," he said. "I hear you, I really do, but please don't let this thing with Ava drive you away from me. I hate that she and I are dumped in your face by the media. Catherine set us up. She chose the restaurant we'd be having dinner at and then leaked the location to the tabloids. Paparazzi swarmed us as we left dinner and the next morning, we were front page news. It was meant to be a publicity stunt. Another way for Catherine to make more money off me."

"It's hard for me to see you with her. It turns me into a jealous teenager, but I guess this is how it'll be for now." She changed the subject. "How's the film coming along? What do you think about the location?"

He exhaled and she imagined him raking his hand through his hair.

"Vancouver's a great city," he said. "It's just very far from everything and everyone I know."

"You sound exhausted. What's up?"

"It's the role. This guy I'm playing is a real challenge. I can feel him leaching into my head. Stewart was very dark. The malicious things he did to those classmates… He thought it was fun. I think the realization of it is getting me down."

A top selling investigative journalist's latest book, *College Bound*, was a true crime novel based on the life of convicted murderer Collin Stewart. At the time of his arrest, Stewart was a college student in Ohio. His intellect and cunning enabled him to hide the fact that he was a serial killer. He targeted his peers—young adults—making his crimes that much more heinous.

"This role is turning out to be a real test of my ability. I'm worried about pulling it off without looking like a laughingstock. Maybe I should've quit after *John Magnum*." There, he said it. The raw truth he could only tell Lyle. His fear of failure. Immediately he felt his worry was halved.

"You've made so many successful movies," she said. "You've moved from fluffy romantic leads to the hard-hitting roles. This is what you've always wanted. Should I remind you, you won a very prestigious award recently?" She chuckled. "Michael, you've already played some very complex characters. No one doubts your ability to portray Stewart except you. I know you can do this, but if it's overwhelming, maybe you should take a break. Get away from it for a while."

"Baby, thanks for that. I do have a hiatus coming up. You and I are definitely getting together then. It's been raining here all month. It's nothing like Bonaire," he said, filled now with melancholy. "It's good to hear your voice. Speaking of getting in my head," he chuckled, "how's your therapy coming along?"

"Dottie was just here. I think she came because I'm feeling alone. I know she wasn't really here. I just imagined her because I needed someone to talk to." She paused to think about what she'd just said. "The fact that I realize that is huge. Danesha would say this is very positive."

"You can always call me if you need someone to talk to. Now that you're aware you imagined Dottie is amazing. You're making progress.

I can hear it in your voice. You sound happier, lighter somehow. I wish I could be there to help you through all of this."

"You know Victoria would never let me go through anything alone. She's driven me to every appointment. She waits for me and takes me home again. Speaking of which, she should be on her way here soon. I'll tell her you said hello."

"I miss you, baby. Let's talk again soon."

Twenty-Seven

Lyle moved her finger up and down her coffee mug, wishing Danesha had offered her a cocktail instead. The sessions with her therapist were helping but the work was tiresome. Instead of feeling the relief she hoped would come, she was struggling with saying good-bye to her lifelong friend. Should she let Dottie go? Everyone around her encouraged her to do so, but what did they know? Dottie was the one who'd gotten her this far. What would be the harm in keeping her around a while longer?

Danesha listened.

"She's fading. I see her less and less," Lyle said, with raw despair in her voice. "Does Dottie know…" She shook her head and started again. "I just hope Dottie knows that…" She stumbled over the words. "I feel bad for her. I'm betraying her after all these years. She's always been there for me and now I'm abandoning her."

"It's natural to be confused about who Dottie is," Danesha explained, "puzzled by your relationship with her. Have you been keeping your diary?"

She patted the journal on her lap. "I've been jotting down my memories of Dottie, like you asked. I'm writing about how she's made me feel. To be honest, reminiscing about her is making it harder to let her go. All the happiest times in my childhood included her."

Danesha scrawled a note then put down her pen. "This is where I'll ask you to have faith in the process. The memories, good and bad, are all part of the progression."

"It's hard to trust it when, in the end, I'm hurting my best friend. But I'm doing what you've asked me to. I'm beginning to imagine how my life will be without her. Doing these journaling exercises, I've realized something. Looking back, some of my memories of Dottie don't add up. I distinctly remember her in my fourth-grade class at Saint Mary's. She stayed behind with me when Sister Meredith wouldn't let me go on a class outing."

Danesha tilted her head, and she continued. "Our class was going on a field trip to the zoo in Syracuse. It has a small aquarium. My teacher, Sister Meredith, noticed my permission slip was signed by my mother's boyfriend, Roy. She wouldn't let me go. The slip was supposed to be signed by my guardian, my mother."

"Okay. Go on," said Danesha.

"The class loaded onto a bus and left. Dottie stayed back with me." She shook her head. "But it doesn't make sense. I'm sure she didn't go to Saint Mary's. I was there on a scholarship. Dottie's family could never have afforded it."

"That encounter certainly does fit the pattern. You felt hurt. You were sad and about to be left behind. Dottie was fabricated to comfort you that day. Read back through your notes. Dottie appears to you when you feel vulnerable or have a concern or are scared by something or someone."

"I do recognize that," said Lyle. "She's always been there for me. Or rather, I should say, I've always taken care of myself."

"And why is this? What have we learned?"

"Because Dottie is me."

"That's very positive. Keep reminding yourself that Dottie is, in fact, you. As you come to accept that, your need to rely on the creation of her will diminish. You'll learn how to trust yourself instead."

Twenty-Eight

Although it was the first time Lyle had been invited to Grey's home, she no longer needed her GPS around Pearl. She had learned the main roads and cross-streets and found his home easily. The low-slung house—built to withstand the hurricanes that whipped through every few years—was more than one hundred years old. She walked up the steps to a covered front porch where she saw Grey's boots. He must've removed them before going inside. She knocked on the heavy wooden door and waited.

Grey's body filled the frame. He offered only a slight smile, the one she had grown to love.

"There's my Crocodile."

When he kissed her something deep inside unwound. There was no question she felt lighter when she was with him. His calmness flowed to her and eased away her stress and worry, leaving peace where her anxiety had been. She was back in Pearl and together again with Grey. She was home.

She stepped inside and into the living room where the walls were covered in pale blue shiplap. A sofa and recliner both had hand-woven blankets draped over the backs of them. A massive stone fireplace took up much of the far wall. The high-tech television and audio system looked out of place in the old house. The mouthwatering aroma of roasted beef and spices came from the kitchen.

"Did I ever tell you my mother used to call me Crocodile? Dottie still does." She dropped her eyes when she heard her slip but Grey generously ignored it.

"It's too easy a rhyme," he said. "I'm afraid I'm not that imaginative, but it does suit you."

"Thanks for the dinner invitation. Something smells delicious." She smiled up at him as he wrapped his arms around her. She lifted her lips to him and they enjoyed a slow kiss. "Something tastes delicious too."

"How'd your session with Danesha go?"

"I think it went well. I'm taking baby steps. She's helping me to trust myself and give credence to my inner voice."

"Moving forward slowly will get you to the same finish line as the person running next to you. This isn't about how fast you go. It's about how well you travel. You'll get there."

"I think so too. Danesha explained a lot of people suffer from self-doubt, so at least I'm not alone there."

"Let me show you around." He took her jacket and gestured to the room where they were standing. "Welcome to my home theater," he joked. "Well, I'm working on it. Right now it's just the TV, some gaming equipment and a monster of a sound system."

"It's nice. I can see the possibilities." She followed him into the kitchen.

He put on mitts, opened the oven, and slid the lower rack partially out. He lifted the cast iron lid of the Dutch oven to check the stew. A chunk of well-seasoned meat fell apart under his fork. "Perfect." He then placed the heavy dish on the stove. "Let me put the rolls in. I'll finish the tour while they bake."

Lyle ran her hand over the massive wooden table that took up most of the room. "This is beautiful. Looks old. Have you had it long?"

"My grandfather made that. Hand-carved out of downed trees from his property on the outskirts of Pearl. It's too big for this kitchen but I couldn't part with it."

"It's gorgeous," she said. The contrasting mahogany and crimson streaks of wood were speckled with dark knots of varying sizes. "I like how he left the edge natural. People pay a lot of money for these live-edge pieces."

"That's how it was done back then. No need to smooth it out."

"You must miss him."

"I do. I think of him every day," he said, while closing the oven door. "I'm surrounded by memories of him. When he passed I sold his home. It was too far out of town and too big for me to take care of alone. I packed up the things that meant the most to him, bought this place, and brought them here. It's hard to believe he's been gone over ten years."

"The house has just two bedrooms." Lyle thought she saw Grey blush as she followed him out of the kitchen. "Only one bathroom. It's an old home, not a lot of luxuries. I thought about finishing the attic but with the gabled roof, there's hardly enough room for me to stand." They walked down a short hallway. "I added an extension onto the back." Grey opened another door. "This is my office."

Three oversized computer monitors arranged in a half circle sat on a desk, with a comfortable-looking office chair in front. Tangled electrical cords ran to a professional grade printer, almost three feet across, on a nearby table. External hard drives stacked on top of each other on a shelf above the desk had gathered dust. They all had been labeled with dates and various family names.

The office was covered in photographs. Huge corkboards held dozens, and when he had run out of room on the boards, Grey had thumbtacked pictures directly onto the walls.

She circled the room and studied them closely. Hundreds of people smiled at her while posed on the beach. Crystal clear sky, deep blue ocean, and honey-colored sand provided the backdrop to these portraits. She had seen similar photos before; North Carolinians loved to have their families photographed on the beach.

All dressed in white and smiling at the camera, a husband and wife knelt behind their four small children. Another family dressed the girls in light pink and the boys in baby blue. The colors worked perfectly on the sand. A beautiful bride, veil caught in the breeze, held a bouquet of pink flowers. In the distance her future husband stood in a black tuxedo.

"You're a photographer?" she asked.

He sat on the edge of his desk, stretching out his long legs and crossing them at the ankles. "I like to think so. It pays the bills. Unlike tattooing, photography is more prolific."

She browsed the room, astounded by the hundreds of pieces hanging there. What caught her attention were the older subjects pinned up among them. As she continued around, individual black-and-white shots of the senior members of the families jumped out at her. Grey had, unbeknownst to them, photographed the elderly up close.

"Tell me about these." She pointed at a snapshot of an older man clearly caught off guard, every wrinkle on his face, every imperfection, captured forever in print.

"The oldest folks are my favorite subjects," He explained. "Look at those faces, those contours. The wrinkles tell their story." He stood and took a photo off the wall. A Native American gentleman looked straight at them. "The deeper the lines the more powerful the lifetime story. This man led a good life. I believe he told a thousand tales in his time." He had deep grooves in his skin but still, Lyle saw something familiar.

"You look just like him. Who is he?"

"This is my grandfather. This is the one I told you about. He passed soon after I graduated high school." He returned the photo to the wall. "How sad it would be for someone to die with no lines. With only a few stories to tell—smooth, young skin."

"You loved him. I hear it in the way you talk about him."

"Yes. Very much. I feel him around me still." He became lost in his thoughts and after a moment continued: "He was instrumental in the state's conservation efforts. He worked with the wildlife federation here. His focus was the dwindling red wolf population. Their numbers have plummeted. They're almost nonexistent in the wild. They can only be found on the Albemarle Peninsula here in eastern North Carolina. Nowhere else in the world. We have such a huge responsibility. We can't let them die off."

"The eagles we saw on our hike. You told me you've been keeping an eye on their nest. That sounds exactly like something your grandfather would do." She smiled and gestured at the size of Grey. "You can be a bit intimidating on the outside." He grinned at the remark. "But your words are kind and sweet, like the eagle's song."

Twenty-Nine

Grey pushed open a door and switched on the overhead light. "And this is my darkroom."

Lyle walked into the cramped, windowless room. A strong and tangy odor hung in the air. "It looks like a chemistry lab." She picked up a glass cylinder. "I didn't think photographers used film anymore, let alone developed their own images."

"We're a dying breed. I love the smell of the chemicals. I enjoy the precise measuring required to mix the developer and fixer. It takes me back to when I was a student learning the process for the first time. The anticipation of watching an image reveal itself as it floats in the solution." Drying clips hung from a wire above. Thirty-five-millimeter rolls of film lined the shelves. "It's a slow and cumbersome process. Paying clients won't put up with it. With all the new editing software, our options now are unlimited. People want instant results. Actually, they want perfect, immediate results. And they want it in their in-box within the week. I could never do that with film. But I prefer to use it for my own projects."

He flipped the switch on the light box illuminating negatives clipped there. He handed her a loupe for closer inspection. She put the small magnifier to her eye.

"Our eagles!" She searched further. "Are these the babies? I see two little tufts just above the nest."

"It took some patience but they both raised their heads long enough for me to get the photo."

"Film is alive and well," she said. "It can't be killed by digital photography."

"It's making a comeback. Just like vinyl records. Give people time, they love the nostalgia. Unfortunately, it's impossible to compete in today's market using film."

As they returned to the front room someone knocked on the door.

"I'm sorry," he said. "Whoever it is, I'll be quick. There's a bottle of wine on the counter. Please help yourself."

From the kitchen she couldn't help but overhear the conversation.

"Hendrix, what's up?" Grey sounded annoyed. "I've got company. This isn't a good time."

She searched through two drawers then found the corkscrew.

"I won't take a minute," Hendrix said. "I need a favor."

The men lowered their voices. Words became muffled, but the tone of the conversation was clear. The unwelcomed guest sounded desperate. He became louder and she heard him say, "A few thousand. You know I'm good for it."

She decided to make her presence known and walked in the room. "Hendrix," she said with a grin. "Nice to see you again." It was a lie, but she would be polite to Grey's friend. She could smell cigarette smoke that clung to his clothes like week old fish.

He gave her a closer look then recognized her. "The chick from the shop?" he asked Grey. When he didn't respond, Hendrix went to the front door and opened it. "I'll see you at work tomorrow. Think it over. I'll repay you with interest."

Grey shut the door behind him. "I'm sorry about that. He's mixed up in some real shit. I want to be mad but a part of me feels bad for him."

They returned to the kitchen where he filled two bowls with beef stew. As he took dinner rolls out of the oven, he nodded at the bottle of wine. "I'm not a big drinker. I hope I did okay."

"You chose well." She read the label. "This is a nice pinot noir."

The beef fell apart under her fork. Coins of carrots, chunks of potatoes, and whole mushrooms swam in the seasoned stew. She covered her steaming hot dinner roll with a generous amount of soft butter which soaked into the airy bread. She tore off a piece, dipped it in the thick gravy, and took a big bite. "Grey, this is delicious. Thank you. I owe you one."

"If you mean it and you're not busy this weekend, I could use an assistant on a photo shoot I have scheduled."

"I'd love to. How can I help?"

"It's a family with three small boys. How're your herding skills?"

Thirty

Arriving at Wrightsville Beach late in the afternoon, Lyle and Grey parked the car and left their shoes on the floor mats. She opened the back door and draped two heavy camera cases over each of her shoulders. She followed Grey as he plowed through the deep sand with a keen eye. He checked the position of the sun, scanned the seagrass growing in scattered patches, and settled on a location. She carefully placed the equipment on the ground.

They waited in the dunes one hundred yards from the water. The sun was low in the western sky, still providing plenty of light but not so glaring that one would have to squint. Swimmers and sunbathers had left for the day and the beach was relatively quiet. A lone surfer rode the crest of a wave until it brought her close to shore. She then carved out a turn and paddled back out. Half a dozen people had dropped fishing lines from the gigantic pier off in the distance.

Grey's clients arrived right on time. They watched as a shining SUV parked near their car and out poured four adults and three children: Lyle's charges. The young boys eyed the surf and started off toward the beach at a lively step. Their mother frantically called out to them, and they rejoined the family. She waved at Grey as they all approached.

"I'm Grey Locklear. We spoke on the phone." He shook the woman's hand. "You must be Rachel."

The family all wore crisp matching sherbet-green button-down shirts and brilliant white shorts. The boys' hair was styled with gel and their shirts were tucked in at the waist.

"Nice to meet you, Grey," she said. "This is my husband, Jake."

Jake and Grey shook hands as Rachel introduced their kids: "These are our boys. John is nine, Paul just turned seven, and our youngest, Nikki, is five."

Each boy squinted up and gave a quick "hi". The boys were finding it a real challenge to be still. With the ocean so close, their attention was fully on the water. They spotted the lone surfer and their excitement doubled.

"And these are my parents, Joan and Ray," said Jake.

The older couple grinned. Their graying hair looked fabulous against their green shirts. Lyle was already imagining how spectacular the family's portrait would look once completed.

"It's nice to meet all of you," Grey said, shaking hands.

Nikki looked up at him with wide eyes. "Wow! You're big. How high are you?"

"How about I show you?" He asked, looking to Rachel for an okay. She responded with a broad smile.

"Okay!" screeched Nikki.

He lifted the boy by his waist. "I'm tall enough to send you to the sun!" He held him over his head and moved him about. The boy spread his arms as though flying through space. He giggled and flapped his arms until Grey put his feet firmly back on the sand.

"Lyle will be helping me today," he said to the family. She smiled and greeted them. "I thought a few shots surrounded by the seagrass to start." The tall blades of feathery green grass swayed about, a perfect complement to the family's chosen wardrobe.

Grey checked the position of the sun and then guided the family members where to stand. He took photos of them informally gathered together. Then he had the parents' place their hands on the boys' shoulders, casually looking at each other and then toward him. The youngest boy stood next to his grandfather and rested his cheek on his leg. He then passed his camera off to Lyle who put it in its protective case. She opened the second bag and handed him the other one that had a different lens.

He photographed just the parents, then had the children join them and they all sat in the sand. The boys then circled around their grandparents as they relaxed in the seagrass. The love between them was easy to capture. The boys hugged and held hands with their beloved grandparents without ever needing to be prompted. Grey knelt and his camera whirled.

"Let's move down closer to the shoreline," Grey said. "Why don't y'all go ahead and take off your shoes. We'll get some casual shots."

The boys threw their shoes aside and charged toward the shore.

Rachel yelled, "No! Not in the water!" They put on the brakes, sliding to a stop, then looked back at their mother, dejected. "Boys, we're not done yet. We're just taking off our shoes. Don't you dare ruin your hair and clothes. Do *not* go in the ocean," she repeated. "We're just going to stand near it, understand?"

The disappointed crew dropped their shoulders and the three sauntered toward the water's edge as the rest of the family joined them.

Lyle watched Grey work, with daylight fading and shadows stretching over the sand. Golden rays of sun illuminated the family. Their hair and complexions seemed to glimmer. He had timed the session perfectly. As the family stood near the water, the sky behind them glowed candy pink. It was clear that this was what Grey loved doing. Lyle basked in his tranquility, sure his over-abundance of peacefulness was spilling into her.

The family murmured to each other, smiled, and laughed. They were at ease under Grey's watchful eye. He quietly caught it all, the family lit now by the impeccable light.

The smell of salt in the air and the pummeling waves called to Lyle. She wasn't needed at the moment, so she placed the camera cases safely in the sand, far from the swash, and walked a few feet to the shoreline. Water spread over the sand and sent chilly fingers swirling around her toes. She left footprints as she waded in a little deeper. The surf broke against her legs, and a misty spray reached her face. She fought every urge to dive in and take a swim. Now was not the time.

When she turned to rejoin everyone on the beach, a rogue wave crashed over her back. She stumbled forward but was able to regain her balance. But as the swell retreated, the undertow pulled her feet out from under her and drug her toward the open ocean. The power of the surf was too great and she fell backward, landed on her behind, and sat there in chest-deep water.

"Oh miss!" The grandfather was jogging toward her with unwarranted urgency. "Hold on, miss, I'm coming!"

She waved her hands, warding him off. "No need. I'm fine." But the man kept coming. She smiled at the absurdity of the moment. There she sat, soaking wet, the sea swirling around her. Just as he entered the water and reached out, a second wave came in, throwing him off balance and sending him floating about. Lyle and the octogenarian were tossed around like children in a bounce house, their arms and legs flailing uncontrollably in the shallow water.

"Granddad!" yelled Nikki.

All three brothers came running. Perfect hair and pressed clothes, they charged straight into the surf.

"Oh! Boys!" He tried to gather them up out of the waves only to be knocked off his feet again.

Lyle stood and dragged herself out of the water.

The soaking wet kids laughed and splashed their grandfather and each other. They made circles around him, kicking up a storm as he pretended to try and catch them.

She stood next to Grey as he captured the moment she knew would be cherished by generations to come.

Thirty-One

Lyle was thriving living at the beach. Being able to help Grey with his photo shoots gave her a sense of purpose. She continued the drive back to Raleigh twice per week in order to keep her meetings with Danesha Clark. Victoria had insisted, from the very beginning, that she accompany her to these sessions. After all this time, she hadn't missed a single one.

"Victoria, I really appreciate you coming," said Lyle. "I don't know what I would've done without you. Thank you for finding help for me." They sat in Danesha's reception room awaiting Lyle's appointment time. "I never would've done this on my own. I certainly wouldn't have seen the need. Maybe that's the craziest part of all of this. I didn't know anything was wrong."

"I have a colleague who was having some trouble," Victoria said. "She worked with Danesha and spoke very highly of her. I'm just relieved she's been able to help. I was so worried about you."

Lyle noticed her friend's smart outfit: tailored pants, slimline jacket, and kitten heels. "You're on your lunch hour. I'm sorry for hogging up all your time."

"Don't be silly. You got me out of a meeting with an impossible-to-please client. I'll grab something later."

Danesha opened her office door. "Lyle, I'm ready for you."

"I'll be right here," said Victoria.

Danesha sat behind her antique desk and picked up her pen. She crossed her legs and straightened the legal pad in front of her. "Good morning. It's nice to see you again. Tell me, how have you been doing with the assignments I gave you?"

Lyle told her about the many journal entries she had written and assured her she was doing the meditation exercises recommended.

"That all sounds great. Have you had any visits from your friend?"

"I've seen Dottie once this week," Lyle said. "But she's changed back to a little girl again. She looked exactly as she did the time we first met."

"Tell me about that day, when she became your friend."

"It was so long ago, but I know I was alone outside, hiding from one of my mother's boyfriends. She always called them her boyfriends, but I realize now they were customers. I think it was getting dark, I remember being so scared." She twisted her fingers. "Dottie found me and sat with me until it was safe to go back inside. She's been with me, one way or another, ever since."

Danesha scribbled down some notes.

"Do you think she's going to need—" Lyle pursed her lips and then started again. "Do you think Dottie will want to... damn. I feel like I get it, but then, she was so clearly a part of my life. Dottie was real to me. It's not only confusing but frustrating too. Everyone around me can see the truth, and yet, I lived it. She was a living, breathing person to me. And at times, she still is."

"She's been with you most of your life. She isn't going to leave instantly," Danesha said. "You still have a lot of unfinished business. If you recall, when we started this journey, I told you it would take some time. Dottie's been a friend for most of your life. She's always looked out for you. She comforted you when you were alone." She flipped back through the pages in her notebook and scanned previous entries. "It becomes very clear when we review the journal entries you've made. When your mother's addictions kept her from caring for you the way a mother should, Dottie shows up time and again to step in." Danesha put down her pen and crossed her arms over her chest. "We've delayed talking about her for about as long as we can. I know this is going to be difficult for you, but I think the time has come. I want you to tell me about your mother."

"She was..." Lyle stopped and thought a moment. She had spent most of her time trying to forget about the mom who clearly wished

Lyle was never born. Nightmares of growing up with that woman, during both waking and sleeping hours, haunted her. "When I think of her, I remember that she was strung out on drugs or drunk most of the time. She didn't give a damn about me, it was the alcohol and pills that were important to her. We lived in a tent when I was three, maybe four years old. A two-person tent. Who does that to a kid? We stayed in a campground. During the summer it was kind of nice, it was fun. I played with kids who were vacationing with their families. But come fall they all left." She paused. "We didn't go anywhere. The two of us stayed in that flimsy shelter all winter. I thought I'd never be warm again. The worst part was when she'd leave me alone in the evenings to go…" The memories were becoming too painful. She clenched her fists and looked at Danesha, now contrary. Her voice rose and she snapped: "There's no way to change the past. Telling you about it won't fix it."

"You're right, but we must be able to face it." She tented her fingers. "I think it's time for you to go see your mother."

"No! I can't. I never want to see that woman again. I won't go." She glanced at the door to the reception room and sat up, ready to leave. "You don't understand. I went to New York with my friends. We were helping my mom get enrolled in programs for people like her, people with no money and even fewer prospects. The morning we were supposed to meet with her, I freaked out! I couldn't go. Rick ended up seeing her without me. I stayed back at the hotel. I don't want to go to New York. I can't. There must be a way for me to deal with this without having to contact my mother." She shouted: "You're the therapist—think of something!"

"I'm afraid that without facing your past, Dottie may never leave you completely." Danesha's voice was soft. "We both agree your mother played a dark role in your childhood. It's going to be difficult, but I strongly recommend you do this. Dottie's been attached to you for so many years. It's time you're set free, only you can unburden yourself. Thank her for being there for you but let her go. It's the only way you'll be healed."

Danesha stood, then Lyle did the same.

"Go to New York, Lyle. Meet with your mother. There's no set agenda. No goals or tasks to complete when you get there. Just talk, stand face to face with her. She may not be the person you remember her to be."

Thirty-Two

"You're going to see your mother?" Michael asked over the phone. "Are you sure about this?"

"I'm not sure about anything. I really don't want to go," she said. "I only know Danesha said I have to do this in order to get better."

"If she thinks this is a good idea, you should go. She wouldn't ask you to meet up with your mom if she didn't feel it was important. We've trusted her so far and you really seem to be doing better."

"You're right," she said. "It's a no-brainer when she asks me to journal each day, keep my appointments with her and do some self-evaluation. It was much harder to agree to go see that woman. But I agree with you. Danesha seems to know what she's doing."

"Damn it, baby, I wish I could be there. I'd love to be the one holding your hand. Is Victoria traveling with you?"

"No, she's not coming. Michael, I'll be okay. I won't be alone."

After a few long seconds it clicked: "The new boyfriend, shit!" He paused a moment and calmed down. "Keep in touch with me. I mean it Lyle, no radio silence. I won't be able to function until I know you're okay."

"Danesha thinks seeing my mother will help me finally be able to…" She took a breath. "I need to say goodbye to Dottie." She whispered, "I'm supposed to let her go."

"Oh, baby, I've never felt this helpless. This fucking movie. First it fucked with my head, now it's fucking with my life. I miss you endlessly. If I could do anything to be there with you I would. I'd move a mountain for you, you know that, right? I want to stand by you through all this tough stuff."

"I know you do. It does help, Michael, knowing you're support-ing me. You really care what happens to me. I realize that. Danesha's techniques have worked so far. I need to trust her on this. I need to go see my mother."

Thirty-Three

Their flight arrived under cloudy skies at Syracuse Hancock International Airport. Lyle and Grey picked up the rental car and drove east on the New York State Thruway toward the little town where she grew up, where her mom still lived. Although it had been programmed into the GPS, she held a crumpled paper with her mother's address scrawled on it.

After exiting the highway, they eventually passed a sign that read, *Chittenango 3 miles.* She absentmindedly played with the note in her hands and her toes beat up and down inside her shoe. Grey's legs had been cramped for the duration of their flight. Now he was driving a compact car with his seat slid all the way back. The tension in the vehicle was thick as curdled milk. She wanted to ask him to turn around and take her back to Pearl. This trip had obviously been a huge mistake, a fool's errand. She glanced at him and it was as though he had heard her thought.

"It's going to be okay," he said. "I'll get you through this, I promise."

"I hope so, but I'm a lot less sure about this than you are. Thank you for being here with me. If she's really bad off, or totally out of sorts, just get me out of there, okay?"

"I won't let her hurt you." And with that, the atmosphere calmed.

"Did I ever tell you I grew up in Oz?" she asked.

"Oz? As in *The Wonderful Wizard Of?*"

"This is it," she said as they drove toward the main area of town. "I'd like to show you around if you don't mind. Then we can find my mother's house."

They followed signs directing them downtown. Soon they saw one saying, *Welcome to Chittenango.* And several yards later another one:

L. Frank Baum, author of The Wonderful Wizard of Oz, *Chittenango's favorite son.*

Quaint shops lined the main street of the charming village. People looked into storefront windows and casually strolled along the sidewalks. Grey slowed the car as the road circled a park with a stone fountain at the center. They continued over a bridge where a river ran through the town. A sign pointed the way to Chittenango Falls.

It was hard to miss the yellow brick road crowded with visitors shopping and taking photos. He grinned and pointed at Auntie Em's Pie Shop and The Emerald City Grill as they drove past. The All Things Oz Museum had a line out front. The enchanting surroundings were a tourist attraction to many, but to Lyle they held only painful memories.

"Chittenango is seriously proud of L. Frank Baum," she explained. "He was born here in 1856, and his book was published in 1900. Sadly, Baum died before his novel was made into the famous movie in 1939."

"Oh, really?" Grey lifted his eyebrows. "1939? 1856?"

She giggled. "We studied Baum in school. I had to memorize the dates. I guess they've stuck with me."

"Okay. You win. You actually did grow up in Oz."

"Well, yes, it's the fairy-tale Oz come to life. But it isn't exactly where I lived. Let's go see my home, if it's there." She directed him down Genesse Street. He watched as the fantasy town diminished in the rearview mirror and reality appeared before them.

Thirty-Four

They had traveled just a few miles when Lyle sat up and pointed out the window. "See that turn on the right? Drive in there."

They left the smooth blacktop and drove down a bumpy gravel street. Grey advanced cautiously, trying to avoid deep potholes. The tires spit loose stones behind them as they crept along.

She held onto the dashboard and studied the landscape, surprised by how familiar everything looked. "Pull in there." She indicated an overgrown dirt road and Grey shot her a look. "Slow down, this is it, go in here."

"Are you sure?" he said. "It looks more like the forbidden forest than Oz."

They drove past a rusted gate that had fallen off its hinges long ago. They crawled into the ominous woods, where low-hanging branches encroached on their path and blocked out the sky. Old mobile homes, tossed appliances, and abandoned cars littered the area.

"Over there," she said.

He pulled up to the mobile home, parked, then sat staring out his window. This was where she had lived as a child. This was the past she struggled to forget. He was overcome with sympathy; clarity fell upon him. When she didn't make any move to leave the car, he turned off the engine.

She stared at her home still propped up on cinderblocks. All the windows were broken out, and the white siding was covered with rust and moss. The roof had collapsed in over her mother's bedroom. Trees and weeds now invading the small space. She got out and studied the long-abandoned trailer. Her feet wouldn't move, trapped in the realization that she was back. She'd forgotten Grey was with her until she heard his door close. He came around the vehicle.

She took his hand and whispered, "Will you go in with me?"

Standing on the first wooden step, she stopped and touched the railing. "Men from Catholic Charities built these stairs. I don't know how they found us. They just knocked on the door one day." She smiled. "I remember when they pulled the old set apart, I thought my mother and I would be stuck inside forever." She ran her fingers over the rotten wood. "After they rebuilt them, they stayed and talked to her. They offered me a scholarship of sorts, to their private elementary school in town. The teachers there made sure I had a hot lunch every day." She glanced at Grey. "There wasn't always food in the refrigerator here. I didn't know it at the time, but they changed my life, gave me opportunities I never would've had. My homelife was so unstable, but I could count on my school. It gave me routine, safety, and a decent education."

She climbed to the top step. "Mind the gap." She walked just inside the door and stopped, wide-eyed.

The dilapidated trailer had been ransacked and the vandals were thorough. Nothing of significance remained. Mold was growing where sheets of the linoleum floor was missing. The air was thick and smelled of rot and tortured memories. The walls that remained were covered in graffiti. Dew drops fell from the surrounding trees. They exploded on the metal roof sounding a rapid-fire of pinging above them.

"Lyle, I don't think this is a good idea. This floor looks dangerous."

But she didn't hear him. She went to the kitchen and touched the warped countertop. The cabinets and sink were long gone, leaving only shadows on the wall and a hole in the counter. "My mother used to smoke her cigarettes in here. She never had an ashtray and would wash the ashes down the drain." She tilted her head back and inhaled. "I think I can smell the smoke." She sniffed the air again but the scent was gone.

She left the kitchen then stopped and peered into a tiny space with a single window. "This was my room. A mattress on the floor"—she pointed—"just there. My mother's boyfriend Roy said it was in case I fell out of bed I wouldn't have very far to go." She chuckled. "Funny, but I remember this room being a lot bigger than this."

Grey looked past her into the revolting bedroom. A threadbare mattress now soaked in grime and mold was pushed up against the wall. Once Lyle's own bed, now home to scurrying rodents from the woods. He was speechless.

As the hard memories seeped back, she unexpectedly felt a sense of calm. Perhaps Danesha had been right. By facing her past, she now felt strangely in control of it.

Grey was ready to leave but Lyle seemed contented to stay and remember her life there. He cautiously walked with her, checking the floorboards as she explored. She stopped in the main room recalling the old couch and folding table and chairs.

"Roy lived with us for a while," she said. "My mom wasn't home much, so I was glad to have him around. He made sure I did my homework and had something to eat. I imagine he was a lot younger than I am now." Her voice filled with melancholy. "One day he was just gone. My mother never said why he left. Maybe she didn't know." She took his hand. "Are you okay? You've been quiet as a church mouse. You haven't said a word." She didn't wait for a reply. "Come with me, I want to show you something."

After one last look she walked outside and down the steps. He followed her around to the back of the trailer. The clouds were increasing and under the canopy of trees it looked like dusk.

Lyle pointed to a gap between two cinderblocks that held the old home up off the ground. The hole was just big enough for a small child to crawl in under the trailer. "That was my secret hiding place. When my mom's boyfriends scared me, I would hide in there." She bent down and tried to look into the dark opening, but it was covered in cobwebs, and she could only see shadows. She smiled, remembering. "Can you imagine? I must've been no bigger than a groundhog. One day I came home from school and some guy tried to grab me. I heard my mama yelling, 'Run Lyle, run and hide!' I flew out of the trailer so fast he couldn't catch me. I ran back here and hid in there." She nodded, indicating the black void. "A few minutes later Dottie came and sat with me. She stayed until we heard the man get in his car and drive away."

Lyle stood gazing at the area where the cement had broken away. She contemplated what she was saying and suddenly understood. "That was when I met her—the initial time I conjured her up. The very first time I needed a Dottie. I was six years old."

Grey knelt and looked into the dark crevice between the cinderblocks. His stomach turned as he felt the horror that must have overcome her at such a young age. She'd been so terrified of being hurt by the man that she found solace in this frightening place. It was here Lyle's mind changed. She found a way to save herself.

"I'm sorry," said Grey, standing. "I had no idea. We never should've come here."

"What do you mean? This was the best home I ever had growing up. Before this trailer my mother and I lived in a tent."

He rubbed his eyes, placed his hands on his hips, then blew a stream of air out of his pursed lips.

"Before you brought me here I wasn't sure," she explained. "I didn't know if this was real. I'm discovering that parts of my childhood that I thought actually happened, were invented by me. All this time, although Dottie was my imaginary friend, this trailer—my house—was real. Thank you for coming here with me. I had to see for myself. I needed to know that my home was real." A brilliant smile brightened her face. "I didn't imagine it."

Thirty-Five

Lyle: *I'm in Oz*
Michael: *Have u seen ur mom yet?*
Lyle: *Next stop*
Michael: *Wish I could be there. U got this.*

Lyle couldn't remember the last thing she ate, but she was thankful for her empty stomach. Her nerves were such that she worried about defiling the pristine rental car. She was on her way to see her mother after all these years. What could possibly be left of her? She was always such a frail person. The drugs and alcohol had eaten away at her, leaving only the scraps behind. Lyle remembered how clothes hung on her boney frame—not much different than if they had been suspended on a hanger in the closet. How her skin appeared translucent. Thick blue veins ballooned out and ran up and down her arms. She was always holding a drink in one hand and a smoldering cigarette in the other. The trailer was perpetually heavy with smoke, and the woman's hair was a frizzy mess. Lyle remembered her trying to tame it in an elastic band at the back of her neck. No matter how hard she tried to calm it, a brown nest of hair circled her skeletal face.

They drove into a neighborhood of single-family homes, built in the 1940s, to accommodate World War II veterans returning from overseas. Like lines of soldiers standing at attention, they were equally spaced apart and each sat the exact same distance from the road. Despite the efforts of homeowners to add unique accents to their porches and contemporary landscaping, each house looked just like the one next to it.

"Number thirty-four," she said, feeling every beat of her heart. "It must be up here on the left."

Grey parked the car at the curb across the street from the home. She tried to give him a reassuring smile, but all she could manage was a nod.

They held hands as they approached the front stoop.

He gave hers a squeeze. "Ready?"

"Give me just a minute." She looked down at her shoes and placed a hand on her stomach trying to settle the butterflies that took flight there. She glanced at the rental car, a perfect means of escape, and contemplated making a run for it. Grey squeezed her fingers a second time, and she knew she had to stay. She knocked.

They heard the knob turn. Someone tried pulling on it then slid the deadbolt and yanked the door open.

Lyle stared at the stranger before her. They had the wrong house. This wasn't her mother. This person's brunette hair was in a neat, high ponytail, with soft gray hairs sneaking in among the darker tresses. She had brilliant blue eyes that twinkled like gemstones from her striking face. This lady's frame was lean but not the emaciated figure Lyle knew her mom would undoubtably suffer. She wore a pair of straight-legged jeans and a simple flowered blouse tucked in neatly at the waist. Lyle had prepared herself to find her mother looking much older than her sixty years, but this woman looked exactly that age. She rechecked the number displayed on the door's frame. Thirty-four.

"Lyle," she said in a soft voice. Her bottom lip quivered and she placed her hand on her heart.

"No," Lyle whispered.

For a moment, time stood still. She searched the face before her: pink cheeks glowed, and tears pooled in baby blues. She glared into this person's eyes searching for an ounce of recognition. Then there it was, in the nervous expression that creeped onto her face, Lyle detected something familiar.

"Mama?" Just a whisper. "Mama, is that you?"

"Yes, Crocodile, it's me." She wiped a tear from the corner of her eye with her finger. "My own daughter don't recognize me it's been so long. I can't believe my little girl has come home."

An awkward beat of silence, then Grey said, "I'm Grey. I'm dating Lyle."

She drew her eyes off her daughter as though looking away could cause her to vanish. "So nice of you to come see me." She nodded at Grey then stepped back and motioned for them to come into the home.

Lyle stood frozen, silently studying the stranger.

Grey put his hand on her back, encouraging her to step inside. Shell-shocked, she couldn't move or speak a word.

"Are you okay?" he asked her quietly. "We can leave, just say the word. Do you still want to do this?"

She nodded once, then stepped into the house never taking her eyes off the woman. In the front room, she was hit from the past with the smell of cigarette smoke, an odor she had always associated with her mother. The multicolored shag carpet was worn flat in high-traffic areas. Mismatched pieces of furniture were arranged for optimal TV viewing in front of the blaring television. A lady sat on the couch there, smoking, her leg was in a cast propped up on the coffee table. She lifted her chin at them as they walked past. No one offered an introduction, so they simply nodded back.

"That's my roommate. She ain't workin' right now. She's temporarily disabled. But the state helps us with the rent. And I got my job at the car wash." She nervously ran her hand over her head, pressing her already smooth hair. "Let's sit outside since it ain't rainin' yet. The bugs haven't been too bad this year."

They followed her through the kitchen. Stark white appliances and counter tops gave the room an institutionalized feel. Green bananas, apples, and sweet potatoes filled a plastic bowl on the counter. Lyle looked at the linoleum and thought of the moss covering the floor at the trailer. She wondered how many years it would take before mold would cover this one too.

The woman led them out the back door to a cement slab, where she motioned to a plastic outdoor patio set with four matching chairs. "Sit down. I'll get us something to drink."

Lyle watched as she disappeared into the kitchen. Grey put his hand on hers, but they both remained silent while they waited. She watched the door until her mother returned with three sodas. She popped the tops and placed cans and napkins in front of them. Lyle thought it rude the woman didn't offer one to Dottie.

Thirty-Six

Was this the same person who raised her? This stranger who didn't have a cocktail or a cigarette in her hand, this individual who drank diet soda and ate fresh fruits and vegetables. This woman who looked… like Lyle.

Grey shifted in his chair as the two continued to gaze at each other. "Your daughter seems to be speechless right now."

"I can see she's going to need a few minutes. That's quite alright. I've got all the time in the world." She extended her hand to him. "I'm Claire Cooper."

Lyle glanced at Dottie, who put her index finger to her lips. "Shhh." Her feet didn't reach the ground. She sat in the extra chair and swung her legs back and forth.

She nodded at her young friend then returned her attention to the woman claiming to be her mom.

"Grey, you and I can talk while Lyle takes a little time to think about all of this." She grinned at him but couldn't take her eyes off her daughter. "I ain't seen my little girl in twenty years. A lot has changed since then. The day she graduated college she moved south to take a job in Raleigh. That's in North Carolina." Her familiar eyes turned teary again. "It was all my doin'. I was so weak. I had a terrible time with drugs and alcohol. The devil had me. Wouldn't let me go. I had little Lyle to raise on my own." She swiped a tear with the back of her hand. "My prayers are answered today. My girl, here with me."

"Your daughter struggles with memories of her childhood," Grey said. "Her therapist recommended coming here to visit you."

"I'm glad she's come, whatever the reason."

"Of course."

"She had some troubles growing up." She looked at Grey. "Is that why she's seeing a therapist?" Her gaze returned to her daughter. "She had an imaginary friend for some time. When I figured it out, I went to her school and asked her teachers for help. She had me so worried."

Dottie nodded. "She did, you know. She tried to get you help."

"Lyle was so clever," said Claire. "She'd go and sit and talk to the counselor once a week. She had the man convinced she was just fine and there was no secret companion. Always so smart, Lyle was." Her mother grinned.

"Claire, there are many pieces of the puzzle we don't know," said Grey. "Can you tell us how you ended up here?"

"After I lost my daughter to her new job, I hit rock bottom. With no one around, no family, not a single friend, with the light of my life havin' moved away, I had nothin' to stay sober for. I ain't lyin' when I say I gave up even tryin'."

Dottie stilled her swinging legs.

"I thank God, really." Claire continued. "He's the one I praise for sending people to help me. They knew me and Lyle from the school and put me in the rehab program in town. Came and got me and drove me there each time. Invited me to come to their church service on Sundays. They had a nice meal in the hall afterward. No charge." She looked admiringly at her daughter then continued. "God gave me Lyle too. I'd call her and she'd send me money. I told her it was for rent or food. I'm ashamed to say a lot of it went to drugs." A tear escaped her eye. "The devil had me good and didn't want to let go. I had a bunch of starts and stops. I'd do well for a while and then slip back into it." She shook her head. "It ain't been easy, but with God's help, I've been clean and sober for a good time now. Lyle and some of her friends got me set up on a free food program and one that pays part of the rent. That's helped me a lot."

"That is something, you know," Dottie, now a grown woman, said to Lyle. "You need to give her credit for finally getting help and pulling herself together. Some addicts never do."

"After you became sober," asked Grey, "did you think about reconnecting with Lyle?"

"Oh no. I couldn't do that to her." She looked proudly at her silent daughter. "She'd made a good life for herself. She went to college and got a job. How could I explain it to her? I didn't do good as a mom. I knew she'd never forgive me."

"She's probably right," said Dottie. "We've been so angry with her. We wouldn't have spoken to her if she had reached out to us."

"I did the best I could," said Claire. "I was on my own. My girl is sweet as sugar though. I do appreciate all she's done for me, even if we only spoke when I called askin' for money."

"Where was your family all those years?" Grey asked. "You must've had parents or a sibling somewhere. Was no one willing to help you?"

"My older brother left home years before I did," said Claire. "We never did find out where he went. I ran off as soon as I could. I was a teenager, so young. I figured I'd be better off alone than living with such hateful parents. They were cruel people. I fell asleep many a night wondering why they ever had me." She sat back in her chair and twisted a napkin in her hands. "We lived in a nice two-story house. It had a small yard out back. From the outside my life looked perfectly normal. No one knew the secrets we hid." The napkin fell in two. She put the worried pieces on the table. "But that's neither here nor there. After I left, I wasn't alone for long." She nodded at Lyle. "This one came along soon after. My family never knew I had her."

Dottie squeezed Lyle's hand. "Now's your chance to talk to her. You can get all your questions answered. Come on now, you can do this. You have Grey and I here for support."

"But Mama," Lyle cleared her throat. "We were on our own. Once Roy left, we had nothing. Your parents could've helped us, or at least helped me. You should've told them about me. We were freezing at night and starving each day."

Claire reached for her daughter's hand. She held it tightly and looked directly into her mismatched eyes. "No, Crocodile. I couldn't put you in front of your granddaddy. He was a wicked man. From as early as I can remember we all feared him. My mama included. She'd stay out of his sights as best she could. She left us kids to face him." She released her hand and straightened her back. "She knew what he was up to. She sacrificed her kids to save herself. I had to keep you hidden so you wouldn't experience the pain that man put upon me my entire childhood."

"It sounds like she was running away from something awful," said Dottie. "Maybe she was trying to protect you like a good mother would. She wanted to be a better mom to you than the one she had. I think she was trying to keep you safe."

Lyle considered Dottie's words. *Could it really be so simple?*

"But Mama, you sold your body—"

"Yes. I'm so ashamed. Yes, I did." She looked down at her lap. "Men would promise me things. Sometimes food, sometimes drugs or money. I tried to keep you fed but the devil had me by the neck. I admit it. I bought drugs before I bought groceries."

Lyle looked at her mother and for the first time, really saw her. She wasn't evil or frightening, not a ghost from her past who hovered about in her present. She was simply a woman trying to make the best of her life. She couldn't easily overcome the horrible circumstances she'd been dealt, but she eventually recognized that she needed help. She had been struggling to fix herself, and even though it took her decades, she was eventually able to do just that.

"Of all the things I've been through in my life, losin' you was the hardest," said Claire. "I always thought I'd sober up and we'd have a better life together. But I lost you before I had the strength to get right. And then it was too late."

"What about my father? Mama, do you know who my daddy is?"

"Oh, Crocodile, you've known him all along," said Claire. "Roy's your dad."

Roy's face flashed in her mind. He lived in the trailer with them sporadically over the years. He could be counted on to make her a meal and tell her to do her homework. She remembered him being at home with her while her mother was out dancing with the devil and paying dearly for every tune. What she recalled the most was Roy on the couch, watching the television and waiting for Claire to come home. There was nothing about him that was particularly good or bad. He was just a man she never gave much thought to.

"Roy?" Lyle whispered. "I thought he was just a boyfriend of yours. He's my daddy? Roy's my father? Why didn't you ever tell me?"

"He took off shortly after I told him I was pregnant," said Claire. "He came and went after you were born. When you were old enough to talk, you just started callin' him Roy. I figured he'd be gone again soon enough, so there was no sense in correcting you."

"I've known my father all along," she echoed.

"That's right, honey," Claire said. "He wanted us to get hitched, be permanent. He had one condition though. He wouldn't marry me unless I gave up the drugs and drinkin' and quit the prostitution. At the time, it seemed like an impossible thing. I always thought I had time. I'd think, 'Next week I'll quit the liquor and Roy will marry me.' A month would go by, and I'd say, 'Tomorrow I'll stop usin' the drugs. We'll get hitched and Roy will take care of us forever.'" She forced a grin and all the things she'd lost in her life Lyle saw on her defeated face. "He loved you. He tried to stay, he tried to help take care of his little girl. One day he finally had enough of me. He stormed out and never came back."

"He left me, with you." The sky darkened, threatening rain.

"I don't know that he could've given you a better life," Claire said. "He was always one for roamin'."

"Do you know what became of him?" Lyle asked.

"Oh, I'd hear stories when he came back to town. By then he'd given up on me and didn't come to call. He's at rest now in the cemetery on the hill. He had a weak heart. Passed before he turned fifty."

Thirty-Seven

The sky was misting as they walked up a slight incline. Grey led the way, holding Lyle's hand as she lagged a step behind. The cemetery was quiet and the grass below them grew damp.

"She said we would find him over there." He jutted his chin at a row of tombstones. "If I've counted right, he should be just down here." He searched each stone as they walked between the graves. He stopped. "Here. This is Roy. He's here." He released her hand. "I'm going to give you some time alone. Will you be okay?"

She nodded and he wandered away. She stood by the modest grave marker and waited for the courage to look down at it. Clouds darkened overhead and the mist turned to rain. She leaned her head back and let the gentle drops cover her face, but as she did, the downpour intensified and began falling heavily over her. When a crow cawed from a nearby tree, the unwavering cry roused her from her spell.

She looked at the flat stone at her feet. Rain poured from her hair and over her face, picking up her tears and washing them onto her father's grave. In simple type it read, *Roy Lyle Masterfield*, with the dates of his birth and death etched below.

"Lyle." She smiled. "I was named after my daddy."

A grown woman still, Dottie placed her arm around her waist. "He was a good man. He took care of you the best way he knew how. I imagine it wasn't easy for him. Lyle, your daddy loved you."

"Roy, I didn't know it was you. I hope I was a good kid." Crying, she wiped at her face. "I'm sorry she ran you off. I would've liked to have had you in my life." She spoke through her sobbing. "We're not always in control of our lives. Sometimes we have to do things we don't choose to do. We have to make our own way. That's what Mama was trying to do." She looked at Dottie, both of them drenched, and took a shuddering breath. "Roy had to finally choose his own path. He couldn't wait for her any longer."

"It's time to forgive her," said Dottie. "In your heart, release your mother, Lyle. It's the burden you've been carrying. Anger, hurt, resentment: let it all go."

Dottie took a step back. "I have to go now. You've come so far. This is where I leave you. It's time for you to go on without me. Look to the future, Lyle, and forgive your past."

———◆———

Grey stood behind her holding her as she sobbed, his body shielding her from the storm. He comforted her in silence as she grieved all she had lost.

She cried for the mother who had done the best she could because she loved Lyle, not because she didn't. She cried for the father who had been there all along but was now lost to her forever. She cried for that voice inside her that saved her and made her strong. The voice that always had the answers and encouraged her to go on. The voice that came from so deep within, it took on its own identity.

She cried for Dottie.

Thirty-Eight

"I got you." Grey held Lyle's waist and steadied her as she stepped into the bathtub. The room was filled with steam, the mirror fogging and the air comfortably warm. Water poured from the faucet and filled the tub. He knelt next to the bath and spoke quietly: "Lean back, I got you." His hand cradled her neck as she moved under the falling stream. Soaked from the pounding rain, she had shivered the entire drive to the motel. The hot bath warmed her and the trembling subsided.

She closed her eyes as he shampooed her hair and thought only of this man's fingers as they massaged her scalp. The familiar smell of the suds reminded her of being home in Pearl. With her mission now completed, she was eager to be back there again. He caught water in his cupped hand and drizzled it over her head, rinsing away the lather. Her shoulders relaxed. The load she'd carried her entire life had lifted, leaving her somehow lighter.

She'd never felt so free. Her burden was gone, and her mind was clear. By forgiving Claire, Lyle unfettered herself from the anger she had held onto for far too many years. By releasing her mother, she had liberated herself.

When he was done with her conditioner, the tub was full, and he turned the knob off. "I found this loofah and body wash in your bag." He worked methodically as he poured the flowery-smelling soap, lathered her back, and then rinsed it away. He added more and rubbed the loofah over her breasts, circling each one and covering them in slippery suds. She lifted her chin, enjoying the soft and scratchy feel. He then dropped it in the tub and rinsed her, the bubbles sliding down into the water.

"Come with me." He stood and extended his hand to her.

Once out of the water, he wrapped her in a short towel that barely covered her. As hard as she tried to adjust it, her body was mostly exposed.

"They make them cheap so we won't want to steal them," he said. "Here, have a seat." She sat on the toilet lid as he untangled the cord to the motel's hair dryer. She dropped her chin and closed her eyes against the powerful stream of air. He brushed and dried her hair until it flew around her head.

They left the steamy room and she turned down the comforter. She dropped her towel to the floor and crawled into bed.

He stood next to her and began taking off his clothes. He slipped off his shirt then slid the zipper on his jeans down and removed them.

She regarded his naked body and felt an ache grow inside as he stretched his arms overhead and breathed a soft yawn.

"Please stop with the expert exhibition and come in here with me." She patted the mattress.

He climbed in next to her and inhaled the scent of her freshly washed hair. "You smell like a spring garden." They kissed slowly, both dog-tired from the emotional and physical events of the day. He moved above her and held himself deftly over her, placing most of his weight on his arm resting above her head. He held her calf on his hip and moved slowly until he couldn't any longer.

The bedframe squeaked with each movement, and the two couldn't help but snicker at the absurdity. The bed's silly whine soon turned to a heavy thump and all laughing ended. They lost themselves in each other, each needing the comfort willingly given by the other.

———◆———

Their bodies now depleted, Lyle threw her arms over her pillow and Grey wiped the sweat from his forehead. Both exhausted, they sank into the sheets while they worked to catch their breath.

He covered them with the blanket. She nestled her head in the crook of his neck. His eyes grew heavy, and he was nearing sleep.

Her voice awakened him: "What a day," she said. "I actually met my mother. I really didn't want to, but now I'm so glad I did. Thank you, Grey. I never could've done this alone." She paused, thinking. "I was frozen. My feet wouldn't move. I couldn't even speak to her. I just stared like I was seeing a ghost. She must've thought I was some sort of lunatic."

"You were great," he said, his voice peaceful. "You did a really tough thing today. I'm proud of you."

"You're proud of me?" She grinned. "I'm pretty pleased with myself. I'm totally worn-out both physically and emotionally. Remarkably, this complete exhaustion feels really good, like I've finished searching and I'm finally home. I think a cloud has been smothering me all these years, and today, the sun started to shine for the very first time. It's a new feeling for me. I'll have to get used to it."

"You know what I think?" he asked. "You deserve a vacation, a chance to take your mind off everything you've been through. We should go somewhere and relax. You need some time to replenish your energy."

"I think I know a place."

PART THREE
Michael Miller

Thirty-Nine

"Let me get this straight. We're going to Bonaire for a well-deserved vacation." Grey cringed. "And your boyfriend is meeting us there?"

"Yes, exactly," Lyle replied. "Michael has a short hiatus from the film he's working on. We'll already be on Bonaire by then, and he'll just meet us there."

"And you don't see anything kind of off about this whole thing?" His eyes narrowed.

"I know it's a lot to ask of you." She slumped on the sofa in her apartment. "I'm hoping you and Michael will understand what I'm going through and consider things with an open mind. I'm embarrassed to say it, but I love both of you. I need each of you equally right now."

"And what exactly does that mean? Are you going to sleep with him?"

She knew the answer was yes, but let her silence respond for her. She thought of Michael and remembered the passionate time they had spent together. His touch, his smell, his mischievous grin, all filled her with great anticipation. But a deep sense of foreboding was just below the surface. She was putting it all on the line and could end up losing everything. There was a real possibility she could leave Bonaire alone.

"Shit, Lyle. I won't make any promises," he said, standing. "I'll meet him since it's so important to you, but after that, we'll just have to see." He kissed her begrudgingly and stomped into the bedroom.

She opened her laptop and reread an article. She had been vacationing on Bonaire with her friends and had met, and fallen in love with, Michael Miller. As her return flight touched down, she had turned on her phone and found a newspaper report about a tourist who had been killed on the island during their visit.

It was late, but she couldn't sleep. Her thoughts bounced between the excitement of returning to the island she loved, and the worry that Michael was meeting them there.

Their flight was scheduled to leave early the next day. From her computer screen, the blond-haired man stared back at her. Only now he had a name: Lawrence Brumfield.

Several days before the body was found, Michael had pulled that same guy off Lyle and beat him to a pulp. Not wanting any publicity or involvement from local authorities, they decided not to report the incident. She now wished they had; the man may still be alive, and she would be fast asleep.

Man Murdered on Bonaire
With a population of just over 22,000, the usually peaceful island of Bonaire is waking up to reports of a brutal crime. Lawrence Brumfield's body was found late Wednesday afternoon. Brumfield suffered blunt force trauma to the head, but police are reviewing security footage and cause of death has yet to be officially determined. He was last seen in a restaurant in Kralendijk, where witnesses say he appeared drunk and was alone at the time. Brumfield, a Michigan native, was vacationing with a friend when he was reported missing. The friend is being questioned by police.

The article was brief with minimal detail. It was the only information she had found regarding the murder.

She could still smell the liquor on his breath and vividly recalled struggling with him at Captain Jack's Restaurant. She shut her laptop and picked up her cell.

"Hi, Michael," she said quietly, not wanting to disturb Grey. "Sorry to call so late. I'm fine. Our flight leaves in the morning but I can't sleep." She listened as he responded. "I'm glad you're finally getting away. I can't wait to see you. It feels like forever since we've been together. A lot has happened, good things." She moved her phone to her other ear. "Oh, he's pretty upset but he's willing to give it a try. I think you'll like him." She flushed. "Please don't be like that. I really need the two of you to get along. Do this for me?" She grinned. "Okay, meet me on the island. Let's go back to Bonaire."

Forty

Lyle and Grey lifted their faces to the warm Caribbean sun. They were enjoying the pool, leaning back on the edge, and letting their legs float out in front of them. Other resort guests relaxed on inflatable rafts and in lounge chairs circling the sparkling water. The Beach Boys, piped through hidden speakers among the palm trees, played a surfing song.

She had stayed at Bon Adventure Resort several times while on Bonaire. The resort catered to scuba divers, offering daily boat trips out to the reefs. Guests had twenty-four-hour access to trucks and air cylinders for diving from the shore, night or day. Its brightly painted motel-style buildings were only two stories. The rooms all opened to a walkway directly outside. Flowerpots overflowing with red blooms lined the courtyards and outdoor stairwells. A gravel road ran through the center of the resort and ended at the oceanfront. Divers could find all their equipment at the dive shop on the dock. After a rigorous day of diving, guests frequented the pool bar and enjoyed live music under a thatched-roofed patio.

"Are you sure you'll be happy here with someone who doesn't dive?" asked Grey. "I'd be glad to entertain myself if you want to get some scuba diving in."

While listening, she noticed that women and men alike were glancing at them. She accidentally made eye contact with a gentleman sitting at the pool's edge, soaking his feet in the water. They both darted their eyes away quickly. She then peeked down at her favorite bathing suit, an emerald-green two-piece with a golden anchor between the breasts.

Grey closed his eyes as he bathed in the sunlight, his tattoos glimmering, splashed with drops of water. His wavy hair had been worked into two long braids. Leave it to him to be wearing a black bathing suit. She often teased that it was his signature color.

"Grey, I think we're the it couple. People are staring at us."

He squinted at the guests enjoying the pool. "You're imagining it."

"No, I think they're gawking at us because we're so cute together."

"People have been staring at me my entire life," he said. "I'll bet they don't see many Native Americans around here. Trust me, we're not that cute."

"Well, no one's ever looked at me. I think it's this bathing suit. Come on Grey, let me have this one thing. Look at how pretty this top is."

"Did it ever occur to you that they might be staring at that masterpiece I created on your back?"

"Maybe. Maybe they're all wondering why it has holes in it."

He placed his huge hand on top of her and dunked her. Bubbles burst above her head, and she came up laughing, flailing her arms and gasping for air.

"I'll give them something to stare at." He lifted her by her waist and tossed her into the air. She squealed and tried to swim away only to be caught and thrown again. The man sitting by the edge jumped up trying to avoid the splashes. An older woman hopped off her float and climbed out of the water.

Once their game ended, Lyle pushed her hair back off her forehead, water streaming down her face. "After that show, we're definitely not the it couple anymore. Now we're going to be shunned by all the other guests and barred from using the pool."

"Let me know if you want to take me up on my offer," he said. "It's a shame to be staying at a resort that caters to divers and not go. I'll find something else to do."

"That's just it. There's a lot more to do on Bonaire than just scuba. Besides," she said excitedly, "Michael will be here in a few days. We'll dive a lot when he gets here." She saw him wince. "What if we take a tuk-tuk tour or go hiking? They have windsurfing down at Lac Bay if you want to try that."

They got out and found two free chairs on the pool's deck. Grey opened the turquois sun umbrella and angled it for shade. Lyle again noticed the attention he was attracting. With his back turned, the magnificent tattoo of the eagle was gaining curious fans. She gave the stink eye to the older lady who had left the pool earlier.

"Should I be worried?" he asked, taking his seat. "About Michael coming here?"

"I was wondering if that would come up."

"I thought this would be a good time," he said gruffly, "now that his arrival is inevitable."

"Michael's very important to me. I don't keep any secrets from him. He knows everything about you and me and our relationship. I've told him all about Dottie and my sessions with Danesha. In turn he shares things about his life with me. He's open about the woman he's been dating. We allow flexibility, in order to be… realistic."

Grey's knee jumped up and down.

"It would be counterproductive—we both would be miserable— if we expected the other to be alone because we're so far apart. We never officially discussed it, but we've fallen into our own type of relationship, not exactly traditional." She added quietly, "I hope you'll be agreeable to this. I don't want to lose you over Michael."

"An unconventional relationship?" He looked at her from under his brow. "What does that mean? It sounds like you've already agreed to it and I have no choice but to go along."

"Grey, it's not so cut and dry. I want you to meet him and then get to know each other. I'm really hoping you like him. My wish is that you'll see the possibility of making this work. If it's something you are dead set against, we can talk about it again and go from there."

Forty-One

The peaceful quiet was an unexpected bonus. The sounds of the island were often hidden, lost in the clamor of everyday life. Lyle and Grey sat in the third row of the electric tuk-tuk, his arm draped around her. They had stashed his camera case near their feet. Three additional tourists sat in the seats in front of them.

Their tour guide was Ancel, an older gentleman whose accent gave away the native Bonairean. He encouraged the five passengers to remain still and listen to the music composed by nature. The shiny green-and-white open-air vehicle glided silently over the roads, allowing the song to be heard. They could hear the waves landing on the coral beaches to their right. Calls from the birds in flight overhead and the gentle winds coming onshore lulled the passengers and conversation was at a minimum. In addition to being environmentally friendly, the electric tuk-tuk was ideal for creeping up on unexpecting wildlife.

She had surprised him and booked them on a three-hour photo-safari tour. As they traveled south the music changed. High trumpeting horns and slow chatter grew louder and echoed over a flat pond. Grey and the others steadied their cameras as Ancel inched closer to a sea of flamingos.

"The proper term is *flamboyance*," Ancel said quietly. "This is a flamboyance of flamingos."

Lyle studied Grey as he took multiple pictures and then flashed her his rare, brazen smile. She knew she would never tire of looking at Grey.

She was glad that the other photographers were a little older. The mature crowd didn't give the younger couple a second glance. They were all there for the same reason. The island held a plethora of possible images just waiting to be captured by the photography enthusiasts. The tuk-tuk stopped in front of the thousands of bright pink flamingos wading in a shallow salt lake. The water was so still the birds cast a mirror image of themselves on the surface.

"Michael would love this," she whispered to herself.

"The Caribbean flamingo is the most colorful of all the species," said Ancel. "This is due to an abundance of tiny rosy brine shrimp that make up the birds' diet here."

Grey stepped outside the vehicle and held his camera steady.

The guide continued: "Bonaire designated this area as a refuge for all species of birds to use for migration and mating. Our government office won't allow even us curious photographers into the sanctuary. It's a safe, pristine place for the wildlife only." Cameras clicked away. "Luckily for us, the view from here is spectacular."

"There's so many of them." A man commented while adjusting his focus.

"At any given time, we are home to ten thousand flamingos," said Ancel.

Grey snapped dozens of photos, adjusting his camera as he did so. The birds flaunted many shades of pink feathers, the different hues blending like ribbons of taffy being mixed on a pulling machine. Their S-shaped necks were graceful and fluid and elegantly long. The pink-and-white beaks, jet black at the tip, faced downward, giving the birds a shy appearance.

Hundreds of them began to run across the top of the water, causing the others to stir and then follow. Their impressive wings on full display as they took flight. Grey aimed his camera skyward and followed the birds as they passed just overhead, exposing coal-black feathers under their pink wings. He held his finger down and the camera whirled and captured shot after shot.

"Lyle, are you seeing this?" he asked, looking up. "This is sick! They're so incredible! And the light this afternoon is perfect." He handed her his digital camera and she passed him the one loaded with film.

She peered up at the cloud of pink and black. A site that left the group gasping and refocusing in a complete tizzy.

———

They returned to the tuk-tuk and traveled on. Grey ran his hand up and down Lyle's thigh and, when he knew they wouldn't be caught, leaned down and kissed her deeply. She grinned at him and snuggled closer as Ancel drove them to the next stop.

"You can't truly say you've seen Bonaire until you hear the story of our slave huts," said Ancel.

Lyle had driven past the structures, found in different locations on the island, but had never taken the time to explore them.

"Most of the tangible reminders of this story have been carefully removed around the world," he explained. "Humankind has tried to erase the truth by destroying the past."

The silent vehicle came to a stop. The group gathered their equipment and climbed out. Grey lifted his camera and took some quick shots. Lyle noticed his height gave him an advantage; no matter where he stood, he simply aimed over the heads of the other photographers.

Ten stone buildings, each the size of a modern-day storage shed, faced the coastline in two straight rows. Painted an egg shell white and with black wooden roofs, they had no windows and only short entryways. Even at the pitch, the houses were less than six feet high— any tall person would have trouble standing up inside. These were the homes of the slaves that populated the island in the eighteen hundreds.

"We're not proud of this history, but we must remember it," Ancel said. "The Netherlands National Antilles foundation chose to preserve these huts so future generations will know."

He strolled toward the subject of his lecture, and the group followed closely behind. "The shelters were built in 1850 to house African slaves, who were forced to work in Bonaire's salt pans. The walls are made from coral stone. The original roofs were thatched, but for ease of maintenance, we've restored them with marine plywood."

The group solemnly advanced, the weight of the history lesson not lost on them.

Grey snapped photos as they walked toward the structures permanently fixed in the sand.

"Working in the salt pans was hard and painful work. Sea salt on Bonaire is unique—the crystals can be very large. The salt had to be pickaxed, shoveled, and transported in wheelbarrows. The tropical sun we've come to cherish and seek out, is the same sun the slaves had to endure." He paused as the group took pictures. "This history casts a shadow over all of us, across all mankind. But in the Caribbean, our bright sun leaves nothing hidden."

Grey turned his camera toward the guide. The artist in him was unable to resist Ancel's distinctive face. He quietly stole memories of this man, and of this day, on Bonaire.

Forty-Two

During her previous visits to Bonaire, Lyle became accustomed to a killer schedule. Most days, her alarm went off well before the sun rose. She and her friends entered the water pre-coffee. They finished their first dive just as sunlight began to bathe the island. A hearty breakfast was a must before leaving the resort for a day of scuba diving. Heavy equipment, irritating salt and sand, and negotiating tricky dive site entrances made for full and tiring days.

Vacationing with Grey was different. How funny it felt to sleep in and wake at her leisure. They hadn't set an alarm since leaving North Carolina. She wasn't sure if he was trying to facilitate her mental healing, or if he simply craved a relaxing vacation as much as she did. They didn't follow any agenda—they were in no rush to get out of bed in the morning.

She stretched and eased her body into the new day. She felt sun-rays pushing at the edges of the curtains. They had removed the blanket and comforter sometime during the night. She was never cold with Grey. He kept her warm in and out of bed.

His curls laid haphazardly about the pillow, so soft and shiny, it was as though he had feathers of his own. He slept on his back, arms thrown over his head. With his elbows bent, he looked trapped by the nearness of the headboard. She couldn't resist his flawless complexion and slightly parted mouth. She placed a gentle kiss on his lips then laid her head on his shoulder. When she smoothed her palm over his chest, he shifted. She traced the edges of his tattoos with her finger, beginning on his shoulder and working her way down to his waist. This had become a comforting practice for her. Outlining his tattoos, trying to connect them together with imaginary lines from her fingertip. He stirred again, then placed his hand on hers, capturing it and ending the tracing game. His eyes remained closed as he slid her hand further down his torso.

He wanted her to play a new game. She ran her fingers over him, toying with him, teasing him and awakening him fully. He placed his hand on her shoulder and rubbed his thumb back and forth.

Sunlight peeked inside and brightened the room. Outside, the resort was coming to life. Laundry carts rolled past their door. A rapid knock preceded "Housekeeping." The knob turned. Someone pushed the door open only to find the latch had been set, keeping the intruder at bay.

Grey arched his back and held onto the headboard as the door was pulled shut again.

Forty-Three

Breakfast at the resort long ago became Lyle's most anticipated meal. Bon Adventure provided a generous buffet each morning for all their guests. It was served on the covered patio overlooking the docks. With the dive boats tied there, it was always entertaining to watch the crew and excited divers preparing for the day. Klein Bonaire, an uninhabited island offshore, could be seen on the horizon.

The fresh air and sunshine awoke her appetite like nothing else could. The smell of freshly baked croissants, sizzling sausage, and strong brewed coffee put a grin on her face as she entered the dining area. She filled her plate with pancakes bathed in warm maple syrup and strips of bacon. Eyeing the sliced mangos and pineapple, she planned her return visit as they found a table for two. Guests mingled below. Some were hauling their dive gear onto a boat, others jumped in the water from the deck. Lyle wanted to be one of them. The sea life she knew was hidden just below the surface called to her. She reminded herself she would be diving soon, when Michael arrived.

"What do you think about snorkeling?" She sank the side of her fork into the stack of pancakes. "The water's so clear here, we'll be able to see a lot from the surface. We can borrow a mask and snorkel from the dive shop if you're interested."

"That sounds like fun, but I might need a lesson. I tried it once as a kid. I was in the shallow end of the county pool. There wasn't much risk of floating out to sea or being eaten by a shark."

"You'll do fine, it's easy. I'm sure you'll catch on quickly." She put a week's worth of pancakes in her mouth. She wiped maple syrup from her chin and took a sip of hot coffee. Her eyes closed when she swallowed the deliciousness. She took a second drink, washing the mouthful down. "With just a few small items we simply float along the top. No cumbersome equipment to contend with." She stood. "I'm going back for fruit. Can I get you anything?"

"I'd love some of those mangos."

She returned with a heaping plate and took her seat. Under the table, an unseen dalmatian pawed at her thigh. Lyle lifted the tablecloth. Dark eyes and a wet nose looked up at her. The dog was so excited her tail seemed to wag her entire body. Lyle's voice went up an octave: "Hi Calypso." She looked into the dog's kind face and gave a scratch behind the ears. She spoke to the canine in a baby's voice: "How are you, girl? I'm so happy to see you again." Never far apart, Lyle searched the patio for Calypso's owner.

She spotted Captain Maartin, who ran the resort's dive operations, standing at the coffee urn. Though in his late fifties, he already had deep wrinkles on his face, no doubt the effects of constant sun and wind exposure. Silver hairs peppered his shaggy beard, but his eyes still sparkled like a child's. He looked for Calypso and spotted his dog at Lyle's table.

"Goedemorgen, Lyle," said the captain. "Welcome back to Bonaire." His accent was fading, but he never failed to greet the guests in his native Dutch. "And with a new companion, I see." He extended his hand to Grey, who stood, and they shook.

"Captain Maartin, I'd like you to meet Grey Locklear," she said. "Grey, this is Captain Maartin. The captain's in charge of all scuba diving at the resort. Bon Adventure wouldn't be the same without him."

"You're too kind. We all know it's the island that's the true gift. We're all privileged to be part of it."

"It's nice to meet you, Captain," said Grey.

"I'll see you both on *Mi Dushi*." He looked at Lyle. "This is good. You needed a change."

She flushed and gazed into her coffee mug. After spending time with Lyle and Michael during their last visit, Captain Maartin made it clear he didn't think Michael was a good fit for her. Perhaps he had seen the inappropriateness of their relationship. She couldn't know for sure.

"I'm afraid I'm not a diver," Grey said, taking his seat, "but we've been exploring your island by land and really enjoying it."

"We've already visited the flamingo reserve," she said, "and got a history lesson and tour of the slave huts. Next, we plan to get in the water and do some snorkeling."

"Ahh, wonderful," said the captain. "Grey, you'll do fine with Lyle as your guide. Our island is known for the reefs surrounding her, not everyone knows that Bonaire has many magical places on land too. Be sure to book a tour of the caves while you're here."

Grey spread soft butter on his toast as Captain Maartin spoke quietly to Lyle. "When you were here last," he said, "we found a body on the northern end of the island, at Karpata. We tried to keep the location quiet, but this is a small island and news travels like a fast train—bad news, like a bullet."

Lyle pictured the blond-haired man's face looking back at her from the article she had read.

"We've not solved it yet," he said. "But the police found a clue at the crime scene that could tell them who the murderer is."

Lyle's stomach turned as the captain continued.

"They are a patient lot, our police officers. They continue to question people of interest. The list is extensive, but they'll get through it."

"It's in everyone's best interest to see that the murderer is caught," said Lyle.

Captain Maartin patted his leg and Calypso came out from under the table. "Enjoy your stay. If you want to dive, Lyle, come on board *Mi Dushi*. We can find a partner for you." He left the patio with his dog by his side.

Forty-Four

The resort provided the guests with white dual cab pickups to easily get around. They were roomy enough to carry four passengers in the cab and all their dive gear and air cylinders in the bed. The vehicle felt like a living room with just Lyle and Grey inside. They traveled over the narrow island roads, following the directions the man at the reception desk had written down for them. The day was still pleasantly mild, with rare clouds scattered in the sky.

They found the tour company and were introduced to their guide, Marco, who would accompany them through the system of caves. He placed a heavy canvas backpack in his Jeep as Lyle and Grey climbed into the back seat.

Once outside of town, he veered off the main road onto a dirt path. The Jeep crept over the rough terrain, making slow progress. Grey held Lyle's hand as they bounced against their unforgiving lap and shoulder restraints that effectively held them in place.

Marco glanced at them in the rearview mirror with childlike excitement on his face. "Are you ready for an adventure? Today you will walk, crawl, swim, and hike. This is the all-inclusive tour." He winked. "There are over four hundred caves on Bonaire. Some are dry, others are completely flooded. If you're divers, you can access the underwater caves, but I do recommend having a guide go with you. We hate to lose the tourists," he said with a spirited grin.

They came to a stop at a random location that seemed to be the middle of nowhere. Small cactus dotted the sandy earth from one horizon to the other. After exiting the Jeep, Marco handed them each a green, military-style canteen, with a crossbody nylon strap. They were full of icy-cold water. The clouds had passed, and now the sun beat down on them.

He hefted the backpack onto his shoulders. "We'll start with the hiking." There was a rise in the landscape a distance away. He nodded toward the incline. "It's not too far, just over a mile or so, but the temperature is climbing. We'll take it slow." With Lyle and Grey behind him, he followed a faint trail worn into the earth. It weaved between rocks, brush and prickly plants just the right height to leave scratches on their shins as they trekked by.

The central region of the island was quiet as a dead man. The quasi-desert landscape was a surprising change from the plush tropical surroundings they were used to. Sandy rich earth tones underfoot, pale green cactus and scattered stones combined to create nature's sandbox. The hikers disturbed two mature-sized iguanas who scurried out from behind a large boulder a few yards ahead of them, desperate to flee from the upright dangers approaching.

Something shiny near her foot caught Lyle's attention. "Marco, take a look at this." She pointed to a tiny reptile basking on a rock in the sun. "What is this little guy?"

"You have a good eye," he said. "That's a silver snake. It's the only snake species on Bonaire."

"Is that a juvenile?" asked Grey.

"No, an adult. The silver snake only grows to a few inches long. It feeds mostly on insects."

The animal slithered off the rock and disappeared into the sand. They continued their hike, getting closer to the hilly area Marco had pointed out as their destination.

As suggested by the tour company, Lyle wore her bathing suit under her shorts and shirt. After walking over a mile, she was covered in sweat and wondered if someone had mistakenly misled her with the advice. She felt ridiculous, there wasn't a drop of water in site. They arrived at the intended area and Marco stopped. Removing the backpack's shoulder straps, he let it slide down the length of him until it hit the ground with a heavy thump. It landed next to a rickety fence-like structure that was flat on the ground.

"We made it. Have some water before we head in," said Marco.

Confused, Lyle scanned the barren landscape. Looking around them, a sudden awareness hit her. "This is the cave?" She pointed to a three-foot crevice in the ground covered by the worn barrier. Peering down, she saw only darkness. "This is where we're going exploring? I don't know if I can do this. It looks very tight. Honestly, I was picturing a big opening where we could mosey on in."

"Captain Maartin recommended we go caving," said Grey. "I'm sure it's perfectly safe. Where's that sense of adventure I've always seen in you? Surely you didn't think a day of spelunking was going to be a walk in the park."

Marco removed long ropes and heavy carabiners from his bag. "Give me a hand with this, will you?" All three grabbed ahold of the barrier and slid it off the cave's opening. "We've set permanent bolts into the side of the entrance. We'll use them to rappel down." Grey helped him as he organized and then dropped several lines into the cave, securing them as he worked. Satisfied with his rigging, he asked, "Who wants to go first?"

Lyle didn't remember volunteering, but there she stood with a harness snug around her hips and a bright yellow caving helmet with an attached headlamp. Grey helped her put on elbow and knee pads and wiggled them into place. A sturdy pair of leather gloves had seen better days, but she gladly slid her hands into them. Grey then donned his own equipment and, once secure, strapped on his headgear.

"I think you're ready," said Marco. He flipped on her headlamp and clipped a sturdy flashlight to her. "You'll descend through a shaft-like space through the rock for about ten feet. Once you've cleared it, the cavern will open up. Then you're nearly there. I've got you all roped in. I'm going to have you turn around and step backward into the entrance. There's a rock shelf just out of sight that I want you to stand on."

She caught Grey smiling at her. "You look very smug for someone who gets to go next."

"Turn the lights on for me," he said. "I'll be right behind you."

"See you down under." She knelt and shuffled backward toward the mouth of the cave. Cool air rose from its depths. Scooting on her belly, she lowered herself and stood on the unseen stone ledge.

"Hold on to this orange cord," Marco explained. "You're going to sit back into the harness and then feed the line upward in order to move down."

"Sit back?" she asked, unsure.

"You're all rigged in," he said. "The ropes and harness will catch you. Once you begin to descend, stick your legs out and walk backward down into the cave." He pinched the bright line between his fingers and wiggled it. "Remember, it's the orange rope."

She was soon descending through the tubelike cavity. "I'm rappelling into the great abyss and no one's even holding a gun to my head." When she realized they couldn't hear her she yelled upward, "I'm entering a black hole!" Her voice echoed off the wall and boomed around her. She looked below, the site of her orange rope disappearing into the pure blackness was unnerving, so she concentrated on just her hands. Goosebumps formed as the cool air blew up past her. The headlamp provided only a narrow beam of light. She spoke out loud to herself: "I really hope there isn't anything down there waiting for me."

She finally made it through the narrow tube. Turning her head, the helmet's light revealed an expansive cavern. Gaining confidence in the rig that held her, she relaxed her death grip on the line. She again hollered toward the narrow opening above her, "I can hear running water!"

After descending another twenty feet, her soles hit the ground. She immediately found, then switched on, the heavy flashlight Marco had clipped to her. She turned in tight circles, illuminating the otherwise pitch-black cave. As instructed, she unfastened herself from the lines and, aiming her light up at the entry point, yelled, "I'm in! Marco, I'm in!" Her voice thundered, and she heard a beating of wings in the darkness. "Bats. Of course."

Forty-Five

Once Grey and Marco joined her at the base of the cave, they began their exploration.

"We'll advance slowly," Marco said. "Watch your every step, and please be mindful of the formations. These stalactites and stalagmites took thousands of years to form. We don't want to damage anything. Follow me closely. I know the clearest path."

He turned and aimed his flashlight deep into the blackness. The going was slow. The cave narrowed, the group ducked their heads and then crouched and duck-walked to pass through. Dripping water echoed throughout the damp cave as they advanced.

"Hanging above us are stalactites formed by drops of water carrying minerals over thousands of years. They are quite hollow and brittle."

They looked like icicles hanging off a roof in winter. They were solid white but porous, resembling bone more so than rock. Drops fell continually from them, keeping the cave's floor slick.

With his flashlight, Marco pointed out the same type of formation growing upward from the floor of the cave. "These stalagmites, or cave mountains, have formed from where the drops of water have landed, depositing elements over a great period of time."

"This is beautiful." Lyle thought, *Michael would love this.*

As the passageway became too narrow to stand, they crawled forward on hands and knees, thankful for their protective pads. Their lower legs were exposed and would later show the sacrifices of inching across the cave floor. Their helmets shielded them as they inadvertently hit their heads. Darkness followed like an unwanted companion as they progressed deeper into the cavern.

Lyle was relieved when the tight space opened up and they were able to stand again. They took a short break and drank more water.

"You two are doing great," said Marco. "How do you like the tour so far?"

"This is really something," said Grey. "We have caves back home but they're pretty dry and the quarters aren't so tight."

"It's all a little intimidating at first," said Lyle. "But I think I'm getting used to the lack of light and the unforgiving surface. Although my legs may never be the same again." She ran a hand over her scratched calf. "It's so quiet down here, and we're out in the middle of nowhere. It's hard to imagine anyone finding this place."

"Oh, but find the caves they did," Marco said. "For centuries, humankind has used caves. Research tells us that they were crucial for mankind's survival. Not just on Bonaire, but on most continents. They've been used for housing, shelter in a storm, storage." He pointed to his ear. "You can hear the stream we'll soon be getting to. The caves were a reliable source of water and food." He screwed the top of his canteen on tight. "Follow me, I'll show you some artwork."

They were able to stand more upright, but Grey's height was a real difficulty and he had to walk hunched down.

"You're going to need some aspirin when we get back, and maybe a massage," she said.

"I assume my ancestors used caves the way Marco described." He shook his head. "I can't imagine how. This helmet is taking a real beating for me."

They came to the area Marco was most excited to show them: ancient artwork on the wall and extending up onto the ceiling. He shone his flashlight on the images. "We believe these drawings were left here by the native people of Bonaire. The Arawak Indians most likely settled here over a thousand years ago. Archeologists deduced they used pigment from the dyewood tree to create these reddish-brown designs."

Crosshatches and random dotted spirals filled the cavern wall. Some were clearly fish, but most were impossible to interpret. Lyle lifted her hand, readying to trace the images on the wall with her index finger.

"We ask that you not touch the petroglyphs. They're very fragile."

"Oh, of course," she said, quickly snatching her hand away. "I'm sorry. I wasn't thinking."

"Arawak Indians?" Grey asked. "Are their descendants living on the island?"

"I'm afraid not. When early settlers founded Bonaire in 1499, they all but eliminated the Arawak tribe. The few who survived emigrated off the island."

"Bastards."

"As I promised you earlier, you have hiked, walked, and crawled. Now you get to swim and relax."

"Swim?" Lyle gestured at the surrounding stone.

"Follow me," Marco said. "I know a place."

Forty-Six

They advanced deeper into the darkness relying solely on their flashlights to show them the way. The sound of running water grew closer. Marco stopped and shone his beam over a still, black pool. Droplets fell from the stalactites hanging overhead.

Three lights lit up the area. Shining one directly into the water revealed a perfectly smooth surface and wonderfully clear view to the rock bottom.

"Those flashlights are waterproof so feel free to take them in with you," said Marco.

Grey and Lyle sat on the stone and unfastened their elbow and knee pads.

She pulled off her heavy walking shoes and socks. Rubbing her tired feet, she circled her foot, stretching out her stiff ankles. They placed their helmets on the edge of the pool.

"This is crazy, but I can't say no," Grey said, removing his shirt and shoes.

She placed her clothes and sneakers in a pile and stood in her turquoise one-piece bathing suit. "I can't believe we're doing this. Swimming in a cave in complete darkness—totally wild." She asked Marco: "Is there any sea life we should worry about?"

"You'll see crayfish, maybe small feeder fish, nothing too exciting." He removed his helmet. Sitting down on the cool stone, he leaned back against the cave wall. "The best thing about the swim is the refreshing temperature. Your muscles will thank you. This is your chance to stretch out after trekking through these cramped quarters." He flashed his light toward the back corner of the pool where a shadow could be seen looming under the surface. "About five feet down there's a swim-through. It's not too long—ten feet, maybe twelve. You'll surface just on the other side of this wall into a tiny, magical cavern. We call it Vogelkooi, Birdcage. It's perfectly round. You'll be surrounded by sta-lagmites reaching for the sky." He laid his head back and turned off his flashlight. "Take all the time you'd like. I'm going to rest here."

They sat on the edge of the pool with their feet dangling in the wa-ter. Unseen, Lyle lightly tickled the hair at the side of Grey's neck with the tip of her finger. He swatted at the air, and once he settled, she did it again and got the same irritated reaction. He swiped a third time at the tiresome insect. But as she pushed her luck, he grabbed her hand.

"Caught you, you big pest." He grabbed her by her waist. "In you go!"

"No! No! Don't throw me in! I'm sorry," she said, in a fit of giggles. "I won't do it again."

He let her go but put his massive hand on the top of her head and thoroughly mussed up her helmet hair.

"Marco's right," she said, swirling her legs around, "this feels amaz-ing." She aimed her light at the bottom. "I don't see any fish, just rock."

They positioned their flashlights to shine across the surface. Grey slipped into the pool and Lyle followed. The clear, refreshing water was their trophy at the end of a marathon. It was just what they want-ed and yet they hadn't known they needed it. They swam leisurely in the darkness, taking full advantage of the open space to stretch and relax their tired bodies.

Grey retrieved their flashlights and handed one to Lyle. "Let's find that swim-through." They paddled to the corner where Marco had in-dicated the way. Grey pointed a long beam of light through the water below them. They could just make out a shaded area in the rock.

"That must be it," he said. "Ready?"

"You gotta love a new adventure. It'll be a little like cave diving, only we don't have any extra air, just what's in our lungs." Lyle spoke over her shoulder: "Marco, are you sure this is safe?"

They couldn't see him in the pitch black, but his voice echoed off the rock. "Take a big breath and use your hands to pull you through. Kick your legs like you want to live another day." He grinned.

"Thanks for that, Marco," said Grey, unsmiling.

Both nervous and excited to be facing the unknown, they drew in full breaths of air and descended. Using their flashlights to guide them and feeling the rock with their hands, they found the underwater opening. Lyle swam in first with Grey following her. The passageway, although only a few feet high, was several feet wide. They grabbed rock after rock as they pulled themselves through the underwater tunnel.

Lyle wasn't prepared for the current pushing against her. Each handful of stone was fraught with the current trying to drive her backward. Kicking her legs, she only managed to bang up her feet and toes. She thought she was making progress, but the end was nowhere in sight. She grabbed a rock and pulled, but her hand slipped off and she was driven backward, slamming into Grey. Her lungs screamed, and she struggled to hold her breath. She reflexively began to exhale and watched as the bubbles became trapped under the rock just inches above her head. She frantically reached in front of her and pulled herself forward again. She fought the natural impulse to inhale, all she could think about was taking a deep breath. More air escaped her nose, but this time they floated up beyond the rock. She'd made it to the end of the tunnel. With a strong kick she followed the rising bubbles, broke the surface of the water, and sucked in a lungful. Grey was right behind her. They found the edge of the pool and grabbed on while they pumped air in and out through their mouths.

"We did it," Grey huffed.

"Not as easy as I'd hoped. I wasn't expecting a current." Her voice echoed around them. "But we made it."

"If you'd asked me what we'd be doing on Bonaire, I never would've guessed this," said Grey.

They took a moment to rest, then shone their lights around the rock chamber and examined the tiny cave. Smooth, shining white stalagmites jutted up from the ledge, creating a fence around the pool. From above, stalactites fell and stopped within mere inches of their counterparts. Several of the formations were touching, creating solid columns of snowy bleached stone. Beyond the barrier, a narrow waterfall trickled down the cavern wall, its origin hidden in the blackness above them. They were two canaries trapped inside a sparkling white birdcage.

"That explains the strong current," Lyle said, while admiring the cascade. "There's a lot of water moving through this cave system."

He took her flashlight then snugged both between two rock pillars. The narrow beams did little to cut through the darkness.

They floated on their backs, looking up into the void. Although impossible to see anything, the fluttering of bat wings could be heard high above. Water dripped down the bleached stalactites hanging precariously overhead. Drops fell onto Lyle's face and splashed in her mouth. It had a tangy metallic taste, not the salty brine she would expect.

A swarm of bugs were attracted to the flashlights and soon, a colony of hungry bats came to feast. The fearless animals dove down, fluttered over the surface of the water, caught their dinner, and flapped clumsily upward, disappearing into the highest reaches.

"Crocodile, come with me." Grey took her hand and guided her to the edge of the pool where they could stand. He whispered, "I thought we would take advantage of this time alone. We'll need to be quiet." He grinned. "I don't want us echoing off the walls."

He switched off the lights and the cavern went pitch-black. He removed his shorts and placed them on the rock edge. "I can't see a thing." He slid her suit off her shoulders, then lower, releasing her breasts. "But I have a good imagination." He pushed it over her hips and down her legs then threw it onto his. He lifted her and held her in front of him.

She wrapped her legs around his waist and held his shoulders. They moved carefully but the water around them began to splash. He pulled her closer and soon, the two were struggling to be silent and fighting to keep the water still. She shifted herself higher and closer to him, resting her forehead on his chest. Bat wings fluttered above them. She threw her head back and felt drips pelting her face. She gasped and her body trembled.

Deep panting, beating wings and dripping water. So much noise in this quiet place.

Forty-Seven

"I had fun today," said Grey. "Thanks for the snorkeling lesson. I felt like I was swimming in an aquarium. I can't believe how many types of fish we saw, and damn Lyle, you knew them all."

"I'm so glad you liked it," she said. "Some people find snorkeling claustrophobic, but after the tight cave exploration yesterday, I didn't think it would be a problem for you. Besides, we needed time to recover from all that hiking. Don't get me wrong, the cavern was beautiful. It's just that my legs may never be the same again. The salt water should help heal our scratched-up calves."

"An easy snorkel and a shopping trip into town was just enough for today," he said. "I really do feel recharged."

She sipped her cocktail and licked the salt from her lower lip. "The reefs here start at really shallow depths. When the sun is shining, the coral and fish look so vibrant."

"What's up with that purple lobster we saw? It looked like it was missing a leg."

"That was a spiny lobster. They don't have the large claws you're used to seeing on your dinner plate."

His cell buzzed. He took it from his pocket and glanced at the screen. "Damn Hendrix. Can't he leave me alone while I'm on vacation? I should take this." He touched the screen. "Hey Hendrix, what's up?" He listened and mouthed "sorry" to her as she circled the rim of her margarita with her finger. She put the tip in her mouth and sucked the salt off. "I've told you I'm not getting involved. I can't help you. I'm on vacation buddy. I'm hanging up now."

He put his phone away and tapped his finger on the table. "Hendrix is in some kind of trouble again. He's neck deep in shit. You may as well know he's asking me for money to get him out of a jam. If I had it, I'd help him, but I honestly don't have that kind of cash to loan out."

"I hope he isn't putting Crystal's shop at risk."

"He's been dealing drugs for years," he explained. "Probably since he dropped out of high school. I think he might be using the shop as a cover. He's got a bunch of people going in and out of there and not one of them is getting tattooed."

She noticed the usually ultra-cool and calm Grey seemed a little off tonight even before the call from Hendrix. He shifted in his chair and repeatedly checked the time. She knew exactly what was on his mind: Michael would be arriving on the island soon.

"What time does his flight get in?" he asked.

"He's on the last one out of Atlanta."

Stars were beginning to glimmer above them. She wore her new sundress. It had elegant flamingos circling the bodice. Inspired by the birds they saw on the tuk-tuk tour, she bought it earlier in the day at a boutique in Kralendijk, the island's capital. Grey thought it would be fun to match her and bought a piece of clothing for himself. His new short-sleeved shirt was unbuttoned at the collar. His complexion in the bold pink top was stunning, and Lyle noticed several heads turn his way. She knew he had stepped out of his comfort zone. Her heart melted at the site of him in the daring color.

They noticed two women sitting at the bar who had swiveled their stools and repeatedly glanced their way. They spoke to each other quietly then grinned at Grey.

He nodded at the women then shifted again.

"Grey," Lyle said, "I know you told me people have been staring at you your entire life. I understand it's uncomfortable for you. I'm sorry for asking, but do you think maybe it's because you're such an attractive guy? You're right," she added quickly, "you don't blend in. Your looks are exotic in an ink-everywhere, beautiful-mane-of-hair kind of way."

"No, that's not it. I just don't fit in with most folks. Back in high school kids called me Chief Broom. I was Chief Broom until I graduated."

"I'm so sorry. Kids can be cruel. I'm surprised they got the reference. That novel was published forever ago. The movie was made back in the seventies."

"It's old, but a modern classic. Our American lit class studied it our Freshman year."

"I remember reading that book," she explained. "Kesey talked about mental illness in a whole new way. If you're Chief Bromden—or Broom, as he was nicknamed—who am I?" She became animated. "I mean, really, Grey, I see people who aren't there." She giggled. "One could make a compelling argument that I should be the one locked up with Nurse Ratched."

"I'm glad we're able to find the humor in all of this." He laughed at the absurdity.

"Look at that—a full smile! I rarely see one from you. I usually only get a grin."

A server brought their dinners. He cut into his bloody porterhouse steak. Dipping the rare beef into a butter-soaked pile of mashed potatoes, he then put it in his mouth. He chewed and took a sip of his pinot noir. Lyle had ordered a dozen oysters on the half shell. The sizeable treats were served on a bed of crushed ice. She smelled the salty brine as soon as the delicacy was placed in front of her. Her mouth watered as she squeezed a single drop of lemon on each one.

While they ate, the breeze caught her hair and blew strands into her face. Her fingers were covered in lemon juice, so she tried to push the locks back with her arm.

"I got you." He tucked her hair behind her ear.

They finished their meals and ordered decaf and pecan pie. The dessert was made with melted chocolate and a splash of sweet Kentucky bourbon. The resort served it warm with a scoop of vanilla bean ice cream nestled beside it. When their plates were empty, and Lyle had all but licked hers clean, they finished their coffees.

Her phone buzzed.

Michael: *Meet me @ our beach.*

She looked at Grey and whispered, "I've got to go."

"I don't like this," he growled. "I don't think he's good for you."

"You haven't met him yet," she said, standing. "I thought we—"

"I know, I agreed. I have to trust that you'll recognize what's best for you." He fell back in his chair, nodded once, then watched her walk away from him.

Forty-Eight

Lyle couldn't remember ever driving down the southern road so late at night. She feared she would completely miss her destination. Angel City had long ago become her favorite site on the island. The fish were abundant, and often times, a curious French angel would join her on her dive, following along until deciding it had had enough of her company.

During her last trip here, she introduced Michael to Angel City, and it had become a magical place for them both. It was there, more than anywhere else, they fell in love. Michael saw his first green moray, and later in the week, he'd found her favorite fish, the juvenile yellow-tail damselfish, swimming among the coral there.

She slowed the truck to more closely search the side of the road. Just as she knew she was getting close, the headlights flashed across a yellow painted rock that read, *Angel City*. Her heart raced as she pulled in and crept over the white coral. Her high beams lit up the ocean. She parked and killed the engine. Once she climbed out, she saw him. Just a silhouette, but she knew it was him. Michael, strolling along the shore, shoes in hand, jeans soaked around the ankles. She regarded her lover, her friend. His hair whipped around his face and his shirt rippled in the strong onshore breeze. She closed the door with a thud.

He stopped pacing and waited for her to come to him. He could barely see her in the darkness. The outline of her body just a promise as she hesitated near her truck. It had been so long since they'd been together. She had fought through so many changes since they last touched. He craved her, but he didn't want to rush her now. He remained by the shoreline, salt water swirling around his ankles.

She took a step toward him then stopped. Why was she holding her breath? With her exhalation, she freed herself from reluctance and her body tingled with anticipation. She slid her sundress over her head and left the pretty flamingos on the truck's hood.

Michael watched her toss her dress and every bone in his body wanted to run to her, grab her, and take her there and then. *Why was she moving so slowly?* He watched as her hair blew about her neck and shoulders and she tried to pin it behind her ears. He watched as she hooked her thumbs into her panties and slid them down over her hips, leaving them by her feet. He was getting tired of watching.

The breeze felt like a whisper dancing over her body. It tickled the sensitive skin of her breasts and cooled her shoulders and between her legs.

As she approached, he pitched his shoes to the coral and unbuttoned his shirt, letting the wind carry it away. He removed his jeans, tossed them aside, and stood naked at the water's edge. Building waves sent ocean water rushing over his feet then pulled back out to sea.

She stood before him, remembering his eyes and face and the way he looked at her. She put her hand on his jawline and felt the day-old stubble she knew would be there. She combed her fingers through his always unruly hair then placed her palms on his chest, recalling the feel of him.

It took all of his willpower to be patient and not pull her to him. He waited as she touched him, tantalizing him like no other could. He held her face in his palm and ran his thumb over her lips. Dropping his gaze, he touched her breast, then pushed her hair aside and nuzzled his nose in her neck, deeply breathing in the scent of her.

His breath gasping on her skin, the heat and moisture stirring her, she rolled her head to the side. He kissed her neck, tasting the saltiness he found there. The surf crashed behind them as he pulled her tightly to him. How long had it been? Weeks, months, years? At this moment he was sure an eternity had passed.

She collapsed to her knees and he fell down on his. She raked her fingers through his hair as he found her lips with his. He laid her back and salt water swirled around her. She too had hungered for this magical moment. They were finally together again. They made love in the sand as waves washed around them and each sought the pleasure they'd been dreaming of for far too long.

"Fucking finally," he huffed.

Forty-Nine

After their sweet reunion at Angel City, she and Michael returned to his room. Covered in salty ocean water, they showered together and then climbed into crisp sheets. Although they communicated most every day, still, they had a lot of catching up to do.

As they talked, she straightaway noticed a change in him. The once boastful and overly self-confident star was subdued. She wanted to bring up the death of the blond-haired man. She needed to know if he had any part in it. But their reunion night wasn't the time. Tonight, they would embrace and make love and pretend, now that they were together, all was right with the world. Though they'd only known each other a short while before they had had to say goodbye, they had amassed a rich history. They would have plenty of time to talk about the murder that took place on Bonaire. She was sure he would have some feasible answers and would easily explain that the crime had nothing to do with him.

They talked for hours before sleep finally took them.

———◆———

The feather pillow hugged her, and the sheets rippled from the breeze drifting in through the sliding glass doors of the balcony. Lyle stirred, alone in bed. It was quiet, and she had a sense the sun had risen long ago. She squinted and pushed her arms and legs against the sheets.

"Good morning, baby. I didn't think you'd ever wake up," said Michael.

Her heart burst with love for the man standing next to her. His hazel eyes were as bright as she remembered. His hair was longer with dark highlights for the character he was playing. He rarely shaved on vacation, and she knew the shadow on his face would only darken with time.

"Maybe your fans won't recognize you so easily with the new hair color," she said, her voice scratchy with sleep.

"I'm afraid they found me at the airport yesterday. I was hardly on the island fifteen minutes."

"Damn," she said, deflated.

"At last, I can see you in daylight." He pulled the sheets off her and climbed on the bed. "Just as beautiful as ever. I almost forgot your eyes. They're sparkling at me this morning. I wonder why."

He trailed his hand down to her hips and over her thighs. He rolled onto her and nuzzled his nose under her ear, taking a deep breath.

He kissed her neck, his lips moist, and with an uncontrollable urge, he nipped the sensitive skin under her jaw.

Pinned under his weight, she placed her hands on his shoulders and spoke quietly in his ear. "I love you, Michael."

"Lyle," he said, his body going weak. He began to sob.

Fifty

At their table, Michael pulled the brim of his baseball hat down to block the encroaching sun. Their empty breakfast plates had been whisked away. A scattering of crumbs dotted the white tablecloth. Three yellow Gerbera daisies in a glass vase offered them a bit of cheer, tempering the tense atmosphere. Resort guests could be heard on the deck below, their excited voices trailing off with the breeze.

Lyle slid her sunglasses from the top of her head to the bridge of her nose. They had discussed this meeting a million times. There was nothing left to say, so they sat quietly while they awaited his arrival. Michael drummed his fingers incessantly on the table. The constant beat he played elevated the tension and irritated her to no end. She glanced at the time on her phone. A minute later, she checked again.

"Are you sure this is a good idea?" he questioned for the third time.

"No. I'm not sure. Please stop asking me that. This could totally blow up in my face."

"It's not *you* I'm worried about. Should I have a backup plan? I mean, in case this goes south and I need to get out of here fast?"

"Backup plan? Like in a movie? No, there's no backup plan. Let's just see how this plays out."

She felt him before she saw him; there was something in the air. The other diners stirred. Or was that only in her imagination? She and Michael turned at the same time. She sensed that the entire restaurant was looking too.

There stood Grey.

No longer in the pink shirt he had worn the previous night, he was once again dressed in all black, as she knew he would be. Not even a pair of shorts—jeans and heavy leather boots. He raised his chin and scanned the crowd, searching for Lyle. He was a grizzly bear on its hind legs hoping to appear even bigger. The effort was working.

"Holy shit. Is that him?" Michael looked from Lyle back to Grey. "I definitely need a getaway plan." He peered over the railing and judged the distance to the deck below. If he had to jump, he might walk away with a bruise or two, or he may not walk away at all. "Maybe we should do this later. Tomorrow might be a better time."

"It's going to be fine." She raised her hand and caught Grey's attention. "It has to be fine," she added through gritted teeth.

Like smoke filling a room, Grey billowed through the dining area. Darkness crept between the white tablecloths and yellow flowers. The bright sapphire sky and the sparkling blue ocean seemed more brilliant next to him. He moved forward and the rest of the world stood still.

Now at their table, he stopped and stood in silence. He looked from Michael to Lyle and back again. He bent down and touched her cheek then lifted her jaw and kissed her deeply.

"Good morning," he said. "I missed you last night." He shot a deadly warning at Michael who seemed to shrink into his chair.

She put her sunglasses on the table and plastered a huge grin on her face. "Grey Locklear, this is Michael Miller. Michael, this is Grey."

As Michael stood, his chair squeaked on the tile floor. He craned his neck and squinted up at the massive man. He extended his hand. "I've heard a lot about you."

"I'm sure you have."

Grey gripped Michael like a vise and they shook.

"You have a lot of nerve coming here," said Grey. He released his hand and took a seat.

"Nerve has nothing to do with it. Lyle wants me here, so I came." Michael sat back down.

"You abandoned her when she needed support, but here you are, free as a bird when it comes time to go on vacation."

"Buddy, you are way off base. You have no idea—"

"Michael, please. Let's not start like this." Lyle's grin faltered.

"Mr. Hollywood conveniently has a movie to make when you need him, but he's easily able to show up on Bonaire."

"Grey," she warned.

Michael's voice shot up an octave: "You know nothing about me." Realizing he was attracting attention, he adjusted his hat then slumped back in his chair.

"Guys, please."

"Do you even know what she's been going through?" asked Grey. "All the hard work she's doing trying to get better?"

"Guys." Her voice was now stern.

"Yes, I do. I've been with her a lot longer than you have, dumb ass. I know exactly what she's been through, and I've been more than supportive of her."

Grey glared at him. He was done talking.

"Okay, take a breath and let's all try and relax," said Lyle. "You're here to meet each other not to pick a fight. This is no place for a rumble."

"But he said—"

"Now guys," she interrupted, "listen to me. Neither one of you is right nor wrong—"

"He can't just come in here and—"

"Let's see if maybe we can just start over." They resigned and heard her out. "The fact is, you've both been instrumental in my recovery. Michael, you were with me during the crazy days," she said, with a wince of anguish. "I was hallucinating, but you never judged me. You saw me through rose-colored glasses. You loved me despite knowing the truth."

"Grey, you knew I was struggling right from the start. You recognized my reason for getting the tattoo was delusional. My thoughts were irrational and yet you chose to go on this journey with me. You helped me come out the other side."

She took each of their hands in hers. "I love you. Both of you. Because of some wild coincidences, the two of you are joined, through me. I know neither of you asked for this and I'm sorry, but here we are. I can't pick one or the other. Please don't ask me to. It would kill me to lose either of you."

The table was silent. She stood and put her hand on Grey's shoulder. "Let me get you coffee and breakfast. I'll give you guys a minute to talk. Where we go from here is up to the two of you." She left the table, leaving them dangerously unsupervised.

"Shit."

"Fuck."

"I really ought to toss you over that railing and hope you land on your head. Problem solved," said Grey.

"There are literally dozens of witnesses here, dumb ass. But maybe prison suits you, you look like someone who's done hard time."

They refused to look at each other and instead watched Lyle as she dawdled back and forth along the buffet.

"We can't undo what she's done," said Grey. "I mean, her healing, her progress. I won't stress her out when she's come so far, not over this. We can't pressure her into choosing. She obviously needs us both right now."

"I agree. When she's ready she'll decide," said Michael. "I just hope you won't be too broken up over getting dumped by *my* girlfriend."

"What are you doing on Bonaire? I know who you are. The famous Michael Miller. Lyle tells me you're dating a model and yet, here you are. Why did you come?"

"Because I love her," he said. "I need her and she needs me. Since we can't be together full time we have an understanding, which, quite frankly, sitting here with you has me questioning its logic."

While strolling through the line Lyle stole glances at the table. She hoped it was a good sign that they were talking. She returned with a steaming cup of coffee and a plate filled with scrambled eggs, buttery toast, and bacon cooked to a crisp. She put it down in front of Grey.

"Thanks, Crocodile. This looks really good."

Thrown by the nickname, Michael used one of his own. "Baby, I think you should take as much time as you need."

"*We* think. We both agreed," said Grey.

"Romeo here thinks you'll choose him." He winked at her. "Let him dream."

Grey picked up his fork. "Michael, have you ever been windsurfing?"

"No. I haven't had time to try it."

"Good, neither of us will have an unfair advantage. Let's go windsurfing at Lac Bay tomorrow. We'll see which one of us comes out alive and who gets totally pancaked."

"This isn't a competition," she said. "You're simply here to get to know each other."

"No baby, you're wrong. It's definitely a competition," said Michael.

"Windsurfing tomorrow does sound like fun," she said. "But I'm also looking forward to rest and relaxation during this vacation."

"Rest and relaxation?" Michael grimaced at Grey. "What've you done to her?"

"Oh, a whole lot of crazy shit." He lifted one eyebrow and gave a wicked grin. "I've done a bunch of wild stuff to her."

She dropped her head and held it in her hands. At least they were talking.

Fifty-One

After breakfast, Grey begrudgingly changed out of his jeans and put on a pair of cargo shorts and T-shirt. The three now kicked off their sandals and put their water bottles under the bench, out of the hot sun. The resort was quiet this time of day. Most guests were out diving and wouldn't return until afternoon. They had the volleyball court to themselves.

Lyle tossed the ball from hand to hand as she went to the far end of the sand pit. Grey stayed on the opposite side and walked toward the net. Michael joined Grey and stood ten feet behind him.

"What are you doing?" Grey asked, annoyed. "You're teaming up with me? Against Lyle?"

"You've never seen her play. Trust me, Romeo, we need each other."

Grey stood casually near the net, awaiting her serve. Michael, knowing the game would be a challenge, stretched his arms over his head and hopped up and down a few times. He chose his position carefully, preparing for the first serve.

She held the ball and sized up her competition. She knew Grey's bulk would work against him, and Michael was easy to mislead if she feigned the intended direction with her eyes. A sly grin crossed her face as she tossed the ball skyward. As it fell, she hopped up and slammed the heel of her palm into it. The ball soared like a missile over the net and exploded in the sand between them.

"You should've had that. It landed right next to you!" Grey barked.

"No, that one was yours," Michael shot back. "You're playing the net. You should've returned that one."

"Just stay out of my way," Grey said, picking up the ball, then returning it to Lyle.

They were off to a rough start, but she felt certain that if they gave each other a chance, they could end up…okay, maybe not friends, but solid mutual acquaintances. They just needed some time together. She had an idea that would force the self-proclaimed rivals to work as a team.

As the game progressed, she deftly handled the volleyball. Serves traveled like bullets to the opposite side of the net. Most of them hit the sand. Some were returned and the guys found a bit of encouragement. She dashed across the court, easily returning the volleys sent her way. Michael struggled and often ended up on his butt. Grey was powerful but not nimble enough to effectively move through the deep sand.

Lyle had the ball and headed back to the serving position. The guys settled in their spots. Grey forward, nearer the net, Michael covering the space behind him. The ball flew at them and they each lunged for it. Grey tucked his shoulders and power rammed Michael, throwing him backward and landing him on the ground.

"That's for calling me a dumb ass at breakfast." Two volleys later, he did it again. "I seem to remember you using that term twice."

A few plays had past and again Grey hammered Michael into the sand. "And that's for calling me a convict."

"Point taken," Michael said, grimacing.

With the morning sun beating down, the guys fought to stay in the game. Drenched with sweat, their shirts stuck to them like paste and sand clung to their legs. Their muscles cramped with each step, but still, they scrambled to get the ball over the net, neither one willing to give up.

"Game!" Lyle yelled.

"What?" Grey placed his hands on his knees and tried to catch his breath.

"Are you guys even keeping score?" she asked. "That's it. I won."

"Rematch. I call a rematch," Michael puffed half-heartedly.

"Are you sure?" Grey asked him. "She's killing us."

"We can't go down this easy—we'll never hear the end of it. Besides, I think we're finally hitting our stride."

The second game was played in much the same fashion as the first. Lyle was cool and calm, hardly breaking a sweat. Michael and Grey stumbled, missed returns, and fell into the sand. When Grey held out his hand to help Michael to his feet, a glimmer of hope sparked in her.

She sent a volley to the far-left corner, where Michael arrived a second too late. Then she sent the ball to the far-right, where Grey didn't stand a chance. The next two pulled the guys close to the net, then she sent them back again. She went back and forth, near then far, Michael's side, Grey's side, the whole time hiding her smirk.

"Wait a second. Not funny Lyle." Michael picked up the ball. "She's playing us like a couple of dogs." He yelled across the net: "We're taking five. I need some water."

"Take all the time you want," she said. "I'll be right here." She drew her forearms together and bumped the ball over her head never letting it hit the sand.

The guys plopped on the bench and slumped back. Michael found the water bottles and handed one to Grey. They watched Lyle as she continued playing her game. Her tan face glistened from a hint of sweat. Her ponytail danced around her head as she chased the ball across the sand.

"I'd fallen in love with her." Michael mused. "We played badminton here with her friends. Can you imagine? A simple game, but I remember it being one of the best days, because I was with her." She twirled across the court. "Don't let her fool you. She's always looked tough on the outside. Inside is a different story."

"You don't know her anymore."

"You can't say that. You don't know us," he said, irritated. "You understand nothing about our relationship."

"She's as strong as she looks," Grey said. "She's changed. I'll forgive your ignorance—you haven't been around."

"You bastard. Go home to Pearl. We don't want you here."

"She wants me here," said Grey. "I was with her in New York when she knocked on her mother's door and could only stand there, frozen.

I held her at her father's grave while she sobbed like a child. I was there. It was me who helped her through it all and she's stronger for it. You wouldn't understand."

It was all true. Michael couldn't deny it. "I knew her first," he countered.

"No, Hollywood, again, that would be me. I tattooed her months before you ever laid your eyes on her."

Michael shot to his feet, slamming his water bottle to the ground. He grabbed Grey's shirt with one hand and pulled back his other. Grey stood and snatched his cocked fist, stopping the attack.

"Bad idea. Now settle down before you get very hurt." Grey released his hold and Michael shook it off.

"Michael Miller! I can't believe it!" A shrill voice came from behind them and they lowered their hands. "Hey guys, it's Michael Miller!" A pod of young women, all wide eyed and starstruck, approached him. "Michael Miller? I can't believe it!" They all cackled the same phrase over and over.

"Hey there! Good morning, ladies." He struggled to put on a pleasant face.

"Can we get our pictures with you? No one will believe this!" one squealed.

"Of course. I'd love to."

The women bounced up and down and clapped their hands in unison. Their high-pitched squeaks ear-piercing.

Grey sat and watched as each took a turn posing with Michael while another snapped several photos. He'd never seen anything like it. He was a complete stranger to them and yet they acted as though they'd known him for years. He thought it odd that Michael too appeared as though he'd run into a bunch of old friends.

"Sorry for the interruption Romeo," he said to Grey. "Fame, fortune and good looks. You can't compete with that."

"We'll see."

With all the commotion the women hadn't noticed Grey sitting there. But as he stood and slid his shirt off over his head, they fell silent. He tossed his T-shirt to the bench and walked onto the court, revealing the majestic eagle that flew across his shoulders. The women's jaws dropped.

Michael looked from his fans to Grey and back again. "Fuck yes, this could really work out for me."

Fifty-Two

Grey grudgingly offered to get lunch on his own so Lyle and Michael could have time to talk.

They had a nice view of the pool from their out-of-the-way table at the resort's restaurant. An expansive thatched roof covered the diners, providing them with shade.

Guests in colorful bathing suits relaxed in chairs set around the sundeck. Several people sipped cocktails while wading in waist-deep water. Others sat on submerged stools and watched as the bartender created brightly colored frozen drinks. The ear-splitting sound of his blender competed with the upbeat island music playing from hidden speakers.

Michael pulled his hat down low and tried to be inconspicuous. "I never dared to dream that we'd be together again on Bonaire. But here I am, with you. My wish came true."

"You're being sentimental. It's nice," said Lyle.

She looked at the menu then put it aside. She lowered her voice: "Captain Maartin was at breakfast a few days ago. He made a point of mentioning the body they found while we were here last. He seemed to think it was something I should know about. The blond-haired man was Lawrence Brumfield. He was from Michigan."

"That has nothing to do with us," he snapped.

"Only, the captain must think it has *something* to do with us. Why else would he deliberately talk to me about it? He said the police are continuing their investigation. They said he was murdered."

"Why are you telling me all this?" he asked, clearly annoyed.

"Because I think he was trying to warn me. He said they found evidence at the crime scene."

"Wait, slow down. What evidence?"

"I don't know. I didn't ask questions. I didn't want him to think I was interested."

"That was a good idea." He looked out at the pool. "I may be fucked."

"Why do you say that? What's going on?"

"You can't tell anyone—promise me. Not a word." He paused. "My hat. I lost my hat that night."

"Michael, please, start at the beginning. I need to know what happened."

A server arrived at their table.

"I'll have the chef salad and iced tea, please," said Lyle.

"I'll have the same," Michael droned, without ever looking at the options.

"Right away, Mr. Miller." She flashed him a toothy smile before turning to leave.

"From the beginning," Lyle said. "What exactly went on that night? Don't leave anything out."

"It was the night you went to karaoke with your friends," he said, deflated. "I was about to bust a gasket over being left behind, so I went into town looking to burn off steam."

She remembered the day. "We were hiding our affair from my friends. We all dived together that day, and afterward, we played badminton and volleyball together." Once the games ended, one of Lyle's friends claimed that evening as a girls-only event. "You were upset I was going out without you."

"I was furious. With your plans for the evening excluding me, we wouldn't be together that night. I sped out of the resort and stopped at a bar. I thought a few shots would take the edge off, you know, settle me down, but it only got me more fired up. I wanted to spend every minute we had left on the island with you."

"This isn't my fault," she said firmly. "I didn't do this, and I didn't cause it."

"I know, I know. I don't mean to make it sound that way. I'm sorry. I'm not putting this on you. I only want you to understand where my head was that night."

She seemed appeased so he continued. "I was heading back to my truck when I saw the fucker that attacked you in the ladies' room. His face was still black and blue from the first time I beat the shit out of him. He was walking down the street alone." He raked his fingers through his hair. "I offered him a ride. I knew he was staying here, at Bon Adventure."

"Oh, you didn't," she whispered. "You set him up. You planned this ahead of time."

"No! I did not plan anything. I swear to you, Lyle, I never meant for any of this to happen. He had too much to drink and never even noticed when we drove past the resort. He was babbling on about how we should find some hot ass." He dropped his voice. "You have got to promise me you won't breathe a word of this to anyone."

"Of course," she said dismissively.

"No. I mean it. You can't tell anyone, not even Grey. Swear to me," he said with an urgency that worried her.

"I promise, not a word. If you drove past the resort, where did you take him?"

"I went up to Karpata."

"No." Any inkling of hope for a plausible explanation left her. "Captain Maartin told me that's where they were searching for clues. This is really bad." Her soul sank. "You drove Brumfield to the site where his body was later found."

Fifty-Three

"Baby, please, you can't tell anyone I was there. I swear to you I didn't kill Brumfield, but if it gets out that I took him up to Karpata, no one will believe me."

Her heart thumped as she imagined what might have transpired that night.

"We'd dived that site earlier in the week with your friends," he said. "I remembered being told it was deserted up there."

"Here you are!" The cheerful server startled them. "Chef salads and iced teas. May I bring you anything else, Mr. Miller?"

Michael couldn't speak and the bubbly woman aggravated him like a juggler at a funeral.

"This looks wonderful," Lyle choked out. "Thank you."

Dejected, the woman produced one more smile then left them alone.

"Brumfield and I got out of the truck," Michael continued. "I reminded him that he attacked you. I saw the moment he realized who I was—that it was me who left him looking like ground beef at Captain Jack's that night." He ran his hand down his face. "I just started throwing my fists. I got him a bunch of times in the face and gut. He tried to fight back, but he couldn't land a punch. I was way too fast, and he was lit—an easy target. Honestly, Brumfield was so smashed it took the sport out of it for me. He stumbled around and when he finally fell down, I got out of there."

"But Michael, they found him—"

"I know, I know, dead." He took her hands. "I promise you when I left, he was alive. He was sitting on his ass holding his face in his hands. I took off in the truck. I figured he could walk back or hitch a ride once he slept it off. He was alive, Lyle, I promise you. He was breathing when I left him."

She sat quietly regarding the man across from her. The agony on his face stirred something within and she too felt his pain. She knew in that moment that her love for Michael would keep her by his side.

"I believe you," she said. "If you say he was alive, he was."

"Thank you," he said in a breath. "I needed to hear that. You have to be with me on this. The next day, I noticed I was missing my hat. I have no memory of losing it. It stands to reason it fell off during the scuffle at Karpata. If the police found my ball cap and know I was with him, this might go down hard. My ball cap was missing, and the man was found dead. Do you know how hard it's been for me to function day to day with all of this fucked up shit on my mind?"

Their lunches sat untouched in front of them. She drug her fork through the salad moving vegetables around the bowl. Their solemn mood cast a shadow as resort guests nearby splashed in the pool under the bright sun.

"You're far away. What's on your mind?" he asked.

"Nothing, really. I…"

"What is it, Lyle?"

"I was thinking that it would be nice…" She blushed. "Now would be a good time to talk to Dottie. This is just about when she'd show up. I'd tell her the problem and she'd find a way to fix it."

"Baby, I'm sorry. I didn't want to stress you out with this. Fucking Grey. He told me how strong you are now. He doesn't know shit."

"That's not true. I'm so much better. My head is totally clear. I know that Dottie was only an extension of myself. I'm only saying that she's the one I'd talk these things over with. Back then. Not anymore." She picked at her salad with her fork. "I miss her. I know it sounds crazy, but I do."

"She's with you," he said, while stabbing a tomato. "Dottie's been with you all along. Even if you can't see her anymore, she's inside you."

"I guess you're right."

"Baby, I love you. I'd never knowingly do anything to hurt you. It's just that, I've been so stressed out over this. I've never felt so vulnerable. I've always been the one to bang my fists on my chest and yell 'Bring it on!' Now, I feel like my life is in someone else's hands. Both my future and my freedom could be in jeopardy. What if they found my hat? They might already know I was with him that night."

"You didn't kill him," she said. "The evidence will show that. But Michael, if you didn't do it, who did?"

Fifty-Four

After a colorful argument that included grabbing keys, snatching them back, and remotely locking and unlocking the truck's doors over a dozen times, Grey smirked, now sitting in the driver's seat. Michael sulked riding shotgun, and Lyle happily stretched out in the back seat as they traveled toward Lac Bay. The heady smell of salt hung in the air. Leaving the west coast, they turned east and continued on a road crossing the interior of the island. Their view changed from aquamarine ocean and palm trees to sandy, dry terrain dotted with cacti, as they cut across the land.

They approached the east coastline and saw a sign that read, *Breezy Shore at Lac Bay*. Within minutes they were back at the ocean. They parked the truck and walked toward a cluster of one-story buildings. Some were merely sheds with tin roofs. Others were thatched storage areas. The more permanent structures, painted in vibrant shades of fire engine red, turquoise blue, and lemon yellow, housed a dive shop, a restaurant with outdoor seating, and a bar. Huge orange flags snapped in the onshore winds above them, displaying Breezy Shore's logo: a windsurfer in black silhouette.

They strode between the buildings and found an advertisement directing them where to sign in for lessons. Lyle had called ahead and made a reservation. People milled about and could be heard speaking in many different languages, including English with varying accents. The ages of the clientele were just as diverse. A young, free-spirited crowd of twentysomething athletes seemed to blend easily with the older, salt-and-pepper windsurfers. No matter the age, they all moved with a bounce in their step. The energy was high and the excitement in the air swirled around like pixie dust. One thing brought this dissimilar group together: windsurfing.

The three checked in and waited with excitement for their instructor to arrive. Michael stood out of the way and kept his face hidden under the brim of his hat.

"Are you my students today?" asked a tanned woman with an energetic voice. "I'm Estefani." She shook Lyle's hand. "I'm an instructor here at Breezy Shore and I'll be working with you today." She turned to Grey. "Are you ready to fall in love with Lac Bay?" She extended her hand and Lyle noticed the muscles rippling in her arm. She then greeted Michael. "The biggest danger here is never wanting to leave us." Recognition hit her face. "Oh, famous Michael Miller, wonderful." Without skipping a beat, she went on. "You're lucky to be learning here. This location is so favorable, its host to international competitions year-round. Please, come with me."

Estefani wore a 'Breezy Shore' tank top. On the back, in bold letters was the word: *Crew.*

Lyle waited with her while the guys left their shirts, shoes, sunglasses, and hats in a locker area. They then followed her down to the beach. Estefani stood in crystal-clear thigh-high water. The sun bounced off the surface and cast rainbows onto her damp legs.

"Nature is good to us here at Lac Bay," she said. "A sturdy reef protects the bay from the strong seas. The ocean provides onshore winds to fill our sails. And"—she took several steps into the shallow water—"the bay is only a few feet deep, just enough depth to give our boards the lift they need!"

"This is going to be sick!" Grey exclaimed, feeding off her excitement.

Michael held his arm over his forehead and watched the airborne windsurfers speed past. "This area is huge. Those guys are really flying."

"Our lake is over four kilometers across. Once you're out there, it will feel like forty. But as you learn to pick up the pace, you'll be surprised at how soon you reach the other side."

As Estefani gathered equipment, they watched as surfers soared across the lake standing on huge boards. Each person, secured with a harness, controlled their speed and direction by manipulating the attached sail. Once they caught a strong breeze, the board rose above the water and its fin cut the surface like a butcher's knife.

"Is it as easy as they make it look?" Michael asked.

"It can be. The trick is to be a friend with nature—don't fight the wind, just let it carry you. Guide your sail and the powerful breeze will do all the hard work. It will lift you up and take you as far and as fast as you want to go."

"A friend of nature? I totally got this." Grey smirked. "Good luck, Hollywood."

"We live on positive energy here," Estefani said. "This isn't a contest." She motioned for Michael to take the board she was holding.

"Oh, yes it is," Grey said as he grabbed a second board. "Where's Lyle's? We're short one."

"I'm not joining you." She jumped in. "I've made other plans."

"You're not trying it with us?" Michael asked, disappointed.

"No, not today. Remember the rest and relaxation I was talking about?" She motioned toward a shop not far from the shore. A wooden sign read, *Massage by the Sea*. The words were spelled out in seashells. "I made an appointment with the spa when I booked your lessons."

"You're going to miss Hollywood wiping out on his ass all morning."

"My massage is ninety minutes. By the time I'm done you'll both have windsurfing mastered."

The guys turned their attention back to Estefani. "Lesson one is stepping on the board."

Fifty-Five

Lyle willingly followed the heady scent of lavender oil to her happy place. She'd removed her clothes and now lay between crisp cotton sheets. Her massage therapist, Karolina, was a young woman whose English was limited. Lyle explained the type of service she wanted through a translator who worked at the desk.

A privacy fence surrounded the outdoor treatment area. Interwoven palm branches formed a natural cover overhead. A fountain trickled in the corner, babbling water trickling over three leaping dolphins. Warm hands kneaded her skin and worked her tired muscles. Karolina pulled a smooth stone from a bath of steaming water. She inched it down Lyle's back and over her buttocks. The rock melting her like wax tumbling down the side of a flickering candle. Her body turning to Jell-O. The hot stone continued down to her feet, around her heal, up into her arch and finally warming each toe.

Lyle, on the verge of dozing, couldn't stop thinking about Michael. Being with him now was as though they'd never been apart. She'd wondered if the time spent separated would dull their love, but seeing him that first night, alone on the beach, immediately put that worry to rest. Their devotion had grown even stronger in spite of their absence and abstinence.

When she had first made the proposal, Michael had sounded confident at the prospect of meeting Grey. Maybe he thought he would bully and boss her new boyfriend around. Perhaps he planned to make Grey so uncomfortable he would leave Bonaire and go back to Pearl without her.

Michael had tried this with Rick, Lyle's previous boyfriend. He called him names and egged him on until fists flew and the two of them couldn't be in the same room together. She remembered how upset she was the night Michael gave Rick a black eye and bruised rib.

But with Grey, Michael had met his match. Not only physically but emotionally—Grey's easy disposition was hard to rile.

She had been more than a little apprehensive about introducing them. She knew the possibility of losing one of them was great. She thought the probability of losing both of them was even greater. How long could she continue feeling this shame of not committing to one or the other? How could she begin to entertain the idea of choosing between the two men she loved?

Her back popped under the pressure of Karolina's hands.

This entire situation was another problem she would have taken to Dottie. She always knew what to say and what to do. Only now Dottie was gone and Lyle was left to fend for herself. How could it be that she never really existed? Her therapist often reminded Lyle that Dottie was still a part of her. Living in the very fabric of her being. Even Michael had made such a statement. Maybe Dottie would be an inner voice for Lyle, if only she could hear her.

She needed more time.

Grey was the calm in her life she required now. His steadfastness quieted her thoughts. When she was with him, she was home. And home was finally a peaceful, comforting place.

Michael was the excitement she craved. At times he was untamed, and she wanted to explore the wildness in him. He was young and newly wealthy and didn't always see the consequences of his actions. His short fuse led him to irresponsible choices. He needed Lyle—of that she was certain. And she loved to be needed by him.

Yet it was that very impulsiveness that landed him in this precarious situation. His temper frequently got the better of him, but this time it hadn't resulted in just a black eye and bruised rib. This time a man was dead.

How could she leave him when he was going through such uncertainty? She couldn't. She needed more time.

———◆———

After her massage, she dressed and went to the dive shop where she admired a pair of leather sandals. Looking around, she noticed the tourists were the only ones wearing shoes. The employees, in their Breezy Shore T-shirts, all went barefooted. She browsed through the rack of bathing suits settling on a bright orange two-piece with a windsurfer embroidered on the seat. It would forever remind her of the giant orange flags that greeted them as they arrived that morning at Lac Bay.

She carried it through the shop searching for a men's short-sleeved shirt to match it—she knew Grey would be pleased by the gesture—and found just what she was looking for. After another quick trip around the store, she grabbed some men's trunks in the same color and placed all the items at the checkout.

Michael was sure to be jealous, so she continued shopping. There it was: a bright orange ball cap with the same windsurfer on the brim that was on her new bikini. The perfect gift for Michael. She found a sleeveless T-shirt in the same hue as well.

With purchases in hand, she went to the changing room and put on her new suit. She slathered herself with sunscreen and, leaving the guys' gifts in their locker, headed toward the beach. She found a lounge chair by the water and scanned the bay, trying to spot Michael and Grey.

A barefooted server, carrying an empty tray, stopped next to her. "May I bring you something from the bar? Perhaps an iced tea or draft beer?"

"I'd love a diet soda please." She put her arm to her forehead and continued to search for the guys.

"Are you looking for someone?" he asked.

"Yes, my friends are taking a lesson with Estefani."

He looked to the horizon. After just a moment, he pointed. "There's Estefani. She's riding the green sail with the blue dolphin."

Peering in that direction, she spotted the instructor. Sailing along with her were two other boards. "Oh! There they are! Thank you." She relaxed in the chair and watched the antics unfold before her.

They raced each other across the water. She could hear faint voices floating over the surface as they sped along the bay. Challenges and trash talk were being thrown back and forth. They played chicken too, each one heading straight for the other. She peeked between her fingers. "Please guys, don't maim each other. This really isn't worth a trip to the hospital." At the last minute they swerved and reached out to share a high-five.

"Woo hoo!" Michael crowed like a rooster.

"Let's go again!" Grey yelled back at him.

The server returned with her drink. "How're your friends doing? Estefani is one of our most popular coaches. I once saw her get a tiny six-year-old up on the board."

"Really? Well, she's got my friends moving like they've been doing this all their lives." The server left and she sipped her soda and watched as her lovers found a common bond. This day in the sun may not forge a friendship, but for the length of their time on the water, they seemed to have forgotten they were enemies.

Fifty-Six

Lyle sat at a high-top table on the patio of the restaurant. Dressed in a pair of shorts and the pretty new bathing suit top, she swung her bare feet back and forth as she read the menu and waited for the guys. They showered then soon arrived wearing the gifts she had bought them at the dive shop.

"You two look great. We look like triplets." She felt contented, something she had rarely experienced in her life, and couldn't believe her good fortune at being in love with two of the greatest guys on earth.

"Thanks for the hat and shirt, baby," said Michael. "Did you dress us the same so you wouldn't lose us?" He pecked her on the cheek.

"Only for you, Crocodile." Grey kissed Lyle slowly and with passion. "Thanks for my new shirt. I don't think I've ever owned an orange piece of clothing." He then ran his finger down the strap of her bathing suit and glanced at her cleavage. She was tanned and gleaming from her afternoon in the sun. "I like this new bikini. You wear it well."

"Enough, Romeo," Michael warned.

"Michael Miller!" A voice yelled and Michael felt his happiness drain. A group of young women, just out of the water and dripping wet, waved and gave him the thumbs-up. He offered a nod of acknowledgment and the fans strolled away.

"Can it really be that easy?" Michael asked. "No pictures? No autographs? We need to hang out on this side of the island more often."

They ordered the local beer and a sampling of appetizers: shrimp cocktail and crab-stuffed mushrooms. Once dinner arrived—a blackened barracuda, a dish of linguini with clam sauce, and a rare filet—they devoured it all. As they ate, they watched musicians setting up on the beach. The strum of guitars and microphone checks drifted over the patrons eating. Soon the band began to play.

While they finished their meals, a man patted Michael on his back. "Nice job with the *Magnum* movie." And he walked on toward the beach where people were gathering near the live music. Some had begun dancing.

He looked at Lyle, puzzled.

"I don't know for sure," she said, "but I think this crowd is simply interested in other things, like being on the water, and the sport. They're not concerned with Hollywood and gossip. This group comes here to enjoy what they love. Windsurfing, wide-open spaces"—she nodded at the musicians—"great music. Maybe they understand that you're here to do the same."

"I think you're right." He looked around them. No tittering fans, no one staring or sneaking a photo. "I think I've found my squad here at Lac Bay."

They made their way to the beach and joined the others dancing. The three moved to the steel drums and kept beat with the lively music. Several times one of them stole a kiss from her. She thought nothing of returning their kisses and naturally responded with a brilliant smile. It was only when she noticed a woman watching them that she understood how inappropriate the three orange-clad dancers must look to the stranger.

The sun had claimed another day and darkness fell. They had enough dancing and found chairs near the water and sat there. Grey brought three beers from the bar.

"May I join you?" Estefani asked as she approached. She had showered and changed into a lilac sundress that rippled around her legs. Her sun-streaked hair fell freely about her shoulders.

"Yes, please do," Grey said. He stood, offered her his chair, and found another one for himself. "You were really great today," he said. "Thank you for your patience. We had an unforgettable time. It's such a high when you catch the breeze just right. I felt like a bird hunting low over the bay. I hope we didn't give you too difficult a time."

"Oh, not at all. I had fun today as well." She looked to the band and swayed to the music, tapping her fingers on her leg.

In the distance, beyond the crowd of people, there was some commotion. Breezy Shore employees were creating a pyramid-shaped structure out of wood.

"Are you staying for the bonfire?" Estefani asked. "We have one every night. It's become a tradition here. A sort of farewell—a send-off for our new friends."

"A bonfire," said Michael. "The perfect way to end the day. This place is amazing. Say, Estefani, just for the record, which one of us would you say did better today? Getting on the board, taking off, who do you think was really your ace student? Give it to us straight up. Settle a little bet we have."

"Oh, Michael, I'm no fool," she said. "You're both equally good. Advanced students, I'd say." She spoke to Lyle. "Are they family? They fight like brothers. They competed with each other most of the day."

"I wouldn't go straight to brothers, no," said Lyle.

The band played on and the wooden structure, short for this world, began to take shape. Lyle watched Estefani exchanging banter with the guys. An uneasy feeling churned. She could see it clear as day. Everything she held dear, going up in smoke.

"Would one of you like to dance?" She looked at Lyle. "I'm not sure…" She raised her shoulders. "I'm not sure if"—she gestured from Grey to Michael—"one of you is…available?"

"No! No, no one's available," said Lyle. There it was, her world bursting into flame. She quickly caught herself and softened her tone: "I'm sorry, no."

"Okay, then." Estefani stood. "I guess I'll call it a night. It was nice spending the day with you both." She walked off, disappearing into the dancing mass of people.

Grey let out a deep belly laugh, tears forming at the corner of his eyes. Lyle buried her face in her hands.

"Well, that wasn't awkward," said Michael.

"I'm sorry, I overreacted. Of course you can dance with her. I don't know what came over me."

"I'm happy right here, baby," said Michael.

Grey leaned back in his chair and stretched his legs out in front of him. He crossed his ankles and put his hand on Lyle's knee. "We love you, Lyle." He stifled a chuckle. "No worries."

The evening turned cool just as the bonfire roared to life. The band's music morphed into a sweet melody. The heat of the fire grew and spread like a blanket over the crowd. They all got up and joined the people encircling the fire. They stood arm in arm and swayed under a sky sprinkled with stars. The now still bay reflected the moon, and Lyle wondered how long this utopia could last.

Fifty-Seven

"Don't get eaten by a shark, Crocodile."

"We rarely see sharks on Bonaire."

"You tell him, baby."

Grey returned to his room as Michael and Lyle strolled toward the water holding hands under the sparse lights of the resort. All was quiet this time of night. The only noise, their footsteps crunching on gravel. They descended the stairs to the dock. Still wearing their swimsuits under their outfits, they kicked off their sandals and threw their clothes on a bench. They walked to the edge and looked out. The light of the moon shimmered off the dark water and a strong onshore breeze was building.

"There's our boat," said Michael. "*Mi Dushi*. It's kind of where we began."

The *Mi Dushi*, the largest in the resort's fleet of dive vessels, creaked and rocked with the rhythm of the ocean. They could hear the waves splashing against the hull and the pull of the line that stretched to the anchor below.

"I was so aggravated when I saw you on the boat that day," she remembered. "You had been making fun of me every chance you got. The last thing I wanted was to be stuck with you on the crowded dive deck." She chuckled. "We had a really rough start, didn't we?"

"I was such an idiot," he said. "When we first met, I didn't give you a chance. At the time my fame was blowing me up. I couldn't get away from myself. But then I realized the stranger I was being a total dick to was actually one of the most incredible women I'd ever met. You still are baby, you're amazing, and you were so brave. You stood up to that drunk fucker at the dive site—when I watched you battle-ram him to the ground, I couldn't believe my eyes."

"Once you and I lowered our guards it was magical," she said. "We were at our best when we were left alone. It was when we had to be around other people that we struggled. Looking back, I see now that my friends were trying to protect me, from myself."

"They wanted to keep us apart. I understand why," he said. "I was being a complete ass. I was totally out of control on that vacation, entirely wrapped up in myself. They were doing what they thought was best for you."

"Do you remember lying on *Mi Dushi*'s sundeck that day?" He took her hand and touched her cheek. "You told me about your mother and your childhood. When we relaxed in the sun, I saw your tattoo. That blew my mind. As much as I hate to admit it, Grey totally slayed it." He nodded at the vessel rocking in the water. "It was on that boat I realized I'd read you wrong, and I became determined to know you better."

"Race you there?"

"You'll beat me in a race, you always do. How about a nice easy swim?"

After standing in the cool night air, jumping into the water was like being swathed in a sultry quilt, warming them instantly. They leisurely swam through the dark water and once they reached the stern, Michael unhooked the steps and pulled down the aluminum ladder.

"After you," he said.

The boat rose and fell as they clambered onboard. The vessel offered plenty of room, easily accommodating forty divers and eighty oxygen tanks. But tonight it was barren—no dive equipment, no air cylinders, no other people—just Michael and Lyle. He held her hand and led her topside. After climbing the ladder to the sundeck, he took her in his arms and found her lips with his. She returned every gentle kiss as they swayed together with the rocking sea.

"I've missed you. I need you, Lyle," he said, nuzzling her neck. He whispered into her ear: "I want you forever." He unhooked her bikini top and let it fall to the deck. He held her breasts in his hands and kissed the salt water from her lips.

He slid his palms down her slick back and pushed his hands inside her suit.

"Michael," she huffed.

He peeled her suit down her legs. She willingly stepped out and he tossed it aside.

"I love you," he said, looking down at his naked lover. "Every time I'm with you, it's like the first time all over again." The sea picked up and the boat lurched as he took his trunks off. "Even the ocean is getting riled up tonight."

He led her by the hand to the forward deck where the bow was absorbing the brunt of the surf. He fell to his knees and kissed her stomach. "Lie down here with me."

She settled next to him as the waves broke against the hull. She reached over her head and gripped the railing as his lips nuzzled under her ear and his fingers traveled over her. The ocean grew stronger and sent salt water flying, dampening the lovers with a heavy spray. With each pounding wave, she fought to keep hold of the slippery rail.

"Michael, please." She gasped.

Together, they rose and fell with the bow of the boat. Wave after wave swelled and hammered the hull. He found her hands and held on to the bar with her. Now drenched, the lovers moved together with the thrashing ocean.

Fifty-Eight

"Ready to go?" Lyle called from the bathroom. She brushed her hair and swept it into a ponytail, then joined Grey in the other room. "We're meeting Michael for lunch. After we eat, we're driving to the northern end of the island to do a little... sightseeing."

Grey sat on the loveseat near the balcony doors and was thumbing through a paperback.

"What've you got there?"

"I found it in a bookstore in Kralendijk this morning." He held up *Natural Healing of the Mind*. "I thought while you're working with Danesha, maybe adding something holistic could help."

"Really? You're reading that for me?" She sat on his lap and flipped through the pages. "Looks like a lot of good information. Nature's pharmacy—your grandfather would be proud. You're a healer, Grey. You've helped me more than you'll ever know."

"When I first met you," he said, "you were hard to figure out. You told me you wanted a tattoo to carry your nightmares and that it was your friend's idea."

"When I think about that time, I ache inside." She slumped. "I was broken. You must've thought I was crazy. You simply accepted my reason and made me feel like I wasn't alone."

"I wanted to help you. I knew you were suffering. I blamed Dottie for putting that idea in your head."

"I did too." She grinned. "Being with you, just near you... I don't know how to describe it. Your calm nature sweeps over me. It opens my soul and lets peace flow in. I've never known such tranquility, and when I'm with you, I'm washed in it."

"You've come a long way," he said, closing the book. "I am concerned that you've been isolated while going through therapy with Danesha. Between the beach house and my place, you only see Victoria and me. I'm worried about you being with Michael again. From what you've told me, it's not been an easy relationship. We can't take the chance that he's going to churn things up. Not when you're just finding harmony in your life. We can't blindly let him undo all you've accomplished."

"When I was last with Michael," she explained, "I didn't have my head on straight. I've been worried about seeing him again. I didn't know what to expect or how we'd get along now that I'm stronger. But he's changed too and in a really good way."

"Advance with caution, please. And if things go south with Hollywood, I've always got you."

"I love you, Grey."

"You love him too." He took the book from her and placed it on the floor. "Let's go home, Lyle, back to Pearl, just you and me. We have a good life there."

"Grey." She hesitated. "Michael may be in trouble. I can't leave him. Something happened when we were here last. I hope we can explain it all to you soon. But I won't abandon him, not now, not when he needs me. Please try and understand."

"I thought I'd ask. I didn't really think you'd go for it. It's not in your nature. Take care of whatever it is, and then decide. Whatever you choose, be sure it's the best thing for everyone involved, including yourself."

The sincerity in his voice soothed her. He was steady in the way he cared for her. Standing by her side when she was shattered and while she healed. He would be there to make sure she was never broken again. Of this, Lyle was sure.

His mouth parted and he leans in close to her. She kisses him then runs the tip of her tongue over his lower lip.

His voice is rolling thunder: "Take off your clothes."

She stood and grabbed the hem of her tank top. She revealed herself slowly, teasing him as she lifted it over her head. She held the shirt to the side and swung it back and forth before releasing it to the floor. She played with him, covering her breasts with her palms. "Did you want a peek?" She inched her hands downward until she stood there exposed. "Is there anything else you'd like me to remove?"

He pointed at her shorts. "Get rid of those too, and whatever's underneath them."

She hitched her thumbs on the front of her waistband. "These? You want me to take them off?"

"I want them gone." He shifted in the chair.

She turned her back to him and swayed her bottom, wiggling her hips as she gradually lowered the pants to the floor. Stepping out of them, she then turned back to face him. She slid her index finger over the fabric of her satin undergarment. "How do you like my panties? They're so delicate."

"Peel them off, slowly."

She inched them down over her hips and then lower until she stood naked before him.

His eyes never left her as he fumbled with his pants. He motioned for her to sit on his lap. In one easy movement, they were together. She held his shoulders and looked into his eyes. Hands on her hips, he steadied her and gazed back. All attention now on satisfying the other's need, offering their bodies for pleasure.

Fifty-Nine

A rock painted yellow displayed the name *Karpata* in black block lettering. They pulled into the dive site and parked the truck near an abandoned hut wasting away in the corrosive salt air. At such a high elevation, the onshore breeze helped cool the three of them. This northern end of the island was quiet, and the lack of traffic had put the snack shack out of business years ago. As they shut the truck doors, an iguana scampered into the crumbling structure.

During the drive, Michael had told Grey about the blond-haired man, Lawrence Brumfield, and how they first encountered him: the man had put his hands on Lyle's friend and made crude remarks to her. Two days later he had then followed Lyle into the ladies' room at a restaurant and attacked her. But Michael heard her screams for help and stopped the assault before he could go any further. Michael told Grey how he'd ended up on Karpata with Brumfield the night he was murdered.

"Grey, I never intended to tell you any of this," said Michael. "I have no reason to trust you, but Lyle does, and I have faith in her. I'm asking you for your discretion. No leaks to the media, no stollen pictures. Not for myself, but for Lyle. If this homicide gets put on me, my life's going to turn into a giant shit show. When it all goes down the fucking drain, she'll need you."

Grey walked to the edge of the cliff and glanced around, hands on hips. "This is where you brought him? It's pretty remote up here. For such a small island I guess this site is the best chance you had to hide him." He shook his head and raised his voice. "Lyle, I'm telling you, this guy is bad news. He is *not* good for you. What are you thinking, getting involved with a killer?" He yelled: "Now let's get in the truck, go pack our bags, and fly back to Pearl!"

"Grey, please," she said. "Listen to the whole story. Michael didn't kill anyone."

"I didn't bring him here to off him!" Michael shouted. "I brought him here to…" He exhaled, defeated. "I brought him here to take my anger out on him. I didn't waste him. I swear he was alive when I left him here."

"Show us where he was when you drove away," said Lyle.

Michael led them away from the cliff and pointed to an area in the gravel. "When I took off, he was sitting about here. I don't know how he died, but I didn't do it. I sucker punched him in the gut and got in a few shots to his face. He stumbled backward and fell on his ass."

"You better be careful, Michael Miller," said a man behind them. "Some people on this island think you're a murderer."

"Captain Maartin," Lyle said. "What are you doing here? Are you following us?"

He'd parked his vehicle down the road hidden behind a patch of scraggly brush.

"Who, Captain Maartin?" Grey asked. "Who thinks Michael's a murderer?"

"My brother, the chief of police, for one," he said, looking around. "Interesting place to visit, considering you don't have any dive gear with you."

"Your brother is wrong," Lyle said with conviction. "Michael didn't kill Brumfield."

"Tell us why he thinks Michael's guilty," said Grey.

"The last time Michael and Lyle visited Bonaire I had the pleasure of welcoming them onboard *Mi Dushi*." He turned his attention to Lyle. "You came diving twice with us on the boat. Each time Michael tried to hide his identity from the other guests. I distinctly remember him pulling the brim of his hat down low on his face. Over and over, he fooled with that cap. I saw him at the resort fussing with it too, the exact same one."

Two iguanas creeped out from under the old shack. They skittered toward the group and raised their noses.

"On the day we found the body, we organized a search of the entire area here." Captain Maartin reached into his pocket and removed two carrots. The iguanas advanced cautiously as he snapped them into small bits and tossed them to the ground. "We found a piece of evidence: Michael's hat. I identified it myself. With a tangible object linking Mr. Miller to the crime scene, and a history of him and the victim together, we have a great interest in speaking with Michael regarding this situation." He dropped the last of the carrots and the animals grabbed them and scurried away. He then spoke directly to Michael. "We've been planning to bring you in for questioning since you landed on the island."

"Captain, you keep saying *we*," said Grey. "Are you on the police force?"

"No, my brother is in charge of that. But it's a small island, everyone tends to know what's what. He's on his way here now. He wanted to talk to Michael away from curious eyes."

Just then a police cruiser pulled up and an officer climbed out. The man wore a pressed white shirt with embroidered shoulder epaulettes. He looked like his brother but was clean shaven with his hair cut short. He had the same youthful sparkle in his eyes. The men greeted each other with a handshake and pat on the back.

"This is Diederik, everyone calls him Dutch."

If Dutch felt any ill-will toward Michael, he kept it hidden behind his smile as they shook. "Michael Miller, I can't believe it. It's nice to meet you. I've seen all your films. That war movie was really good. Congratulations on the big award." He nodded at Lyle and Grey but didn't offer his hand.

"Thank you," Michael said, plastering a forced smile on his face. "I'm glad you liked it. It's always nice to hear from fans."

"I'm afraid we have a little matter to settle," he said. "Would you be so kind as to answer a few questions regarding a crime that took place the last time you visited us?"

"Sure, I don't know much about it, but if you think I can help, I'll be glad to try."

"During the course of this ongoing investigation we've interviewed Brumfield's travel companion," Dutch explained. "He said your group had an encounter with them at a dive site. Miss Cooper here pushed Brumfield to the ground. This friend is suspicious that one of you beat up Brumfield a few days later, and since we doubt it was Miss Cooper," fake laughter all around, "our attention has turned to you, Mr. Miller. Perhaps an act of retaliation?"

"Honestly, Dutch," said Michael, "Lyle is quite capable of taking care of herself. I had no reason to seek revenge."

"Yes, of course," said Dutch. "I'm sure she is. But as you can see, a lot of the story needs to be cleared up, loose ends, so to speak. I'd appreciate you coming with me voluntarily. It's much better this way. We didn't have the authority to extradite you. After all, you're not being arrested for this crime. It continues to be under investigation. Since you've been in Hollywood's spot-light, we decided to wait patiently to have this conversation."

"I don't think I have any useful information," said Michael, "but I want to get this cleared up as much as you do." He hugged Lyle and spoke in her ear. "Everything's going to be okay, don't worry about me." Releasing her, he turned to leave.

"Why did you return to Bonaire?" asked the captain. "You must've known we had some questions for you."

"Lyle's here. I'm here because she is." He followed Dutch to the police vehicle. The three watched as he opened the backseat door and Michael climbed in. Dutch gave a little wave as they drove off.

"This murder has left our island with a heavy heart," said Captain Maartin. "We only want our home to be at peace again."

The captain always spoke of Bonaire as though it were a person, a woman, perhaps a mother. He'd told Lyle once the island was magical and could heal people. Now he worried she was hurt from a crime committed on her shore.

"Bad juju," Grey said, agreeing with the captain. "This island isn't just a piece of land—it's a living, feeling presence. Captain Maartin believes as I do. We've always held a deep respect for nature and peace. This land, and all life, deserves to be protected."

"Your friend Grey understands. This is why we must end the mystery and imprison the one responsible. When we discover who tarnished our land with such a brazen crime, and we will find them, they will pay their due. We must cleanse her aura and only then will our island be whole again."

Sixty

"You should eat something," Grey said to Lyle. They were sitting at a table near the water. Forks and knives lay untouched, meticulously lined on folded cloth napkins next to water glasses that were never filled. The dinner crowd was thinning and sunlight was dying out. "You haven't had anything since lunch."

"I can't eat, but I'll take another one of these." She pinged her empty cocktail glass with her fingernail. "You should join me. It takes the edge off."

Now at the bar, Grey signaled the bartender.

He returned with two mint Mojitos and sat down. He placed one in front of Lyle and took a sip of his own. "That's good." He stirred his drink and she watched as the crushed leaves swirled around the ice. "You know how I feel about Hollywood. I have so many doubts about his story I could fill Dodger Stadium. But in order to keep you from totally losing your shit over this, I'm going to trust your judgement. If you say he's innocent, then I'll do everything I can to help prove that. I hope you know that I'm on your side no matter what."

"Thank you. I can't believe they're keeping him this long. The wait is killing me." She drank then dabbed the corner of her mouth with her thumb. "You'll see, he's innocent. They must have confiscated his phone," she said, checking her own. "He's not replying to any of my texts or answering my calls. I wonder if he's contacted a lawyer."

"Do you think he knows to ask for an attorney?" said Grey.

"I don't know. We're under the Netherlands' jurisdiction here. I'm not sure how the law's applied on the island. Is now the time someone should bring in a lawyer?"

"Try to relax," said Grey. "I'm sure he'll be fine."

"What's taking so long? He's been gone all afternoon." She took a long pull from the cocktail straw. "Do you think I should drive down there? He may need me."

"Loyal to the end." Grey stood. "It's late. Let's go back to the room. If there's any news, he'll know to find us there."

———◆———

Steam filled the bathroom as water poured from the showerhead and crackled against the plastic curtain.

"I have it set nice and hot," Grey said, stepping in. "It'll help you sleep."

Lyle stood under the soothing stream and leaned her head back, soaking her hair. He turned her, then drizzled shampoo into his palm. He massaged her scalp as he worked it into a foam.

"That feels so good," she said, her eyes closed. "I'm so lucky to have you to take care of me."

After he washed his own hair, they rinsed off. Bubbles tumbled down their bodies then circled the drain.

He picked up the bar of soap and turned it in his hands, creating a rich lather. Standing behind her, he coated her breasts with the flowery scent. She leaned back on him as he continued to move his hands over her chest and down her stomach.

She turned and took the bar from him and ran it over his torso, playing with the pattern of bubbles. She was quiet, contemplating the day, while the shower pounded on her back. "Grey." She regarded her lover's solemn face, an expression that reflected her own concerns. Sliding the soap down over his stomach, she lathered him completely.

He closed his eyes and placed an open hand on the tile of the shower wall. He shuddered and inhaled as her slippery hands washed him. When he had had all the teasing he could take, he lifted her and she clamped her knees onto his hips.

"Lyle," he whispered.

"I need you too," she answered.

Streams of water beat down on them and steam hung thick in the small space. Her fingers clamped onto his shoulders as he lifted her higher and held her against the slick tile wall.

Sixty-One

Lyle put on her summer nightie and Grey a pair of boxers. They climbed in under the fresh sheets. He stared up at the popcorn ceiling, trying to think of a way to keep her from being damaged psychologically. With everything going on, he worried she'd suffer a relapse. What if she started talking to Dottie again? At the thought of that, he decided if she mentioned Dottie at all, like it or not, he'd take her home on the next flight out. Even Michael would have to agree that was best. Tomorrow, he would ask her for her therapist's contact information, just in case.

She lay next to him, exhausted, but knowing she wouldn't be able to sleep until she knew Michael was back at the resort.

They had spent most of the day contemplating his fate. They asked why and what and what if until they had covered every possible scenario. They googled *laws of the Netherlands* and every combination of crime and punishment that might be relevant. Now they lay quiet, spent. There was nothing left to ask.

A soft knock sounded at the door.

"Michael!" She sprung from the bed and threw open the door.

In spite of being outside in the sun all week, he was white as a sheet. His normally bright eyes were dull and his posture limp. He looked like a wool cardigan after the spin cycle.

"Michael. Oh, thank God." She flung her arms around him and buried her face in his shoulder.

"It's okay, I'm here." He held her and rubbed her back. "Everything's going to be okay." His stress melted by half. "What a day."

"I've been so worried," she said. "When I didn't hear from you, I thought they were going to keep you forever. You didn't do anything wrong. We need to make them understand the truth." She stepped back. "Come inside, please."

"You've been gone all day," said Grey, sitting up in bed. "What's going on?"

"I'm sorry it's so late," Michael said, standing by the door. "Dutch just dropped me off."

"Have they been questioning you this entire time?" he asked.

"We broke for dinner. Dutch took me out for something to eat."

"I guess it's a good sign you're calling him by his first name," Grey said. "I also think Michael Miller may be getting some movie star treatment. I don't imagine they take murder suspects out for dinner very often." He got out of bed and put on a pair of shorts. "Come in, sit down and tell us what happened."

Michael and Lyle sat on the love seat and Grey took the club chair.

"They swabbed my cheek for a DNA sample to test against the evidence. I thought if I refused, I'd look guilty, so I agreed to it." He looked at Lyle. "Do you think that was a good idea? I wasn't sure."

"The DNA will match," Grey said. "If they have your ball cap, as the captain thinks they do, it'll definitely be identical."

"Captain Maartin was right. It's my hat. I saw it on a shelf. It was in a clear plastic bag with a label that said *evidence* in red ink. I guess they don't have an evidence room, their system uses a wall of shelves." He grinned. "Really, though, you gotta love this island. Anyway, I stuck to the truth as closely as I could. I'm innocent, I have nothing to hide." He looked to Lyle. "I told them all about how we first ran in to him at the dive site. He was lit and you pushed him to the ground. I told them he attacked you at Captain Jack's a few nights later and how I beat the shit out of him." He took a breath and sank deeper into the chair. "Shit, hearing it come out of my mouth as I spilled it all to Dutch, I sounded like someone who had a reason to kill him."

"What did you say about the night he died?" Lyle asked. "Did you tell them you were with him?"

"No, I already sound like a killer. I'm not going to give them anything else to use to connect me to this murder. Everything took forever." He kicked his shoes off. "We had to wait for a trained officer to take the DNA sample. Then they had to find someone to record my statement. They asked a lot of questions and then asked them all a second time, wanting more detail. 'What time of day was it? Was that on Tuesday or Wednesday?'" He rolled his eyes. "Shit people, I was on vacation. I had no idea what day of the week it was. By the third round, I could hardly remember what I'd originally said."

"I've seen that tactic used on true crime shows," said Grey. "They question suspects for hours to see if their story changes at all. If they had enough evidence, they would've charged you today. The fact that Dutch let you go is a good sign."

"Did you ask for a lawyer?" said Lyle.

"I thought that would make me look more guilty, so I didn't bring it up. Maybe I should've. It was hard to think straight." They sat quietly, all wondering the same thing—Where this was going to go from here?

"It's funny," Michael said. "But the worst part is knowing Captain Maartin thinks I did this. I respect that man. I feel like I've disappointed him."

"You're exhausted," she said, tucking his hair behind his ear. "You need to get some sleep."

"It gets worse." He took Lyle's hand. "I think there's a witness. Not to the…" He started again. "No one saw us at the dive site, but Dutch told me that someone saw Brumfield get in my truck that night." He bared his worry like they were the only two in the room. "I'm scared, I really messed up this time. It all feels so out of control. That person's testimony makes me the last one to be with Brumfield while he was alive. I'm afraid this might be it for me. With the evidence against me and an eyewitness, how am I going to get out of this fucking mess?"

"It's late." Grey stood. "We can finish this conversation tomorrow, when we're rested and clearheaded."

"Do you mind if I crash here?" Michael asked. "I don't want to be alone tonight. I keep imagining them showing up and hauling me off again."

Lyle found an extra blanket and pillow in the closet. "This love seat is kind of small. I hope you're comfortable." She spread the blanket and fluffed the pillow as Michael got undressed.

"Thanks, it looks perfect." He gave her a deep kiss until Grey cleared his throat. Michael winked at her then settled into his makeshift bed.

Lyle and Grey climbed back under the sheets and turned off the light.

In no time at all, they were sound asleep.

Sixty-Two

The morning sun was shining in through the balcony doors. Lyle, cradled in her down pillow and fluffy comforter, woke to an arm draped over her stomach and a heavy leg across her knees. Trapped, she blinked herself awake and let her eyes adjust to the light.

His hair was tossed about his face. She heard a faint snore coming from his mouth. He lay so close to her she could feel his breath on her cheek.

"Michael," she said.

He didn't flinch. She struggled to break free but only managed to scoot a few inches. Then she saw Grey sitting up next to her, scrolling on his phone with a scowl. She wondered how long he had been sitting there building up steam.

"Grey," she said in a faint morning voice.

"I don't remember inviting him into our bed."

Michael stirred, pulling her closer. "Oh, baby. Your body starred in my dreams last night."

"Michael, wake up." She shook his shoulder with some urgency. "Get up, Michael. Grey's really mad."

He squinted at her and then up at Grey.

Grey reached over Lyle, put his hand on Michael's chest, and shoved him off the bed. He landed on the floor like a sack of rotten potatoes.

"Damn, Grey. I'm just trying to sleep."

"Back to the couch if you want more sleep."

"Enough guys." She climbed out of the bed and stepped over him. On her way to the bathroom, she said: "Michael, if you have the slightest ounce of self-preservation, you'll get dressed and skedaddle back to your room."

Sixty-Three

Grey sent the tennis ball flying down the beach. Calypso tucked her body, dug in and flew after it, ears flapping and tail wagging. The ball hit the coral and bounced in the ocean. The dog scooped it up in her mouth and ran splashing through the shallow water back toward Grey. She then dropped it at his feet for the umpteenth time that morning. She could hardly stand still as she waited for him to launch it through the air again.

"It was definitely your hat on the shelf?" Grey asked Michael as he threw the ball. "You're positive about that?"

Relaxing on lounge chairs, Lyle and Michael had been glancing up periodically to watch the endless game of fetch. Lyle, holding a folded newspaper, chewed on the end of her pencil while she studied the crossword clues. Michael pulled his new baseball cap down low to shade his face. All three were wearing orange as if part of an exclusive club, or perhaps, simply an embarrassing coincidence of wardrobe.

"It's my hat. I'm sure of it. It had a label with *Brumfield* written on it and a case number, plain as day. It had the location too—Karpata—and date they found it."

Lyle tapped the pencil on her bottom lip. "What's a five-letter word meaning clumsy?"

"Klutz," Michael said, tilting his head toward Grey.

"Clown." Grey retaliated.

"Oh," said Lyle, as she filled in her answer. "Inept."

Two women in matching bikinis strolled along the shoreline. Both had dark red hair cut into similar bobs and shared the same height and shape. Lyle guessed they were twins.

They slowed as they watched Grey hurling the ball for Calypso.

Michael removed his hat and pushed his hair off his forehead. "Shit, with McDreamy down there being a major chick magnet, I don't need to hide anymore."

The women smiled and nodded at Grey as they walked past him, then continued down the beach. Calypso ran by them, kicking up sand and splashing water, as Grey sent the dog's ball soaring again.

"And you said it's a two-story building, the police station?" He glanced at Michael. "Limited security?"

"What are you getting at?" asked Lyle. "Why all the questions?" She squirted sun lotion in her palm and then passed it to Michael. She smoothed it over her face, neck, and shoulders, then he did the same.

"I'm just trying to picture it." Calypso dropped the ball at his feet. "That's it for today girl. Go find Captain Maartin."

The dog picked up the ball and brought it to Michael. She dropped it in the sand and looked up at him expectantly. She pranced, anticipation building like a spring-loaded Jack in the Box ready to pop free. He stood and tossed the ball down the beach.

Lyle handed out masks and snorkels. "Ready for a swim?"

They walked into the refreshing waves. Standing in water up to their thighs, they put on the masks.

"We should be able to see a lot right here on the house reef," she said.

The water was a predictable 82 degrees. Snorkeling wasn't as adventurous as diving, but it had its advantages. They could easily talk to one another, and with only a mask and snorkel, it took a lot less planning than diving in full gear.

Michael patted Lyle's behind. "Do you think we'll find your favorite fish today? We can make it a contest."

During their first visit together on Bonaire, Lyle had challenged Michael to see which one of them would find it first, and she'd won. The yellowtail damselfish was in its juvenile phase. A dark blue body speckled with glowing sapphire scales and a brilliant yellow tail made the baby fish stand out.

"A friendly competition sounds fun," she said. "What do I get when I win?"

"Me," he said, glaring at Grey, "exclusively."

"In your dreams, Hollywood."

"Really, guys?" She rolled her eyes. "Still at it? Can we try and get through just one day without getting on each other?"

———◆———

The three swam out a few yards, then floated lazily at the surface. The tide moved them along, giving them an ever-changing show of the reef below.

"Baby," Michael called out. "What's this over here?"

She swam to his side and saw a triangle-shaped black fish covered in white polka dots weaving in and out of the coral, its yellow fins quivering like honey bee wings at its sides. It had timid, dark eyes and blew a never-ending kiss. She lifted her face from the water and removed the snorkel from her mouth. "That's a trunkfish. Sometimes they're called boxfish. They're usually really shy—I'm surprised that little one is letting us look at it for this long."

They returned to their peaceful swim, each of them exploring what could be seen just feet below them.

"Lyle, come look at this," Grey called out. "Something's hiding in the sand over here."

She swam over and searched underneath them.

It if weren't for Grey's sharp eye, the stingray may have never been noticed, it was buried so well. She spotted two spiracles, set behind the ray's eyes, just above the sand. Its long, feather-shaped tail and stinger gave away its hiding place. The animal suddenly shook off its camouflage and glided away, avoiding any possible danger that may come from the curious swimmers.

She lifted her face from the water and removed her snorkel. "That's a southern stingray—a really big one. The circular openings allow them to breathe while they're hidden beneath the sand like that."

"Baby, come here," Michael called out. "What's this?"

She swam to him to see what he'd found. Three eye-catching fish milled about the coral, searching for food. Their bodies were such a deep shade of blue, they almost appeared black. What made them unusual was the silvery opalescence at the base of their fins.

"Aren't they pretty?" she said, removing her snorkel. "Those are black durgons, a type of triggerfish. I love that glowing single line."

She inserted her snorkel and just as she was about to submerge, Grey called out, "Crocodile, come see this."

She swam to him. "What'd you find?"

"I'm not sure. I can't tell if it's alive or dead. It looks like a huge slug."

With that description, she had an idea what it was. She put her mask in the water to confirm her hunch. She lifted her head out and removed her snorkel. "It's a sea cucumber. They're really sedentary during the day. They look like a huge slug but actually have little tubed feet for moving around."

"Baby—"

"I'm heading back to the beach," she called out to them both. "You two enjoy yourselves."

"We'll come in with you," said Grey.

"No need. You both stay out here. I'm going to catch some sun," she then mumbled to herself, "and a minute of peace and quiet."

————◆————

She swam toward shore leaving the guys on their own. Once in shallow water, she removed her mask then watched them from the quiet of her lounge chair. Without her there for them to fight for her attention, they seemed to forget they were at odds and searched the ocean together for exotic life.

When she saw them pointing out fish to each other, she thought maybe they would make it through the afternoon without being at each other's throats. She laid her head back and let the warmth of the sun dry her. She fought the sleep that threatened but soon her lids grew heavy. The sound of waves lapping, and the muted voices of her lovers was like a lullaby. With no intention of doing so, she slept.

There was a time not long ago when she feared falling asleep. Nightmares haunted her and memories of a troubled childhood wouldn't relent even if she dozed. Recalling the isolation of her early years, with no one to care for her but her unreliable mother, left her tossing and turning most nights. Countless mornings she turned off her alarm feeling groggy and depleted.

But now, with encouragement from her friends and the aid of her counselor, she felt free from the ghosts of her difficult past. For the first time, she would awaken well rested in the morning with no memory of any dreams whatsoever.

At peace with her past, she now slept deeply on her lounge chair under the warm Caribbean sun.

Sixty-Four

The onshore breeze brought with it voices that nudged Lyle from her sleep. Then high-pitched, incessant laughter pulled her fully back to consciousness. She held her arm over her forehead, blocking the bright sun and gave herself a minute to become fully awake. The guys had given up on snorkeling and were having an actual conversation in waist-deep water. Their body language told her they were discussing something important. Maybe Grey was giving it to Michael for climbing into their bed last night.

More giggling. She squinted and saw that the bikini-clad twins had waded into the water and were making a beeline for her lovers.

"No, no, no," she said softly. "Ladies, don't you dare." But she was too late. A squeal pealed across the water, and she continued the conversation as if they could hear. "Yup. It's him. Michael Miller. Unattainable Academy Award winner. Now move along, girls."

As they looked from Grey to Michael and back again, she thought they might give themselves whiplash.

"They're not for you, now head on down the beach. Come on, girls. Please, leave us alone, please."

Grey and Michael both looked her way. They gestured in her direction, explaining something to the twins. Smiles gone, the women looked to her and then back at the guys.

Something inside Lyle unmoored.

The longer the women stayed to chat, the more uncomfortable she grew. Her chest tightened and her insides sank. She knew she wasn't being fair and that they were simply talking to the girls, fans, probably, but she couldn't stop her wariness from churning.

How could she be so selfish to the men she loved? Stringing both along, unable to make things right by setting them free. Guilt was a pest she'd been trying to ignore.

After a few more minutes, the guys said goodbye and splashed toward shore. The women continued down the coastline, looking back over their shoulders several times as they walked away.

"Sleeping beauty awakens." Grey picked up a towel and worked it over his shoulders.

"Did you have a nice nap?" asked Michael.

Grey sat on the adjacent lounge chair and Lyle pulled her feet back to make room for Michael on hers.

"I'm sorry. I don't mean to string you along like this. I'm not being fair. We need to end our polyamorous relationship. I created it without giving either of you a choice. I'd never choose one over the other, so I need to ask you both to leave me."

"But you've been so happy," said Michael. "I've honestly never seen you this contented. Don't let those women upset you. Say whatever you will—I'm not going anywhere."

"I don't want to hurt anyone," she said. "I feel hopeless because I love you both. Honestly, I do. I'm leaving it up to you guys—if either of you wants out of this... incredibly mixed-up mess, I won't stop you." She took a breath and sat up a little straighter. "I'm going to be okay. I can't continue using my problems as a justification for hurting the men I love."

"Where is this coming from?" asked Grey. "I thought we'd decided already. We're all in this together until the end. We all agreed to wait." He gestured down the beach. "Do you think Hollywood and I want to be with those girls?" He winked at Michael. "Michael, would you rather be with the twins?"

"You mean the ones in the bikinis?" He grinned. "I hardly noticed them."

Grey flashed his rare smile. "The epitome of every young-blooded teenaged boy's dream?"

"Stop it," she chuckled. "You're not funny. Okay, we're in it till the end. The three of us, thank you. I love you, both of you."

Sixty-Five

"Grey, who does *your* tattoos?" asked Michael.

"I've been tattooed by a few different artists. Why do you ask?"

"I'm thinking maybe I should join the club." He ran his hand over his biceps.

"Do you think that's smart?" said Lyle. "I'm just thinking about your career. What if you get a roll playing a man of the cloth or something?"

"I've actually tattooed a priest, so I think his livelihood is safe," said Grey. "I'll do it. I've already come up with a design for you."

"Really?" Michael sat up straighter. "What is it?"

"A weasel," he replied.

Michael squinted. "Why a weasel?"

"Because you are, in fact, a weasel."

Michael balled up his napkin and chucked it at him.

Three teenaged fans approached their table seeking autographs and pictures. Michael easily put on his public face. He sat up a little straighter and raised his eyebrows.

"I'd love to," he said, standing and tossing his hat onto the table.

"I haven't seen the Magnum movie yet," one girl chirped, "but I really liked Summer Time Love."

"That film was fun to make. It took a lot of people working behind the scenes to pull it all together. They made me look good."

They moved to a less crowded area away from diners.

He put on a casual grin as he posed with his fans. To Lyle, Michael now seemed more at ease with his admirers than he had been on their previous trip. He was less pretentious, more genuine, easily natural.

He stood with his elbow lightly resting on the shoulder of an acne covered boy and smiled at the camera.

"It's funny, isn't it?" said Grey. "He seems like just one of us, and yet… he's a celebrity." He looked at the people waiting for a photo. "To them, they might as well be standing with royalty."

A young girl giggled as her father stood with her in the growing group waiting to meet the star.

"Dad, what will I say to him? I can't do this," she said.

"Darlin', you'll never get a chance like this again," he said. "Michael Miller is at our resort. Come on now, just say hello."

"Dad, no." The closer she got to Michael, the more frantic her tittering became.

"Let's get a picture," he said. "Your mother will be sorry she missed this."

Grey nodded toward the young fan. "I imagine she's about my daughter Cece's age. Are twelve-year-olds Michael Miller fans? I wonder if she knows who he is."

"You could score some major points if she does," said Lyle.

"There's so much I don't know about her. My own little girl is a stranger to me."

They watched as the shy pre-teen approached Michael. When he extended his hand to her, she offered a limp-wristed shake and turned beet red. He engaged in some pleasantries as they looked into her father's camera.

"I wonder if she ever thinks about me," said Grey. "Maybe if I told her I vacationed with Michael Miller she'd want to see me."

"I'll say it again, as her father you have rights. You could get legal help. Sure, your visits may be court mandated, but that's a start. Once the two of you spend time together it's bound to get easier. If you want a relationship with her, you'll have to take the uncomfortable first steps."

"I doubt Cece's grandfather would agree to this. He's the type that would put up a big fight. I'm a freelance photographer and tattoo artist. I'm pretty sure I can't afford a lawyer. I'd need some serious cash for that."

The young girl rejoined her father. She hugged him and bounced on her toes as they scrolled through the pictures he'd taken.

"Did someone say something about needing money?" Michael rejoined them.

Grey hesitantly explained his predicament. He told Michael all about Elizabeth and the child they'd had together twelve years ago. "Bottom line is, I'll need an attorney to get the ball rolling on visitation."

"Shit, Grey, I'm sorry," said Michael. "I had no idea. Just let me know. I'd be happy to help you out."

"You hardly know me. I can't ask you to do that."

"It's totally up to you. I'm just offering to foot the bill. It seems a shame to waste any more time. Don't be too proud to accept my donation to your cause. Time…I've learned, it's all about time. We can't really count on how much we have ahead of us. Connect with your daughter. The courts can force Elizabeth to let you see her."

"If you're seriously offering, I'd like to take you up on that." He extended his fist across the table and Michael did the same. "It must be nice having all that money," Grey said. "I wouldn't have a care in the world if I were rich."

Michael put his hat back on. He tucked some loose hairs in at the sides and pulled the brim down. "You would think that, wouldn't you? I feel like I made a deal with the devil and he's coming to collect. I always thought I knew what I wanted. Now that I have it, I'm not so sure. Sometimes it's just too much."

"What do you mean, exactly?" asked Grey.

"When my last movie became a hit, I was under a load of pressure not to fuck up." He chewed on the end of his cocktail straw. "I never saw that stress coming. I'm afraid to be seen in public with the person I love. We worry that my fan base would drop like shit in a cow pasture if they knew I was dating a woman older than me. And then I go and dig myself in deeper. I'm supposed to be in a relationship with Ava

Rookesby, the sweetheart of the tabloids. People would tar and feather me if I publicly broke her heart."

"That's totally messed up," Grey said.

"For the entire two weeks we were here," Michael continued, "we had to hide at dive sites to find any peace. There are cameras everywhere these days." He snapped. "I wish I'd never won that fucking award. I thought the tension was tough back then. Hiding, pretending. And the movie I'm making now is already being compared to *John Magnum*. How do I know if it's going to live up to the hype?" He spoke to Grey: "Nick Park wrote a best-selling novel about this guy, Collin Stewart. When they make films out of popular novels the expectation is always sky high. The suits at the studio presume it's going to be a box office hit. They're so confident, they're paying me a small fortune to star in it."

"You're making a movie about the serial killer in Ohio?" Grey asked. "The college student?"

"That's the one. The story was all over the news when it first broke. He was a truly fucked up son of a bitch." He lowered his voice. "I don't know if I can pull it off. I think maybe I'm a one-trick pony."

"You're overthinking it," Lyle said. "You're putting way too much pressure on yourself."

"It's not only the movie. This investigation is scaring the shit out of me. How long do you think this will stay out of the press? *Michael Miller being investigated for murder*. That's a headline I won't overcome." The realization of what was at stake struck him. "My freedom, our basic human right, may be in jeopardy. I could lose everything," he whispered, "and everyone."

Sixty-Six

"I don't know where Grey is," said Lyle, distraught at Michael's door. "After we finished our drinks last night we went back to our room. When I woke up this morning, he was gone. Why would he leave in the middle of the night without telling me where he was going?"

"Please, come inside. Did you two have a fight? Some kind of a disagreement?" He closed the door behind her. "Is there a reason he would've caught an early flight home?"

"We never fight, we're fine."

"You never argue? What about hashing out petty disagreements?" he asked, perplexed by her statement.

"No, never. I don't understand where he could be. I figured I'd give him a few hours to show up, but it's after noon already." She checked her phone again. "I haven't seen or heard from him at all."

"Let's take a quick walk around the resort. He probably fell asleep in a lounge chair or is throwing a ball for Calypso down by the water. If we don't find him there, we'll drive into town."

"Thank you. I'm sure he just got busy with something and I'm worrying needlessly. It's just that it's so unlike him not to check in with me."

Guests milled about and staff wheeled their service carts from room to room, leaving fresh towels and changing linens. They walked to the restaurant, where employees were clearing away dirty dishes and restocking the salad bar. The tables were full, but there was no sign of Grey.

Next they stood at the shoreline and scanned the sunbathers. But he wasn't among them. They walked back through the resort and into the parking area. After searching the lot for Grey's truck with their corresponding license plate, they discovered it too was missing.

"I'm starting to really worry," she said. "Where do you think he is?"

"My best guess is he took you up on your offer. I think we're going to find his truck at the airport."

"What do you mean? Why at the airport?"

"Yesterday on the beach. You told us both, remember? You said if either of us wants out of this crazy, mixed-up mess you wouldn't stop us from leaving."

"He must've left me," she muttered. "I can't blame him really. I knew I was asking too much and taking a huge chance. Having you both here together was a big risk. It had the potential to backfire on me and now it has. He was in such a hurry to get off the island, he left his things in the room."

"Let's take my truck down to the airport. If his is parked there, we'll know he's left."

They climbed into the vehicle and pulled the doors shut.

"I'm sorry about this," he said. "I really am. Romeo isn't half bad. I was just starting to like the guy."

"I just didn't think he would—"

Michael's lips were on hers, kissing her repeatedly, and all thoughts of her missing lover momentarily vanished. Eyes closed, she let a low moan escape her.

He gave her one last kiss then moved behind the wheel. "Let's go find out what Grey's up to." He started the truck. "If I'm lucky, he's finally decided to leave us alone. But honestly, sneaking off doesn't sound like him. I would've thought he'd at least let you know he was flying home."

They drove the short distance to the airport. It was quiet that time of day, most flights having left early in the morning. They circled the parking lot several times looking for any white truck that may belong to Bon Adventure. Then they began driving up and down the endless lines of cars. Each time they spotted a white truck, Michael stopped and Lyle hopped out to check the plate. After an hour, they gave up the search.

"It's not here," she said. "He didn't leave me."

"He's on the island," Michael said. "Where the hell is his truck? Let's go back to the resort. He'll show up there when he's ready."

"Grey, where are you?"

———◆———

They sat together on the bottom step leading up to her room. She wanted to have a clear view of the resort entrance and the stairs were perfectly situated. Meandering fans stopped to chat and asked Michael for photos as the afternoon wore on. Lyle usually found the attention endearing, but today she imagined using his admirers for target practice.

"Can't they leave you alone for a minute?" she said. "We're just trying to sit and wait in peace here."

"I know you're worried. I'm sure he'll be back soon. He's probably in town buying hair gel, or out taking photos of seaweed." He twisted the top off a bottle of lukewarm water and handed it to her.

She took a drink and then checked the time. She looked toward the main gate.

Michael got up and stretched, trying to ease his sore muscles. "Okay, that's enough. My back is starting to ache from sitting on these cement rungs. Come with me."

She stood and they trudged up the stairs. Housekeeping had made up the room. She sat on the end of the freshly made bed and checked the time again. "This is crazy. Where is he? I keep imagining him in trouble. Maybe he went for an early swim and got caught in a riptide or swept away by a strong current."

"Try not to think like that. Besides, that doesn't sound like him. Leaving in the middle of the night for a swim? He wouldn't do that."

"I'm going to call Dutch at the station," she said.

"I think it's too soon to involve the police. We don't know what time he left or how long he's been gone. Besides, when he comes walking in that door with a plausible explanation, we'll look like idiots." He slid the balcony doors open. "I'm going to relax out here. You should join me. The parrots in the trees will cheer you up."

They sat in white wicker chairs with thick floral cushions. She played on her phone and scrolled through Instagram, usually a huge diversion. But today, even the posts from friends and videos of outrageous strangers couldn't distract her. Michael called Catherine to assure his agent he would be back on set when the production's hiatus was over. Lyle put down her phone and crawled into his lap. She laid her head on his shoulder.

It was approaching dinnertime when they heard a knock.

"Grey!" She sprung to her feet.

"He has a key, he wouldn't need to knock."

She threw open the door and deflated at the sight of a Bon Adventure employee standing there in his uniform. Next to him was another man, wearing a white shirt with embroidered epaulettes on the shoulders and a badge pinned to his shirt pocket.

"Dutch," she said. "What's going on? Has there been an accident?"

The employee cringed. "I'm sorry to disturb you, but the police chief insisted I escort him to your room. The privacy of our guests is always of utmost importance to us. I apologize for interrupting your afternoon."

"Okay Robert, you did your part," Dutch said. "Now leave us alone." Robert turned to go. "Tell your mom I'll be by this weekend for some of her fish dinners." He smiled at Lyle. "His mother sells fried lionfish at the food market in town. Best I've ever had."

"Dutch…"

"I'm sorry to pop in on you so unexpected. May I come in?"

"Yes, please do. Does this have anything to do with Grey Locklear?"

"Or are you here to take me in for more questioning?" said Michael, who had walked in from the balcony. "I've already told you everything I know."

"No, Mr. Miller. No need for any more interviews."

"We're worried about our friend, Grey." She gestured for Dutch to have a seat, then she and Michael sat across from him.

"First and foremost, you should know that he is safe," said Dutch. "He's been held under suspicion of breaking and entering."

Lyle shot to her feet. "What? Are you kidding me? Give me a damn break, Dutch. What kind of an operation are you running here?"

"Lyle," Michael said, "let's hear him out. Breaking and entering what?"

"The police station."

Lyle's eyes darted to Michael then immediately fell to the floor.

The police chief stood and went to the door. "I've been out on a call. I was just heading home when I was told on the radio that he's being released. We don't have any evidence to hold him. Our video surveillance system was suspiciously disabled. I'm sure he'd appreciate a ride home."

Sixty-Seven

They entered the police station and approached the officer sitting at the main desk. Hearing their footsteps on the tiled floor, she looked up at them. "May I help you?" Recognition lit her face. "Michael Miller!" She jumped up. "I heard you were on Bonaire! May I get a selfie with you?"

"No need," Lyle said. "I'd be glad to take some shots of the two of you together."

"You're completely whoring me out right now, aren't you?" Michael asked through gritted teeth.

"You better believe it."

After several photos, they explained why they were there. The officer disappeared into the back of the station and soon returned with Grey and three coworkers.

Lyle ran to him. He scooped her up and carried her to a far corner. She buried her face in his hair. "I was so worried. I thought you got on a plane and left me. What the hell is going on?"

"Shhh. I'm sorry," he whispered. "Not here. We'll talk soon, just not yet." He kissed her neck and slid her down his chest. She wrapped her arms around his waist. Rubbing her back, he pulled her closer to him, and kissed the top of her head. "I'd never leave you like that."

They watched Michael stand for pictures and waited as they exchanged small talk. When the station's staff seemed contented, he made his way toward the door. "It's been really nice meeting all of you. Thank you for your service to the people of Bonaire."

The group yelled their thank-yous and congratulations as the three left the station and climbed into the truck. Tires squealed as Michael sped them out of the parking lot and down the main road.

"Grey, what the—"

"Not yet, Michael. Keep driving. I need to get away from here. I'll explain everything. I just have to clear my head first."

They drove up to the town of Rincon and found a distillery with a few vehicles parked out front. Smiling cactus danced across the establishment's façade. Most of the patrons turned to see who had entered. Someone yelled a standard greeting from behind the bar. Michael lowered his head but quickly realized there was no need. All eyes followed Grey as he and Lyle found a booth near the back. He was conspicuous even in the dimly lit room.

Michael sauntered toward the bartender, purchased a round of drinks, then carried them to the table.

"I thought we could all use something strong," he said, placing three copper mugs on cocktail napkins. "Rum and ginger beer." The golden spirit was served over ice and garnished with a wedge of lime.

"Just what the doctor ordered." Grey grabbed a drink, relaxed back in his seat, and took a swallow.

The walls surrounding them were jam-packed with names, initials, dates and hometowns. Past patrons had carved the memorabilia into the wood over the years. *Randy NC 2022* was engraved near *Ted 1993* on the table in front of them.

"When you're ready, we'd love some answers," said Lyle.

"I'm sorry I worried you. I would've left you a note, but I thought I'd be back before you woke up this morning. I guess I'm not as stealth as I once was. In my younger years, I never would've gotten caught. I thought I could do it." He looked at Michael. "The way you described the police station, it should've been an easy in and out. I didn't consider motion detectors and silent alarms. My mistake. I underestimated them."

"You actually broke into the police station?" she whispered.

He glanced around, ensuring he wouldn't be overheard. "I drove into town, parked the truck behind the ice cream parlor, and walked to the station from there. Michael was right—a two-story building, and I thought limited security."

Michael raked his hand through his hair. "Oh, hell Grey. I never would've asked—"

"I know you'd never ask me to intervene. This was something I wanted to do for all three of us. I came to Bonaire ready to hate you, a famous actor trying to steal my girlfriend. And the fact that Lyle out and out tells me she loves you—well, I didn't have much reason to like you." He takes another sip of the sweet, mellow drink. "Then you confide in me about this Brumfield guy. At first, I just assumed you were guilty. There are way too many coincidences to believe otherwise. But I've heard you proclaim your innocence a bunch of times. Your story never wavers. Honestly, the biggest proof that you're not culpable is the fact that you've come back to Bonaire. No killer is going to show up in the jurisdiction that might charge him with murder. I also have complete faith in Lyle, and she's right. You didn't kill him. Last night, I thought I could get this matter settled once and for all."

"Grey," Lyle said, "tell us what happened."

"Getting in was easy. And like you said, the hat was in an evidence bag sitting on a shelf. I was in and out of there in minutes. Three, maybe four, tops."

"Did they catch you on your way out?" Michael asked.

"No. I started walking toward the ice cream shop. I had parked my truck there. I thought I was in the clear, but I must've triggered a silent alarm or something. I was back at the truck when I saw lights from a police vehicle speeding down the road. No alarm or siren, just the lights. They were definitely searching for someone. I left the truck and started walking in the opposite direction trying to blend into the darkness. I made it several blocks but eventually they saw me. The fact that it was two in the morning and I was dressed in black didn't help. I definitely looked the part. They stopped me and took me in under suspicion of breaking and entering."

"Dutch said they didn't have enough evidence to hold you," said Lyle.

"I think it would be a good idea if I got off this island while I still can." He lifted his glass and drank the last of the rum.

"I agree," said Lyle. "One criminal boyfriend is enough."

Sixty-Eight

They parked in the resort's lot and started toward their rooms.

"Michael, would you do an exhausted man a favor?" Grey tossed him his keys. "Will you go get my truck at the ice cream shop? It's only a short hike from here."

"Sure. It's the least I can do."

"See if my phone and wallet are still in the glove box, will you?" He draped his arm over Lyle's shoulder as they climbed the steps to their room.

She opened the door and helped him inside. "How about a hot bath? Then you climb in bed and I'll look into flights home."

"No need for both of us to leave," he said, removing his shirt. "You should be here for Michael. He's neck-deep in shit." He unzipped his jeans and dropped them to the floor.

Lyle started the tub and put her hand under the running water until it was hot. She stood and removed her clothes just as Grey came in the bathroom.

"You're a sight for sore eyes," he said while reaching for her. "But I'm afraid I'm just too tired."

As he spoke, his body gave him away.

"Let's just take care of this," she purred, "then we'll get you in the bath."

He turned her, stood behind her, and they looked at each other in the mirror, the steam distorting their images. His complexion was pale and dark shadows hung below his eyes. Lyle's face was filled with worry. He caressed her and she felt his need strengthen behind her.

"Come here," he said. In one easy movement, he turned her and lifted her up and placed her on the vanity. He put his massive hands under her behind and raised her to him. He was satiated after just a moment and placed her back on the counter. He stumbled backward.

"Be careful, you're so tired you're about to fall over." She cut off the water and helped him step in the bath. She dropped a towel on the floor and knelt down next to him.

After saturating a washcloth with soap, she started moving it from one shoulder to the other. The dark ink of his eagle tattoo glistened as the bubbles ran over it.

"Lay back and relax. I'll get the rest of you from here."

He closed his eyes as she spread the lather over him. Bending at the knees, his feet resting on the tiles next to the faucet and his arms falling over the brim, the tub could hardly contain him. The steamy room smelled of flowers and kept her naked body warm. She finished by pushing the cloth between each of his toes then dribbling water over them.

"There now, I'm all done. You're squeaky clean. Relax here while the tubs still warm."

"Thanks, Crocodile. I think I will. That felt amazing."

After brushing her teeth and hair, she put on a robe, turned down the bed and grabbed her phone. She was checking the next day's flight schedule when there was a knock at the door.

"It's open," she yelled.

Michael walked in just as Grey was coming out of the bathroom with a towel wrapped around his hips.

"Did you find the truck okay?" asked Lyle.

"Yup, I found your truck," he said, looking at Grey. "Your phone and your wallet were in the glove box along with this." He held up his ball cap, still sealed in a plastic bag labeled *evidence*. With pure amazement he asked, "You got it. How?"

He tossed his towel onto the bathroom counter. "I was already at the truck when I saw the lights of the police cruiser heading my way. I had just enough time to ditch the hat." He pulled boxers from a drawer and put them on. "I started walking down the street trying to draw the cops away from the stollen evidence. It worked. They never connected me to the vehicle parked at the ice cream shop all night."

"I can't believe it," she said. "You got his hat."

"If there's insufficient proof we might be able to create reasonable doubt," said Grey. "You may have a fighting chance. Now we just have to worry about that witness who saw Brumfield get in your truck."

"I can't thank you enough," Michael studied the hat in disbelief. "I never would've thought you'd do this for me. You took a huge risk getting this back. This fucking hat. It's given me so many sleepless nights."

All of these months of worrying. The jarring panic he'd suffered being connected to the murder. The raw fear of what may happen to him, his freedom, and to his career, all slowly seeped away as he stared at the hat. The police no longer had physical proof that he had been on Karpata that night. He fell onto the bed, sat there and wiped embarrassing tears from his eyes.

"What am I going to do with it?" he asked. Anxiety grew in his voice as he realized the consequences of being caught with stolen evidence. "I can't put it in my luggage, I'm sure they'll search it." He jumped up. "I could take it out to sea," he rethought that, "but things eventually wash ashore somewhere. Will you help me bury it? Somewhere it'll never be found."

"Get dressed, Lyle," Grey said, while checking the time. "We're going back to Lac Bay. We can make it just on time for the farewell bonfire and a celebratory beer."

Sixty-Nine

"Crystal's going to pick me up in Pearl," said Grey.

It was early morning when they arrived at the busy airport terminal. Cars and resort vehicles dropped travelers near the entrance. Mountains of luggage were piled on carts ready to be rolled inside.

Michael waited in the driver's seat as Lyle helped Grey pull his bags from the bed of the truck.

"I hate that you're leaving. I'm so sorry I got you involved in this mess," she said.

"Not your fault. I chose to do what I did. For what it's worth I'm glad I did it. I just think it's a good idea that I leave while I still can. Dutch has already put two and two together. I'm sure he knows I'm the one who took the hat, he just doesn't have the proof. And, thanks to our friends at Lac Bay, it'll never be seen again." He dropped his bag on the sidewalk and wrapped his arms around her. She placed her cheek on his chest. They embraced, neither one wanting to say goodbye.

"I'm worried that your indecision is causing you pain." He rubbed her back. "Search your heart and do whatever brings you happiness. Take a good look inside yourself. Find what it is you need." He kissed the top of her head. "I'm afraid I'm losing you. Leaving you here with him is a rookie move, but I think some time alone with Michael will help you with your decision." He released her and picked up his luggage. "If you would just decide to stay with me, we could both fly home right now."

"I have to stay." As she said the words her heart spoke to her. "I won't leave him to face this on his own."

"You'll be loyal to the bitter end." He glanced at Michael. "Hollywood needs you. Do what you need to clear his name. If he's innocent, like he claims, it should be easy."

"But what if…" She let the question drop.

"I've wondered," he said. "If he didn't kill Brumfield then who did? Why don't they have a better suspect?"

"Innocent or not, I'm going to help him through this mess anyway I can."

Grey's phone buzzed. He pulled it from his pocket and answered it. "Hey Crystal, what's up?" As he listened his brow furrowed. "I'm at the airport now. I'll text you when I land. We'll get it figured out."

"Is something wrong back home? Is Crystal okay?"

"I think Hendrix is up to more of the same old shit. Crystals at the shop but the door's locked and people with appointments are waiting outside. A police officer has asked her to come to the station for questioning."

"What's going on? Where's Hendrix?"

"I'm not sure," he said, "Never a dull moment. I've got to go, my flight will be boarding soon." He kissed her. "Goodbye, Crocodile."

She watched him until he was out of sight then joined Michael in the truck.

"He's gone," she said. "Maybe it's just as well."

"I owe him," he said, while putting the key in the ignition. "He may have given me my freedom. The least I can do is help get his daughter back. I told him to hire a lawyer and spend whatever it takes."

"I guess we'll find out soon enough what kind of a fight Elizabeth and her father are prepared to launch." She squeezed his hand on the seat between them. "Now you and I get to see how things are going to wash out here. Grey may not be the only one who needs a good attorney."

"Let's wait and let the local authorities show their next hand. I'm so sorry about all of this. Thank you for not abandoning me."

"I'd never do that. I'm here no matter what happens."

The truck idled while they sat. People milled about, and vehicles drove by. Suddenly, they heard a high-pitched whistle from a man directing traffic. Michael put the truck in gear.

"What do we do in the meantime?" she asked.

"We're on Bonaire. Let's go diving. It's the least suspicious thing anyone does on this island."

In spite of everything going on—the stress of the investigation and having just said goodbye to Grey—the thought of sinking below the surface into peaceful oblivion lifted her spirits. "Let's drive back to Bon Adventure and grab our gear."

She was ready to finally be getting back in the ocean, but she felt more than just a smidgen of guilt. She rolled down her window and watched a plane leave a white trail of smoke as it soared across the clear sapphire sky.

Seventy

They returned to their rooms to organize gear and change into bathing suits. The anticipation of diving with Michael again had Lyle moving quickly. All her gear had remained packed away since she'd arrived on Bonaire. She'd heard it shouting to her many times but had to ignore its call.

She placed the heavy bag on her bed and ran the zipper around to reveal her cherished treasures. She sucked in a deep breath and closed her eyes. When did the smell of neoprene become such an intoxicating fragrance? She then lifted out her wetsuit, held it to her nose, inhaled again, and grinned. Could she be imagining the scent of the ocean? Salt water and sunshine. The aroma brought back dozens of memories. Her first dives, when her equipment was brand-new and lacked the briny bouquet. The dive trip where she met Victoria. She recalled the oceans across the globe where she had explored the undersea worlds. They were all right there, lingering in the heavy material of her wetsuit.

She put on her new navy-blue one-piece with a cute ruffle across the chest. Checking herself in the mirror, she wasn't surprised to find the sparkle in her gem-colored eyes had returned. Her tanned face attested to the time she'd spent out in the bright sun. She covered up with an oversized T-shirt, pulled on a pair of board shorts, and slipped her feet into some flip-flops. She was back.

She gathered all she needed for the afternoon. It was a practiced skill to carry and balance the heavy load in her arms. She made two trips up and down the stairs and piled the gear at the bottom. She shut and locked her door just as Michael pulled up.

He hopped out and helped lift everything into the bed of the vehicle. He wore only swim trunks and sandals. His bronzed skin was showing the effects of the sun and his messy island hair shone with highlights. He flashed her a brilliant smile. This routine they knew, and the familiarity of it put them both at ease.

After swinging by the dive shop for air cylinders, they drove south along a road running close to the shore. The sky was cloudless and the sun's rays poured into the truck.

"I feel like I'm living on borrowed time so let's make the most of it," he said. "Dutch could show up and drag me off again at any minute."

"I think Grey was right," she said. "If they had any concrete evidence, they would've arrested you by now. Diving should take our minds off all the ridiculous drama. We've looked forward to this for so long—let's try and enjoy it while we can."

"You say that like our time together is limited," he said. "Like maybe I'll be in prison soon."

"That's not what I meant. You're not going to be locked up because you didn't kill Brumfield. Dutch will figure this whole thing out. We have to have some faith that he'll find the truth about what happened that night. Now let's go get lost at sixty feet below."

"Vanishing from Dutch and his crew sounds good to me. Let's find a site that isn't crowded with divers. I want you all to myself."

They drove with the windows down and Buffett blasting from the radio. In between shifting gears, he held her hand on the seat between them. She couldn't help but notice his grasp was strong.

"Alone at last," he said, turning down the music. "I could get used to Grey, but if he's going to vacation with us, he's going to have to learn how to dive. Oh, and by the way, I checked out of my room. I'll move my stuff in with you when we get back." A grin crossed his face. "I asked that housekeeping change the sheets."

"A little bold of you don't you think? Maybe I like having my own room." She grinned. "I know it would mean more rest for me."

"Baby, you never say no to me. And since when are you looking for a relaxing vacation? This is the second time you've said that. Last time we were here, we were up before the roosters and dancing at the resort while one day changed to the next."

"I guess I've learned to appreciate the slower pace." She thought of the previous days spent with Grey. They took a tuk-tuk tour, went caving and hiking. She taught him how to snorkel and showed him the island. "Or maybe I'm just worn out from the busy week I had before you arrived."

"I got here as soon as I could."

"I know you did, and I'm really glad you came. It feels right that we're back together on Bonaire. This island is like our home. I promise I'll catch my second wind soon." She watched as they passed several sites, each sprinkled with a fair number of divers. "Thank you for helping Grey. It means more to him than you'll ever know."

"I'm glad to do it. I must admit, he's become a friend. I like Romeo. I hope it all works out with his daughter."

"He likes you too. I was hoping he would. It's important to me."

They slowed as they traveled through town. People looked in store windows and tour groups followed their guides along the sidewalks. Cheerfully painted buildings lined the road and welcomed interested customers. As they drove past the art gallery and glass specialty shop, Lyle made a mental note to visit them before leaving the island.

"This is going to be different for us, isn't it?" she asked. "Just the two of us being alone here." They had never stayed in a room together, and during their prior visit to Bonaire, were often accompanied by her friends or his sister and brother-in-law.

"If by different, you mean awesome, then yes. I finally get you all to myself. No ex-boyfriend getting in the way and no current boyfriend stealing your time. Honestly Lyle, this is exhausting for me. You really need to settle on one guy.

Seventy-One

Town was soon in the rearview and they continued down the narrow, barely two-lane road. The salty air blew through the truck as he navigated the tight lanes. He slowed as they approached Bachelors Beach.

"Looks like only a few divers are here." He glanced at empty trucks parked haphazardly on the coral. "Most of them are in the water already. I might have to stand for one or two pictures if someone spots us before we're in. Is that okay with you?"

"Of course. We can't hide from your fans completely."

He dropped the tailgate, and they began the arduous task of assembling and putting on equipment.

Lyle pulled the unforgiving neoprene suit up her legs. The thick fabric fought her for every inch. She then climbed in the bed and began assembling gear. She attached air cylinders to buoyancy compensators, or BCs, they would wear. The vests would be filled with air, enabling them to float, and lead weights in the pockets helped them sink. It was a skill to find the balance between the two, but once attained, they would glide effortlessly over the reef. She ran lines from the tanks to the mouthpieces and double-checked the valves.

Once Michael had his wetsuit on, he joined her in the back. She passed the BCs to him, and he sent compressed air through the systems then rechecked the pressures. He made sure all the connections she had already made were secure. The extra inspection was a safety precaution, something she would expect him to do.

After sliding the heavy equipment on over their shoulders, and with masks, snorkels, and fins in hand, they walked into the water.

When they were in chest deep, they put air into their vests—a few short bursts and they were floating. She held her long fins above the surface and struggled to angle her foot into them. She flailed on her back as her feet and fins waved in the air. It looked as though she was trying to hail a cab in rush hour. After finally winning the skirmish, she fastened the strap around her heel.

"That's one on," she said, panting. "I feel like I haven't done this in a while. First, my wetsuit wouldn't cooperate, now my fins."

"You looked so cute with your legs sticking up in the air, fins waving," said Michael.

"I'm out of practice," she huffed. "Besides, the first dive is always a little clumsy."

"Don't worry, by the end of the day you'll be looking like a pro again."

———◆———

It was midafternoon when they began a leisurely swim to the buoy marking the reef. The water temperature was a perfect 82 degrees and kept them comfortable under the assault of the blaring sun.

"What do you think is down there?" She rinsed her mask, washing away the fog on the lens.

"I don't know," he said. "Maybe an eagle ray? A green moray eel? There are so many possibilities. I hope we find your yellowtail damselfish. That would make your day. But it all depends on what's swimming in this exact area in this enormous ocean when we descend."

"Wow. Maybe your over-thinking it."

"I'm just wondering what memories I'm going to take with me when I leave here. After our last visit, I kept catching myself daydreaming about our dives and all the incredible things we saw." He grinned. "Which would've been a good thing, if I wasn't supposed to be working and learning my lines. I thought about that trip, and you, constantly. I still do."

"I'm afraid all our phone calls and texting only made me miss you more," she said. "Even with you facing all this trouble, I feel selfish for saying it, but I'm so glad you came back to Bonaire."

"Romeo doesn't stand a chance. Baby, we're meant to be together," he said defiantly. "When he got on that plane this morning, he may as well have thrown in the towel. He tucked tail and ran. You're going to be mine. You just don't realize it yet."

"There's the self-assured, overconfident guy I remember." She laughed.

Grabbing her vest and pulling her to him, he kissed her. With her chilly lips, she kissed him back. She wished the moment would last forever. When Grey left the island that morning, he took with him the guilt that had poked at her since Michael's arrival.

"Let's go make some more memories," he said.

They inserted their mouthpieces and put their masks on. Together, they sank below the surface.

At ten feet down, Lyle checked that the computer she wore on her wrist was working. At twenty feet below, she confirmed the amount of air in her tank. At thirty feet, she looked at Michael. But instead of following his own procedures, he was watching her. She pointed to her wrist indicating he should be keeping track of his numbers. He checked his computer at fifty feet, just as the colorful coral came into view below. They slowed as they reached the bottom and leveled off.

Cerulean, mauve, and golden corals offered protection for the vast array of colorful fish that lived among them. They hovered at sixty feet, sunlight glistening off the reef around them. Cutting through the water, they watched the show that nature provided.

They were joined by a curious female pufferfish who swam alongside them with a much smaller one in tow. Their cow-like eyes gave the fishes an innocent expression. They held their mouths slightly open and looked as if they were smiling at the divers. The mother seemed to be losing patience with her little one—she nipped at the baby's tail fins, urging it to move along. The little fish instantly puffed up to the size of a baseball. It wiggled its tail and deflated as it moved forward, only to have its mother nip at it a second time. The baby once again inflated and hurriedly swam ahead.

Michael shook his head at the funny little fish then lightly pinched Lyle's bottom, just as the mama fish had been doing. Her smile broke the seal of her mask and water seeped in. She pushed her mask tighter to her face as she continued to laugh.

He had drifted dangerously close to the fish. She put her hand on his chest to stop him. As adorable as their chubby cheeks and harmless expressions made them appear, she knew the bite of a pufferfish was even stronger than a piranha and that its spines contained a toxin deadly to both fish and humans.

He backed away, unaware of the danger but confident that she knew something he didn't.

She made a mental note to explain the secrets of the charming fish to him once they surfaced. The fish swam away, searching the reef for snails, clams, and krill. The hard-shelled diet kept their ever-growing teeth in check.

They let the gentle current move them down the reef. Except for the sound of bubbles being released from their mouthpieces, they floated in complete silence.

As they drifted over the beautiful coral, Lyle noticed a reef fish had taken up residence under Michael's midsection. Using him as protection, it swam along, patiently waiting for an easy meal. It suddenly darted out from under his stomach, caught bits of food, and then retreated back to the safety of his belly. Michael studied the reef, oblivious to the little stowaway.

After forty-five minutes, their air was getting low, so they turned and swam back toward the buoy. Lyle saw it first. The yellowtail damselfish was hard to miss. The glowing sapphire scales and bright yellow tail glowed as it dashed in and out of the coral. Measuring just a few inches long, the juvenile fish was dazzling. What it lacked in size it made up for in coloring and radiance.

As they watched it, Michael decided this was his favorite fish too. Once it disappeared into the reef, Lyle clapped her hands, removed her mouthpiece, and smiled broadly. She then put her regulator back in her mouth and they continued to the buoy.

After leaving the site, they headed south, searching for the next place to dive. They had two more full tanks of air. As they drove, Michael slowed down and Lyle scanned the beaches, checking the number of trucks and divers already there. If Michael started taking pictures with fans, signing autographs, and answering questions, he wouldn't have much time to dive.

"Pull in here!" Lyle said, as they reached a site with no trucks parked on the beach. "Oh, this is great! You're going to love this."

He read the name on the yellow-painted rock sitting near the road: "*Hilma Hooker*?"

"I think it's time to expand your skills. Let's make a wreck diver out of you today."

Their truck leapt over the white coral and came to a stop near the water.

"I've already seen some shipwrecks," he said. "Remember that boat that sank in front of our resort?"

"This ship's going to make that one look like a bathtub toy."

Seventy-Two

Lyle and Michael had the place all to themselves. They floated to the buoy that marked the sunken ship. Looking directly below, they could just make out its shadow, suggesting an intimidating size. Its blackness was a menacing sight. The day turned eerily quiet as dark clouds formed in the distance. The water was becoming milky and the wind picked up.

"The *Hilma Hooker* sank here in 1984," Lyle began. "She's a two-hundred-thirty-foot-long cargo ship."

Michael put his mask in the water and looked down at the colossal vessel. "What was this huge ship doing in such shallow water?"

"Her story is folklore, you'll never hear the same tale twice. The way it was told to me was that in 1984 the ship had mechanical problems off the coast of Bonaire and was towed into port here. After sailing endless nautical miles in her time, she had fallen into disrepair. The crew didn't have the proper paperwork for the cargo on board, so local authorities got suspicious. They searched and found a false hull filled with more than twenty thousand pounds of weed. The crew was arrested. The authorities really wanted to find *Hilma Hooker's* owners."

"Twenty thousand pounds? Damn." He again looked at the resting ship. "Total respect, *Hilma*."

"Oh, it gets better. It turned out Interpol and the FBI had been tracking the *Hilma Hooker*. When they heard she was on Bonaire, they ordered the ship be held for evidence. But she was so decrepit, the crew in port had to constantly pump water from the hull in order to keep her afloat." She watched a school of giant barracuda circling the bow of the wreck. "People started to talk about sinking her and creating an artificial reef. They knew that a ship that size, sunk conveniently near the shore, would be quite the draw for divers to come to Bonaire."

"I guess so. Where else can you swim from shore and have access to a wreck like this?" said Michael. "What's amazing is that from the beach you'd never even know a cargo ship was here."

"Everyone thought sinking her sounded like a great idea, but the FBI and Interpol wouldn't allow it," she explained. "They said they needed the *Hilma Hooker* in case the owners were found not guilty in court. If so, the ship would be returned to them. Of course, nobody ever claimed it."

"No one in their right mind would show up and tell Interpol they owned the ship full of illegal drugs."

"Exactly," she said. "And keeping her afloat became really difficult. If a ship that size were to sink while in port—it would be a logistic nightmare—so they towed her here and kept pumping the hull. After five days the water won out and she sank to her final resting place in only two minutes."

"Wow, two minutes?"

"Some people think divers sabotaged the pumps—they wanted that artificial reef and lost patience. Others believe the owners had a hand in making sure she sank, leaving any evidence one hundred feet deep. Only the *Hilma Hooker* knows for sure, and the ship took that secret to its watery grave."

"What a killer story. A bit of history come to life."

"Knowing how it ended up here makes for a more exciting exploration." She put her mask on. "Now let's go say hello to the *Hilma Hooker*."

Seventy-Three

Dark clouds had advanced and blocked out much of the sun. Releasing the air from their vests, they sank below the now choppy surface. They clicked their flashlights on as they approached the wreck and the murky water revealed its secret.

The massive vessel was now serving the purpose bestowed upon it all those years ago: it had become a true, albeit artificial, reef, protecting its charges from strong currents and unrelenting predators. Tall purple tube sponges had grown from many of the port holes and were surrounded by brain and star corals. Sergeant majors, a species of damselfish with yellow bodies and black vertical stripes, swam in small circles over the ship, guarding patches of plum-colored eggs they had lain on the hull. Although less than a foot long, the fish were aggressive toward divers who swam too close to their clutch, darting and nipping at them, hoping to annoy them enough to leave.

They relied on their flashlights as they made their way around the resting goliath. With the storm clouds rolling in and no sun to light up the wreck, their visibility was limited. The *Hilma Hooker* rested on its starboard side. The mast, still in one piece, pointed westerly toward the open ocean, perhaps indicating the direction it wished to travel. The wheelhouse was intact, but the ship's wheel was losing out to encroaching rust. Only half the original helm remained. Michael followed Lyle as she swam to the stern of the ship. They circled the enormous propeller and found that the rudder was, remarkably, whole.

She caught his attention and pointed at the ship. She then made a swimming motion and lifted her shoulders. He enthusiastically nodded and followed her toward the eerily dark and sleeping giant.

She carefully maneuvered through an opening into the ship with Michael trailing close behind. Once inside, they swam through a long hallway past windows and grates. They relied on the light that cut through the blackness as they held their flashlights out in front of them. They advanced down the cramped passageway then jumped when a green moray came from behind and took its time swimming past in the tight quarters. Its ribbonlike body rippled and disappeared into the darkness ahead. She looked over her shoulder to see him clapping his hands at the close encounter.

Coming to the end of the corridor, she swam through a second opening. It was a practiced skill fitting herself and all her gear through such a narrow hole. Sharp metal edges could puncture her vest or cut her air line—an accident that could prove to be fatal. Once on the other side, she guided Michael safely through.

They found themselves in the cargo hold. Their flashlights were no match for the massive space. They creeped into the unknown. As they progressed, they could just make out remnants of the ship's infrastructure. Lyle wished she knew where the false hull was. She wanted to see where the marijuana had been stashed. They continued searching the darkness until an opening came into view just feet in front of them. It was large enough to pass through with little difficulty.

Now out of the vessel and in the open ocean, they checked their computers and discovered they had enough air left to circle the outside of the wreck one more time. Many tarpon, whose shiny silver scales reflected the limited light, joined them on their swim. Two spiny lobsters hiding under the mast, flailed their antennae, warding against any predators while keeping their bodies well protected.

After a thorough inspection of the ship and the surrounding reef, their air was low and it was time to end the exploration. They made a slow ascent and broke the surface at the buoy. The clouds were now directly overhead and a heavy rain was falling.

Lyle pulled her mask down under her chin and wiped water from her eyes. She spoke up in order to be heard over the shower. "That was great! I'm so glad we had the chance to dive here. So, your first true shipwreck. What did you think?"

"Totally amazing," he shouted. "Thank you for bringing me here."

They swam on their backs and paddled toward the shore. The rain picked up and pelted their faces. It exploded off the surface like tiny hand grenades as they swam side by side.

"I'm surprised the ship is in such great condition," he said. "I can imagine her powering through the ocean, crashing over waves, and leaving a huge wake behind. To see her lying here, well, it's a little sad."

"I think she's lucky," said Lyle. "She gets to live on Bonaire forever."

Seventy-Four

The sky darkened and the downpour continued as they made a dash from the parking lot to their room. Michael put his arm over Lyle's shoulders, ushering her toward the stairwell.

"I can't possibly get any more soaked!" she yelled.

"It's not the rain that worries me," he said. Just then, a lightning strike lit up the sky directly overhead. A moment later, thunder rumbled and shook the very ground they walked on. "We need to get out of this storm."

They took the stairs two at a time. Rain blew in and pelted them as she fumbled with the key to the room. Once opened, they ran inside. Out of breath, she slammed the door shut and leaned against it.

"That storm came up quick," he said. "You're shivering."

He draped a bath towel over her shoulders as she inched her soaking wet bathing suit to the floor. Peeling off his suit, he found a second towel for himself. They dried off and turned the heat on. The storm continued to rage as she sat on the bed and towel-dried her hair.

"Come lie with me under the blankets," he said. They tossed their towels to the floor and got in bed. Their body heat warmed them faster than anything else could.

He ran his fingers through the wayward strands of hair that pooled about her head. "Your face is flushed. I don't know if it's from the sun or the wind or if you're just excited to be with me."

"All of the above." She cuddled closer.

His kiss was familiar and the storm was soon forgotten. Their lips melted and their bodies moved together like the pair of long-lost lovers that they were.

He covered her and she kissed his neck and chest. He tasted like ocean water and her desire grew. She inhaled his salty smell and waited for his urgency to overwhelm him. Rubbing her hands over his back and chest, she then wiggled her pelvis, sure that he would take her now. She let out a low groan and waited for him to demand the release she knew he would soon require. She lifted her chin and thought only of his lips and tongue as he trailed them from her ear down her neck and to her breasts. Growing impatient, she wiggled her hips again and waited.

"Choose me," he whispered. "Choose me, Lyle. I can give you everything. I'll give you the world."

He then took her and moved himself with complete control.

Lyle inhaled as he stirred slowly and deliberately. The usually frenetic lover now performed with control and compassion. With her eyes only half open, she gazed up at him. Every unhurried motion he made felt like a thousand tiny movements.

Michael watched the face of his lover as her body succumbed to his deliberate execution.

Seventy-Five

"You said you think the *Hilma Hooker* is lucky because she's on Bonaire," said Michael.

Lyle rested in the crook of his arm. They had been listening to the storm as it quieted and moved out to sea.

"No more plowing through the ocean," she said, "fighting waves, being manned by an unsavory crew. It's so peaceful here. Anyone would want to stay."

"I'm asking you to choose me. You don't love Grey like you love me. You and I belong together. I can give you everything. I'll buy you a home here. You could stay as long as you want. You can live here forever."

"Michael—what?"

He was offering her a dream and immediately she felt excited at the prospect. She could stay on Bonaire. She'd never have to cry over the last dive or wait months to return. It was easy for her to imagine it.

"We can start looking for a place tomorrow. I'll fly in as often as I can, and you'd come and meet up with me whenever you like. This will work, it'll be great."

"It sounds amazing, but it's all pretty sudden. And I need to think about…"

They'd never even seen each other outside of Bonaire. She tried to envision life with him beyond the perfect island—it's easy to get along and have a fabulous time in a tropical paradise. How would they do together in the real world? When they'd first met, he talked about the two of them being permanent. He suggested a long-distance relationship if that was what it took. She was the one to squash that plan, but now she wondered if they could make it work.

But if she chose him, what exactly would that look like? Would they continue to keep their relationship a secret? She knew nothing of his life in California. How often would she even see him? And the biggest unknown of all: Michael may be charged with murder.

"You don't need to answer me right away. Just promise me you'll think about it. I'll take care of you while you make a home for us here. Let your dream come true, say yes."

He held her as she drifted off to sleep.

———◆———

Lyle carried a basket of homemade muffins and greeted the woman seated at the desk. "Half blueberry, half chocolate chip. Just how you like them."

"Girl, with muffins as moist as these, you can visit twice a day." She picked up a set of keys and unlocked the gate. The heavy metal slid open and clanked against the wall. "Same place as always." She nodded down a long, narrow passageway.

Lyle kept her eyes fixed on the last room on the right. She flinched as a green moray swam past. A pair of withered hands gripped the bars as she approached. He could hear her black boots on the tile floor. The air became murky, and it was difficult to see. She directed her flashlight toward the cell. Michael's hair was gray, and his beard needed a trim. Shiny-scaled tarpon swam in circles behind him.

"Hi, baby. Just like I promised you. Forever on Bonaire."

———◆———

Lyle shot up in bed and searched the room with wild eyes. Michael was sitting in a chair near the balcony door, a flashlight in his hand.

"Did you have a nice nap?" he asked.

"I had a crazy dream," she said, shaking off her sleep. "You were locked up with tarpon."

"Really?" He grinned. "That's a new one. The storm must've taken out the power. The entire island is dark."

She stretched then climbed off the bed and found a flashlight of her own. She kissed him then peered out the balcony doors. "The entire island is out?"

"As far as I can tell. I don't see any lights outside at all."

"I have a great idea. Get dressed and grab the extra blankets from the closet. I'm going to take these pillows with us." She shone her light around the room. "Let's find the keys. I've got something to show you."

Seventy-Six

The storm had passed but the air still felt eerily electrified and had an earthy aroma. Clouds were solid across the night sky and there was no moon or stars to be found. They threw the blankets and pillows in the back seat and Michael started the engine.

"Where to?" he asked.

"Angel City, of course."

They were the only vehicle on the road as they traveled cautiously down the pitch-black street. They swerved around downed tree limbs and scattered debris. The headlights finally flashed on the Angel City rock. They pulled in and climbed out of the truck. With utter bewilderment they watched the shoreline.

"What's going on here?" he whispered. "It's incredible."

In the black of night and no moonlight to speak of, the ocean put on an extraordinary show. As waves crashed against the coral beach, bright light glowed from the turning water—the luminescence shined up and down the entire coastline.

"The ostracods are showing off for their mates." She removed her shoes and he did the same. "They're tiny seed shrimp looking for girlfriends."

"I've never seen anything like it."

"We lucked out with the storm and the timing. Ostracods are most active a few days after a full moon. With the island's electric out, we have the perfect setup to witness this." She took his hand and led him toward the crashing waves.

"I don't want to step on them."

"Each one is only a few millimeters long. It would be hard to hurt them," she said.

They reached the water and each took a tentative step in. They laughed as the shimmering surf swirled around their legs. They stood at the water's edge until goosebumps covered their arms.

"Let's grab the pillows and blankets and watch from the bed of the truck," she said. "They only glow for twenty or thirty minutes. If they haven't found a companion by then, they're out of luck."

"That's a lot of pressure."

After a haphazard attempt to create a cozy spot, they sat back on the pillows and threw the blanket over their legs. A flashlight beside them cut some of the darkness. The light show continued in the water.

"Today's been totally sick. Finally diving again and exploring the *Hilma Hooker,* and now this." He nodded at the ocean. "Once again, you've amazed me. This island is full of surprises, and I love—more than anything else—experiencing it all with you." He reached into his pocket. "And now I have a surprise for you. I brought you a gift."

Her heart raced when he balanced a small hinged black velvet box on his palm.

"You don't have to bring me gifts." Was that a tremble in her voice? She held the box with two fingers as though it might sprout fangs and bite her. Tentatively, she opened it. "It's beautiful. I love it Michael, thank you."

The ring was a wide gold band covered in black diamonds. Interspersed among the dark stones were sparkling blue sapphires. "It's my fish. You created a perfect representation of my damselfish."

"I knew you'd get it." He took the box from her and removed the ring. Offering it to her, he said, "I had it inscribed."

She took the ring and he pointed the flashlight on it. Turning the wide band, she read aloud: "*Meet me on Bonaire.* Oh Michael, nothing could be more perfect. Thank you." She slid the ring onto the index finger of her right hand.

The stones were beautiful and the thought and execution that went into creating the gift was heartfelt. Yet, her disappointment surprised her. She squelched the thought and admired the gift, chastising herself for acting like a spoiled schoolgirl.

"I have something for you too," she teased with a devilish grin. "It's too big to fit in a box." She pushed the blanket aside and got up. Shimmying, she removed her shorts. "It's really more of an interactive gift." She removed her top and then looked down at him. She waited as he undid his shorts and slid them off. She threw one foot over his legs and stood straddling him. Hooking his fingers into the waistband of her panties, he slid them over her hips and down her legs then helped her step out of them. He extended his hand up to her. She held it and sat in his lap.

He placed his palm on her face. "*Meet me on Bonaire.* When you said those words to me—" He kissed her lips. "My whole world brightened as soon as I knew I'd be seeing you again."

He nuzzled her neck breathing deeply into her ear. She dropped her head to one side, thinking only of his tongue, lips and hands.

The waves crashed and the water glimmered. They moved in time with the surf pounding the shore.

The ostracod's opportunity was up and the lights in the ocean went out.

Seventy-Seven

After completing three dives in the morning and grabbing a quick lunch, Lyle and Michael took it up a notch and dived at more challenging sites. They jumped off a cliff and into the surf at Oil Slick Leap where they stumbled upon an octopus hunting for clams. Keeping their distance, they watched it without frightening the cephalopod away. But once it discovered it was being observed, the octopus propelled over the reef and camouflaged itself as a piece of coral. Even Lyle's trained eye couldn't find the animal again.

To leave the water, they had to climb an eight-foot metal ladder wearing their dripping-wet gear. Worn out and ready to end their dive day, they hopped in the truck and took off.

"Let's drop our gear at the dock." Michael turned into Bon Adventure. "We can shower and get dinner. Do you want to eat at the resort or go into Kralendijk?"

"I'd love to try the lionfish dinner at that market in town."

Spotting a police vehicle parked directly across from their room, Michael slowed as he passed by it. An officer in the driver's seat nodded when he and Michael locked eyes.

"This can't be good," he said. "What do you think the cops are doing here?" Like air seeping out of a balloon, all joy left him. "Shit Lyle, this might be it. Maybe they have enough to arrest me."

She looked out the back window. "He's not following us. They're probably here on some resort business. Besides, Grey stole any evidence they had against you. Let's just take care of our equipment. There's no reason to start acting suspicious now."

They carried the heavy gear down the steps to the locker area. Working in silence, rinsing the equipment and clearing the delicate mechanisms with a water hose. The tension was palatable as he absent-mindedly handled his regulator.

"Give that to me. I'll finish this for you."

He sat on a bench and held his head in his hands while she completed the task.

"I'm nervous too," she said, when the last piece was put away. "But we don't know why that cop is here. Maybe he's gone by now."

But the hopeful thought was soon crushed. As they drove to the parking area, they saw the squad car was still there. They walked back to their room avoiding any eye contact with the officer.

While Michael was in the bathroom, Lyle half expected a knock at their door, but she went about getting ready for the night out. She chose panties from the drawer, found her sundress with the flamingos on it, and laid them on the bed. She heard the water turn off and the shower curtain scrape across the rod. He came out wrapped in a towel.

"Let's stay in tonight," he said. "We can order room service. If he's waiting for me, he can wait a while longer." He towel-dried his hair then put on a pair of sweats and a long-sleeved T-shirt. "Go ahead and get your shower. I'll phone down to the restaurant."

If the police officer came to their door, it would be the beginning of a long night. And if he didn't, they would constantly be wondering if the shoe was about to drop. She was contented to stay in and avoid a public scene either way.

She turned the shower on and moved the temperature up. She let the steamy hot water soak her hair and warm her body. She squeezed shampoo into her palm and worked her hair into a thick lather. The pulsating water and flowery scent relaxed her. She took the time to shave her legs and underarms and thought of Dottie while doing the monotonous tasks. In the past, this exact situation would have her relying on her friend's advice. She would know just what to say to calm Lyle. She'd figure out how to get Michael out of this nightmare. But Lyle had said goodbye to her and now she was on her own.

Holding a towel around herself, she put away her sundress and searched through the drawer for a nightie. The velvet ring box caught her eye. Popping the hinges open, she admired the shiny new stones. She put it on her finger and looked at Michael. He sat against the pillows on the bed and stared at the news broadcasted on TV. She thought it odd; they had never once turned the television on while on the island. She tossed her nightgown on the bed and tried to draw his attention. She dried her breasts and lowered the towel exposing her damp body.

He glanced at her and then back at the television and patted the space next to him. "Put on your pajamas and climb in here with me."

Disappointed with her inability to take his mind off his troubles, she did as he requested. She rested her head on his shoulder, and he held her. They were silent as they watched the news being broadcast in Spanish. They listened to the reporter not understanding a single word.

―――――◆―――――

They both jumped at a knock on the door. Seeing no need to delay the inevitable, she climbed out of bed and opened it.

"Room service." A young man in the resort's uniform stood smiling next to a cart. "I have two dinners—meatloaf with mashed potatoes and glazed carrots—a lemon meringue pie, and a six-pack of Dive O'Clock, our local beer."

"An entire pie?" she asked, as she signed the receipt.

"Sí. As requested."

Lyle stepped aside and he rolled the cart past her and into the room. After taking the receipt, he pulled the door shut and left. She removed the cloches from the china plates then put the dinners and pie on the coffee table. Michael opened two beers. He took a long drink then handed the second bottle to her.

"Is the police car still out there?" he asked.

"It's there."

He picked up his fork but made no attempt to eat. "Damn it!" He slammed his palm on the table and their dinners rattled. "Do you know how many people are counting on me to finish this movie? I'm under contract and they're paying me a fuck-ton of money." He twirled his fork in the mashed potatoes and put his hand through his hair. "I need to call my manager and give her a heads-up. She has no idea what's going on down here." He quieted. "Catherine's going to blow a fucking gasket. The Stewart movie's over halfway done. How are they going to make it without me? The fucking incompetent police on this island could end my career and put me away forever."

"Maybe that police officer has nothing to do with you," she said, reaching across the table and taking his hand. "Maybe something else is going on at the resort."

"Thanks for your optimism, but I'm pretty sure they're here for me." He put his fork down and took another long sip of beer. "It looks like the blade is dropping and it's my neck in the guillotine. Grey will take good care of you. If I end up going away for this—Grey's a good man."

"No, don't say that. Don't you dare give up on us." She turned her new ring around her finger. It sparkled even in the dim light of the room. He stood and slipped his phone out of his pocket.

He was right—Grey was a good man, but he wasn't Michael. What would she do without him?

He put his phone to his ear and slid open the balcony door. She could clearly hear him talking to his manager. He broke the news gingerly, explaining who the dead man was and how the police knew Michael had fought with him after stopping him from attacking a friend. Although he was now implicated in the murder, he declared his innocence.

Lyle noticed he stopped short of mentioning he was with the man in the area where his body was later found. She could hear Catherine's muffled voice as she began to fire questions at him. Stopping and starting, he couldn't get a word in.

An hour had passed when he finally came back into the room.

"She's hiring a lawyer familiar with the laws of the Netherlands," he said. "She's not messing around with this"—he made air quotes—"banana republic." He tapped his phone. "I'm sending you Catherine's contact information in case this gets out of hand. Tell her who you are and that you're a friend of mine. She'll know what to do."

———

The dinners were never eaten and the pie wept. It was near midnight when they climbed into bed. They tossed and turned, both jumping at the sound of the air conditioner kicking on. Lyle finally dozed, but only to awake in the middle of the night to find Michael out on the balcony. She wanted to join him, but he insisted she go back inside.

In the very early hours of the morning, a knock on the door startled her out of a sound sleep. She climbed out of bed and was confused to see Michael, showered and fully dressed, pulling open the door.

"Good morning, Dutch," he said. "I thought I might be seeing you again."

Standing beside him was the officer who had been sitting in the police car all night.

"Mr. Miller," Dutch said, "I think we're close to wrapping this case up. We're expecting the final autopsy report this morning. I imagine it'll prove Brumfield died from the injuries you inflicted. Would you be so kind as to come with us to the station?"

Lyle dropped onto the bed, tears quietly streaming down her cheeks.

"Let me say goodbye first."

He knelt in front of her and wiped her tears with his thumb. "I'm so sorry this is happening. I wish I could put things back to how they were. You asked me last night not to give up on us. Now I'm asking you not to give up on me. I promise you as sincerely as I'm in love with you, I didn't kill anyone." They kissed and then he stood. "Call Catherine if I'm charged. She'll know what to do."

How could this nightmare be happening? Michael was innocent, of this she was convinced. They had the wrong person and couldn't see their mistake. Dutch had spent months investigating this crime and now he was collecting his pound of flesh. Stunned, she watched as they left the room, pulling the door closed behind them.

Before returning to Bonaire, she knew there was a possibility that she'd be leaving the island by herself. Now, it indeed looked as though she would be returning to North Carolina alone.

The space around her was shrinking and the air became heavy. She was trapped.

Seventy-Eight

Feeling liked a caged bird, Lyle paced the room. She'd been told that Dottie would continue to live in her. She sat and closed her eyes, waiting to hear her friend's voice. Searching deeply within herself, she tried to find the strength that was once Dottie.

She saw his bright eyes and heard his fading accent. "Of course." She jumped up, showered then dressed. She had an idea. Not a plan, but hopefully a useful first step. Either way, she was ready to get to work. She left her room and jogged toward the breakfast buffet.

———————

Guests mingled and smiled with hearty food atop their plates. She looked out at the water as her coffee went untouched. She'd been waiting almost an hour when a familiar figure caught her eye. She dashed down the steps to the dock below.

"Captain Maartin, you've got to help me." The captain was preparing one of the smaller boats for the morning divers. "Dutch came to our room this morning and took Michael."

He yelled instructions to the crew and then gave Lyle his undivided attention.

"Has your brother told you anything?" she asked. "Do you know what's going on? Are they planning to arrest him?"

"Slow down, Lyle. One question at a time."

"I'm sorry, I just don't know what to do. Something told me you're the person who can help. Do you think Dutch will let me see him if I go to the station?"

"I'm sure he would, but what good would that do? Take a seat on the bench. Let me get this boat out, then we'll talk."

The sun was starting its daily assault. She found a shady spot and settled in. She rubbed her thumbs together and clenched her teeth as the staff loaded the vessel. If anyone could help her, she knew it was Captain Maartin. She was willing to wait.

Watching the captain stride across the dock and climb on and off the boat helped to take her mind off things. Quieting her wild thoughts, she was able to steady herself and unclench her jaw.

Every few minutes, the captain looked her way, making sure she was still there. As divers began to arrive, he helped them on board and answered their questions.

Finally, the boat was full and ready to leave. He untied the mooring lines and threw them to the crew. He watched as the boat cleared the dock and gave a last salute to the excited divers.

Lyle stood as he approached.

"Come with me," he said, walking past her. "Let's see what we can learn."

Seventy-Nine

The resort logo was painted on both doors and the navy-blue exterior of Captain Maartin's truck sparkled. An over-sized red cooler, neatly stacked air tanks, and an assortment of masks and fins filled the bed. The captain's vehicle lacked the back seat the guests' provided. When Calypso insisted on sitting in the passenger seat with her head hanging out the window, Lyle ended up squished between the captain and his devoted companion. They drove north and she wasn't surprised when he pulled into Karpata.

Calypso trotted off in search of a spot to relieve herself and to sniff out critters to torment. Captain Maartin fished two bottles of cold water out of his cooler and handed one to her. He leaned against the vehicle and took a satisfying gulp.

"I never liked this dive site," she said. "It's always so quiet—it feels like a wasteland. We're so high up on this cliff we can't even see the water from here."

"The hat Dutch held in evidence has gone missing."

She remained silent and waited for him to continue.

"They've been combing the neighborhood near the station to see if anyone saw anything suspicious the night it was taken. Their only suspect—your friend Grey—was questioned at length. You may not know this, but they had obtained search warrants for your room as well as Mr. Miller's. While you and Michael dived the *Hilma Hooker*, Dutch had a team go through both of your rooms searching for the stolen hat."

"They followed us?" Lyle asked, as heat radiated up her neck.

"As Grey went through security before boarding his flight, we had a TSA agent search his luggage and do a body scan. But still, they didn't find it. Personally, I think someone at the station got sticky fingers when they realized who the cap belonged to."

She lifted her eyebrows in response to the remark. It was certainly a plausible idea. She was glad he couldn't see her thoughts as she remembered the roaring farewell bonfire in Lac Bay. The three of them had arrived just as the wooden structure was set ablaze. They joined in the crowd of people encircling the fire. The band was playing and when the singer called for everyone's attention, Michael tossed the hat, plastic evidence bag and all, into the towering inferno.

She and the captain both drank more water as the sun beat down. She imagined Brumfield's body lying dead on the ground and wondered what unlucky soul had found him. Maybe it was a diver excited to be on vacation, unknowingly about to have the shock of a lifetime. They must've been frightened at the sight of the beaten body and would have rushed back to their vehicle to call for help.

"With or without the hat," she said, breaking the silence, "Dutch told us they have a witness that saw Brumfield get in Michael's truck that night." She looked at her feet and kicked at the dry earth. "This is all my fault. The night Brumfield attacked me in the ladies' room, Michael insisted we report it to the police, but I refused." She shook her head. "I didn't want to ruin our vacation. Imagine that."

Calypso ran past them with a branch the size of a small pine tree in her mouth. Her tail wagging, moving her entire hind end in a circle.

"This whole thing has really gotten to him," she said.

"He's scared."

She took a drink of water, but her throat had gone dry, and it was difficult to swallow around the lump that had formed there. "He didn't do this. That witness has no idea what happened that night."

"How many white trucks do you think travel on this island each day—maybe twenty, thirty? Or more?" he asked. "Lots of our resorts supply their guests with that same means of transportation. The witness could've seen any one of a dozen of them on the road that night. It would be hard to prove they saw the exact one Michael was driving."

"You're right." she said. "The island is swarming with them. It was dark at the time, so how can they know for sure Michael was driving that particular truck?" She mumbled, "I wish we had never come to Karpata."

"What was that you said?"

"I said I wish we'd never come to Karpata when we were here last," she repeated. "This place is bleak and depressing."

"Who did you come here with?" He leaned in closer.

"All my friends. During our previous trip here, we had just met Michael." She smiled. "It was the same day we taught him how to jump in at Oil Slick Leap. After diving there, we brought him up here. For as dry and silent as this area is, and as much as I find this site bleak, we've always loved the topography of the reef here. That day a rogue storm blew in. We were caught in the current and taken hundreds of yards out to sea. We made it back to shore exhausted, but we were all okay."

"And I'm sure Michael was wearing his cap that day, correct?"

"I don't remember." She bit her lip. "He might have been. He wears a hat to keep from being noticed by his fans. What are you getting at? Why do you ask?"

"Don't you see? If he had been diving here with you and all your friends several days before the body was found, wouldn't it stand to reason he could've lost his cap that day? It's plausible the hat was already here days before the man was killed. We found it and thought it was related to the murder. I myself identified it as Michael's, but we have no idea when he may have lost it."

"Captain Maartin, that's it!" Her face lit up. "We have reasonable doubt!"

Eighty

Later that day, Captain Maartin accompanied Lyle to the courthouse. The yellow cinderblock building, built in the early 1600s, was originally a fort erected to defend the island. Thankfully, it never saw any aggression. The structure had been restored over twenty years ago and has since served the court.

They were stopped just inside the door and asked to explain what business they had there. Captain Maartin answered for both of them, and they were directed toward the room where the legal proceeding would be held.

"Don't be nervous," he said. "This is only to decide if there is sufficient proof to proceed in the case. And I understand some new evidence has been submitted."

"More evidence?" Her heart sank.

"Dutch has received the autopsy report. We've been waiting months for it. The victim's family petitioned to have the body removed from the island before we could complete the initial post-mortem exam. They called our island backward and unsafe. Such nonsense." He shook his head. "The family didn't think the report would be accurate, so they chose to hire a pathologist in Michigan to do an exam. By law, if one doubts the findings of an initial autopsy, they can hire an independent pathologist to take a second look. Those are the results that Dutch got this morning. It must have explained something. Autopsy reports aren't made public until an investigation is complete."

"So, you're saying the search for the killer is over?"

The captain didn't answer her.

They found a seat in the courtroom. Lyle was grateful the whole ordeal had been kept under wraps. If the press knew Michael was being questioned as a potential suspect in the murder of Brumfield, the room would've been at capacity. She was sure they had Captain Maartin and Dutch to thank for their discretion.

"What did the report say?" she asked.

"That, we find out together."

The judge walked into the room followed by Dutch, Michael, and another man who was dressed formally in a suit and tie. He gestured for Michael to have a seat and then sat down next to him. Lyle guessed this was the lawyer Catherine had hired.

The mood among them seemed tense. When he saw her, he gave her a grin, but his eyes looked dark and unhappy. Everyone took their seats, and the judge began to speak.

"Good afternoon and thank you all for your patience in this case," she said. "Justice isn't swift, but it must be precise. I have a family in Michigan waiting for answers."

"And I have an island waiting for peace!" Captain Maartin yelled out.

"Yes, Maartin," the judge looked over her glasses at him. "I am well aware of the pain the island has suffered." She opened a folder. "Dutch and I have reviewed the post mortem examination and accept this final report." She rifled through the papers and read: "*Lawrence Brumfield, male, aged thirty-seven, one hundred eighty pounds. Upon examination the following is the coroner's report.*" She pushed her glasses up the bridge of her nose. "*Superficial contusions to the left eye and jaw, suggestive of an altercation. Severe head injury indicative of a fall or push from a height onto a hard surface.*"

"A fall or push?" Lyle whispered.

"Let's listen," the captain said.

"*The toxicology report: blood alcohol level of point one nine,*" the judge read, "*confirming that Mr. Brumfield consumed no fewer than six alcoholic beverages the night he died.*"

Lyle nodded. At least this Brumfield lowlife wasn't coming out of this looking like a teetotalling saint. A fact she knew all too well.

The judge continued. "*Other than the substantial head injuries and contusions about the ribcage, there were no additional external wounds to the body.*"

"Do you think they found anything?" she asked. "This report isn't answering any questions."

"Be patient," he said, patting her knee. "The judge is still going through it."

"*Internal examination confirmed salt water in Mr. Brumfield's lungs and airway—*"

"Salt water?" She straightened in her chair.

"*—indicative of respiratory impairment from submersion.*" She glanced up at Dutch and droned, "May he rest in peace."

"He drowned?" Lyle asked, shocked. She jerked her head toward Michael, who had a smile on his face the size of Texas. His lawyer patted him on his back. "He drowned." She lunged for the captain and held him in a vise. "Captain, he drowned!"

The judge addressed the room: "At this time, the court would like to thank everyone who has cooperated with us as we investigated the death of Mr. Brumfield. In light of the coroner's report, no charges will be filed. Michael Miller, you're free to go."

Eighty-One

Dutch propped his feet on his desk, his hands clasped behind his head, and watched as chatter filled his office. The atmosphere was euphoric, but no one was happier to see this case closed than he.

Michael's lawyer stood talking with Captain Maartin near the back of the room. Calypso slept curled in a circle under the police chief's desk.

"I'm sorry we scared you last night," Dutch said to Michael, who sat in a chair next to Lyle. "I had an officer placed outside your room while we waited for the autopsy report. We were planning to arrest you. I felt certain the post-mortem would point to homicide. I'd already discussed with our local officials how this was going to impact us—a murder on Bonaire would drive tourists away. If we were responsible for locking up beloved actor Michael Miller, think of the money we'd lose. People come here to enjoy our natural resources and leave their troubles behind. If they thought for a minute we had a crime problem on the island, they would go elsewhere. Imagine my huge relief when I read the words *respiratory impairment from submersion in salt water.*"

"Dutch, I don't understand. When I left Brumfield, he was alive. I'd punched him a few times, but he didn't have any head injuries. What happened to him? How did he drown?"

Dutch swung his feet off the desk and sat up. "What we believe happened is this: Brumfield had been drinking at the bars most of the night. The toxicology report confirms that. We found his body on the cliff face. In spite of his clothing being intact, the zipper on his shorts was open. I believe that after you left him, he went to relieve himself over the side of the embankment. He misjudged his position and walked off the ledge. When he fell, he hit his head on the rocks and passed out. When the tide came in, he drowned."

"But wouldn't the current have taken him out to sea?" asked Lyle.

"It certainly could have," Dutch said. "The swells are strong that far north. But the way he was wedged between the rocks after the fall, the water wasn't strong enough to pull him free."

"So that's it?" Michael asked. "It's over?"

"You clearly left your mark on him," said Dutch. "But the coroner's report revealed those injuries didn't contribute to his death. We're going to slap a disorderly conduct fine on you, and some community service time, but no other charges will be filed."

Captain Maartin leaned back against the wall, arms folded in front of him. "Believe what you will. The island killed that man. She drowned Brumfield. And it was no accident."

PART FOUR

Grey Locklear

Eighty-Two

Lyle sat with her bare feet tucked under her and snuggled with Grey on his couch. A fire crackled in the hearth. After freshly brewed coffee, the smell of burning wood was about the best scent she could think of. The fire danced and popped in flames of burgundy, gold, and blue.

"I met with an attorney who works here in Pearl," Grey said. "He told me Michael spared no expense and said he told him he expected this matter to be settled immediately. Can you believe that? I have a willing lawyer at my beck and call. He got on it right away and contacted Elizabeth. It's all set. You and I are meeting her and Cece on Saturday."

"Did he tell you how Elizabeth reacted to all of this?" she asked. "Did she, or her father, try to fight it?"

"He didn't say anything about that. This weekend is just an initial meeting. He'll help us when it comes to negotiating future visits. I was thinking of asking for every other weekend and then two or three weeks over the summer." He glanced around the room. "Maybe I should paint."

"You have a beautiful home. The walls look fine. They'll be glad to know you have food in your refrigerator and don't live under a bridge." She took the blanket from the back of the sofa and laid it on the floor in front of the raging fire.

She had his full attention when she stood before him and removed her shirt. Her breasts were swelling over the top of her black satin bra. She opened her jeans and slid them over her hips and down to the floor. In her matching black panties, cut high at her thigh, she turned her back to Grey and teased him with the curve of her backside. Pulling out her hair tie, the locks fell freely over her shoulders and down her back. She then completed the turn and stood facing him. "I know how much you like black. I wore these especially for you."

"You know me so well." He took off his shirt and undid his jeans. "Turn around again. I liked that."

She put her fingers in her hair and lifted up the shining tresses. She lazily started to turn, basking in the heat from the fire. As she spun, she let her hair gradually tumble back into place.

"Again," he growled.

This time, as she rotated toward the flames, she unfastened her bra and dropped it to the floor. She held her hands over her breasts.

"Keep going," he rumbled.

She faced him and removed her hands to fully expose herself. She hooked her thumbs in her panties and began to turn. As she faced the fireplace, she slid them to the ground and stepped out of them. She ran her fingers over her ankles and, before she could rise, he was standing behind her. His cool hands massaged her bottom. She remained still, fingertips on her toes, and let him lead.

He wrapped his arm around her ribcage and pulled her up to him. She laid her head back on his chest as he moved his hands over her. Burning within, she fell to her knees. Grey knelt and held her face as they found each other's lips.

"I got you," he whispered.

He laid her on the blanket. They locked eyes as his hand slid over her breasts and then down to her stomach. Once on top of her, his body overshadowed hers and she surrendered to him desperately. Together, they stirred in the light of the fiery blaze. Firelight danced off their glistening bodies and threw long shadows across the floor. The shadows moved together while logs in the hearth burned away.

———

They cuddled on the blanket in front of the smoldering embers. She rolled her hand, admiring her ring as it sparkled in the firelight. Satiated with Grey and thinking of Michael.

Eighty-Three

Lyle sipped her coffee as Grey placed a bowl of hot oatmeal on the table in front of her. She sprinkled brown sugar on top, mixed it in, and took a taste.

"We're meeting Elizabeth and Cece this weekend. Are you nervous?" she asked.

"I'm excited to see my daughter." He blew on his steaming breakfast. "I can imagine my grandfather smiling down on me. He only saw her once, but he loved her so much. I'm worried Cece won't want anything to do with me. What if Elizabeth is telling her lies? I hear that happens all the time when parents split up."

"From what you've told me, you only have Elizabeth's father to worry about," Lyle said. "He's been in charge of his daughter—and your daughter—for far too long now. It sounds like your lawyer took care of him. He has no choice now but to let you see Cece."

"Thanks to you and Michael, she might actually become part of my life. I'm trying not to think of all the things that could go wrong. Work has been a nice distraction. By the way, I have a new client coming in at noon. I'd love for you to come to the shop with me. You can hang out and help keep my mind off this weekend."

"Sure, I'd be glad to go. I can catch up with Crystal while I'm there."

"Oh, and don't let me forget," said Grey, "I've got something to show you later."

———

Lyle looked forward to going to work with Grey. The atmosphere at the shop had greatly improved since Hendrix mysteriously disappeared. Grey was quite certain he'd gone missing on purpose. Nobody had any idea where he was, and no one was looking for him.

"I'm not worried, he'll be back," he had told Crystal. "He's waiting for some trouble to pass."

Lyle was thankful for the man's absence. Although Grey considered Hendrix a friend, she never felt comfortable around him.

While she was sitting with Crystal behind the counter, Grey's noon client arrived. The college student was having a hard time choosing a design from the flash sheets—a skull or an angel—and her two friends weren't helping.

"Go with the mermaid," one said. "I know I said skull on the drive over, but look how cute this one is. She's got seashells over her boobs!"

"Why would I choose a mermaid? I don't even know how to swim."

"You should get a quote." The second friend suggested. She read from the wall: "*If you can dream it, you can do it.* Disney said that." She looked at the saying again and tilted her head. "Disney was a person?"

"This could take a while," Crystal said.

Lyle heard boots echoing from down the hall. He had set up his ink and gun and was ready for his client.

She hopped off the stool and introduced herself to the new patron. "I have some experience choosing tattoos. Maybe I can help you."

"I'd really appreciate it. There's so much to pick from."

"I was once told"—she glanced at Grey—"that people get tattoos for all sorts of reasons. Maybe if we narrow down why you want one, we'll have an easier time coming up with the design. Is it commemorating someone, or are you celebrating something?"

"I'm graduating next semester. I'm going to be a teacher like my mom." Her eyes filled with tears. "She died from acute liver failure two years ago. She was my inspiration to go into teaching. She was always my greatest supporter. I know she'd be so proud of me. I thought a tattoo would honor her."

"Congratulations on your upcoming commencement," said Lyle. "You're going to be a teacher, that's wonderful. The apple is known as the fruit of knowledge. It could represent you. The tattoo could include your mother's hands, holding you, supporting you forever."

A single tear ran down her cheek. "My mom's hands holding an apple. That's perfect. Thank you."

"I'm Grey Locklear," he said. "It sounds like the two of you came up with a great design. Let me sketch it up and we'll get to work."

Eighty-Four

They stood at the sink in Grey's kitchen. Lyle washed dishes and handed them to him to dry and put away. Being just the two of them, it took only a few minutes.

"Thank you," he said, "dinner was delicious. Chicken piccata is my new favorite. It had just the right amount of lemon."

"I'm glad you liked it. I found the recipe online."

"And I really appreciate your help at the shop today. You were great with the college student. She was so happy with her new ink. I have a feeling her friends will be back for their own."

He put the last plate away while she dried her hands on a dish-cloth. "Come with me. I have something to show you." He led her down the hall to his office. "I have the pictures I took on Bonaire. I finally found the time to organized and edit them. Have a seat, I think you'll like this."

"The ones from our tuk-tuk tour? I've been waiting to see them." They sat side by side as he clicked his computer and opened the file. The first to pop up was of the brilliant pink flamingos as they flew overhead. The bright feathers and blue sky were in stunning contrast to the birds' black-tipped beaks. He advanced through several more images of the birds.

"That was such a memorable day," she said. "You really have an eye for this. Have you ever considered selling your photos? I mean, not just the portraits, the other images too?"

"I'd love to. I've thought about creating a website, but you know how it goes—there's never enough time to actually get it done."

Next, they looked through the ones he'd taken of the slave quarters. Rows of cramped huts, each the same as the other, sat side by side near the shore. She studied an image he'd taken of a small flower growing out of the sand next to one of the huts, perhaps a symbol of resilience.

After seeing the colorful prints, the black-and-white on the monitor was a surprise. The portrait of a friend—Captain Maartin's gaze directed just beyond the camera. Grey had stolen his photo without his knowledge. His dark hair and weathered skin reflected the love of his labors. Deep lines covered his forehead and creeped from the corners of his eyes. Even in monotone, his eyes twinkled all the same.

Lyle touched the screen with the tip of her finger. "He proved to be a true friend." She dropped her hand. "The way he connects with that island—I've never seen anything like it. He loves Bonaire like family."

"His face shows the reward of a life well lived," Grey said. "He has a lot of time ahead of him. And those wrinkles will become deeper with each passing year." He watched her face as he clicked on the next one. Again, a candid shot in black and white. This one, a picture of her.

She couldn't place the day or time it was taken. Faint lines on her face fanned out from the corners of her eyes. Her forehead was smooth but there were soft creases at the corners of her mouth.

"Crocodile, you have a long way to go. Your lines are only youngsters."

"The going so far hasn't been easy for me, but I feel in my heart that's changed now. For the first time, I'm looking forward to what my life may bring." She studied her image in front of her. "Do you think it's possible I'll have a long and peaceful existence?"

"With your recent change of course, you're now on that path."

Eighty-Five

They sat on a wrought iron bench and passed the time by watching kids climb over playground equipment like ants on a hill. It was slightly cool and Lyle wore her fall jacket. Grey unknowingly held her hand in a grip so tight she thought the insides might shoot out the tips of her fingers. She could feel the apprehension pouring out of him. His knee jumped up and down in sporadic rhythm.

She put her hand on his hyperactive leg. "It's going to be fine." She sounded confident but inside she worried. She imagined Elizabeth to be a hardened ex with an axe to grind. Still harboring anger toward the man who fathered her baby and was unable to provide a comfortable home for them. Maybe she'd be jaded, having carried the responsibility of raising a child on her own over the last twelve years. Or, she could be resentful, having to rely on her father for support.

"There she is." He dropped her hand and stood, ramming his fists into his pockets. "That's them," he whispered.

Barreling toward them from across the park, a tall woman held her daughter's hand. The young girl trotted along beside, hardly able to keep up. Elizabeth was cloaked in a camel-hair overcoat. Her curly locks bounced around her shoulders as her long stride brought her closer.

Lyle scrutinized the approaching woman then blinked and looked again. She was astonished to see a brilliant smile on her face and a happy pep in her step. She raised to greet her with a welcoming smile, but Elizabeth's eyes were fixed on Grey. She stopped in front of him, beaming.

Grey had been immediately transported back to high school. Once again, a timid teenager facing a pretty girl. Neither said anything as they stood staring at each other with lopsided grins plastered on their faces.

Lyle noticed an unexpected flush sweep up Grey's neck then bloom over his cheekbones. Looking at the two, she realized she had been anticipating the wrong sort of reunion. She turned to the young girl wearing a pink fur-collared jacket. Her shoelace had come undone. "You must be Cece. I'm Lyle. I'm so happy to meet you."

"Hi," she peeped.

The twelve-year-old looked remarkably like her father. Cece's dark hair fell to her waist. She had Grey's complexion and his jet-black eyes, but hers were almond shaped, like her mother's.

"Elizabeth," he whispered.

"Yes." She giggled and amazingly her smile grew.

He pulled his attention away from her and looked at the young girl holding her hand. He was lost for words. "Cece. So beautiful." He looked back at Elizabeth. "I'm sorry you had to drive so far. But I've wanted to know her for so long."

"Don't be silly. I'm the one who's sorry. I never knew…" She started again: "I was always told…" She shook her head. "We have so much to talk about." She put her hand on the young girl's shoulder. "Cece, this is the man I've been telling you about. Grey's your dad. He's been away"—she looked up at him—"but he's back now."

"Do you like dogs?" Cece asked. "I have a dog named Fagen. He's black with a curled-up tail. We found him on the side of the road."

He knelt down, his eyes searching his daughter's face. His grandfather looked back at him. "I love dogs. Maybe you'll meet my friend Calypso one day." He straightened up. "I'm sorry, where are my manners? This is Lyle Cooper."

Elizabeth threw her hand out. "Nice to meet you, Lyle."

"Would you like to get lunch?" he asked Elizabeth. "There's a diner just a few blocks from here."

"I think lunch is a great place to start."

Eighty-Six

Cece ordered a hamburger, a chocolate malted and fries. The others could only stomach coffee. The conversation ebbed and flowed as they tried to find common ground.

"Grey and I were in love." Elizabeth grinned, explaining their story to Lyle. "But we were so young. We'd just graduated high school and had no jobs or money. I really needed my father's help to raise Cece. I'd lost my mother and my dad was the only family I had. He worried because I wanted to be with Grey." She said, blushing. "You asked me to marry you. I remember saying yes."

"It feels like a lifetime ago," Grey said.

"My father told me I'd only be holding you back. He said no eighteen-year-old wants to be stuck struggling to pay bills and raising a child." She spoke to Lyle: "I tried to convince him that Grey wasn't that way. That's why he moved us to Virginia shortly after Cece was born, to keep us apart. It all happened so fast. He packed our things, sold the house, and I never heard from Grey again."

"I wanted to marry you," he said. "I would've found a way to pay the bills. Then, when he told me you were getting married, I felt like my chance to be in your lives was over, I blew it. He made it perfectly clear you wanted nothing to do with me."

"I never wanted to take Cece from you," she said. "I was just young and confused. I had a hard time seeing my future with a newborn. I was about to be a mom and I'd lost my own mother. I couldn't chance losing my father too."

"After he moved you to Virginia," Grey said, "your father kept in touch with me for a little while. He brought Cece to Pearl twice so I could see her. Looking back, I realize he was trying to appease me. Or maybe he was showing me how much work a baby would be. After he told me you were getting married, the visits ended."

Elizabeth looked at her finger where a ring once was. "I got married when Cece was a toddler. We only lasted a few years. After the divorce, she and I moved back in with my dad. He was sick and needed help if he was going to stay in his own home. Then he passed, and Cece and I have been on our own ever since. We're doing okay—my father left me an inheritance and his home."

"I'd love to take Cece to the shops down the street," said Lyle. "Give you two some time to talk in private."

"Can I go, Mom? Please?" Cece whined. "This is so boring."

They thanked Lyle and, as she slid her jacket on, Grey stood and gave her a kiss. "Have fun. We'll wait for you here."

Lyle and Cece found a bakery and sat inside, enjoying cookies and hot cocoa.

"Chocolate's my favorite," Cece said while dunking her double-fudge cookie into her mug. "I bake at home with my mom, only I like the dough better before we cook it."

Once the cookies were gone and Cece wiped her face clean, they walked across the park to a row of specialty shops. The pre-teen loved the latest fashions and pointed out what was "boujee" and what she thought was "so last year."

They stopped in a shoe store and had fun trying on outrageous styles. They paraded around the store in extravagant footwear until their feet screamed. They went back to the park, where Cece scrambled around on all the playground equipment. Lyle couldn't remember the last time she was on a swing but pumped her legs back and forth until she was flying high along with her new friend.

Once they grew bored of the park, they walked back to the diner.

Elizabeth and Grey had spent the time reminiscing about days past. They decided to table the tough conversations for a later date. He sat in the booth with his arm casually draped over the back, a dirty dish with scattered pie crumbs and two forks on the table between them.

"There they are," he said, cheerfully. He stood and dropped several bills on the table.

"We've got a hotel room for the night," Elizabeth said, while putting her coat back on. "If you're free, I'd love to get together again tomorrow. Give you more time to get to know this one." She rubbed her daughter's head.

Cece ducked from under her mother's hand.

"That'd be great," said Grey. "I've got your number. I'll text you in the morning."

Eighty-Seven

Lyle never tired of watching Grey's creative juices flow when she joined him at the shop. As the tattoos came to life, she could hardly wait for his clients to see them. She began thinking about her own tattoo. With all she had accomplished, she was ready to have this last thing done. She no longer feared the process—she was looking forward to it. If only Grey would decide on those three gremlins, she could finally have the empty spaces filled.

Lyle and Crystal chatted it up at the front desk. Heavily tattooed people sat around a table having power drinks and soda. Many wore leather and had arrived on motorcycles. The establishment had become a hangout for past and future clientele. Lyle brought the shop owner a mocha coffee and pulled up a stool. They began airing their grievances like two old curmudgeons.

The trials and tribulations of Crystal's relationship with her partner closely mirrored some of Lyle's own experiences. Today, Crystal complained that her girlfriend suggested they eat cleaner, and that they should visit the farmer's market more often. Yet she never volunteered to do so herself. "Who has that kind of time? I'd still have to hit the grocery store, and sometimes a drive-thru is the best I can do."

Lyle jumped on the bandwagon and threw Grey under the bus, boots and all. "I mean, his laundry basket is clearly sitting on top of the dryer. For crying out loud, he put it there himself. Why does he pile his dirty clothes on the floor in the closet? By laundry day, I can't close the door."

The screen door slammed. Elizabeth had walked into the shop. Her winter-white slacks and blush cardigan sweater were eye-catching, and her sleek red bag matched her patent-leather flats. She didn't immediately notice Lyle at the desk and looked around, clearly surprised by all the artwork on display and the small gathering of bikers. She approached the counter and recognition lit her face.

"Lyle!" she said with a warm smile. "It's so nice to see you again. I didn't realize you work here."

"It's good to see you too. I'm not working, just dishing with Crystal. We're this close to solving the whole chicken or the egg question." She introduced the two. "Greys in the back, but he should be finishing up soon. You look beautiful. I love that color on you."

"Thanks," said Elizabeth. "I wasn't sure what to wear. He told me we're having dinner tonight at a place called The Crab House. Have you been before?"

"Yes, you'll love it. Be sure to order the clams casino appetizer. The owner told me it's an old recipe from the Oaks Inn on East Hampton. The inn served them when they were a speakeasy during the depression. They broil them with bacon and just the right amount of bread crumbs and lemon. Perfection," she said, with a chef's kiss.

"They do sound good. Aren't you joining us?"

"I'm afraid not. Crystal and I have plans we can't break." The lie slid off her tongue.

Crystal's eyebrows shot up. She plastered a huge smile on her face and nodded like a bobble-head until Lyle elbowed her and she stopped.

Grey finished with his client and joined them. He was suspicious of Lyle's flimsy excuse to get out of dinner but didn't push her on it.

They all yelled "good night" just as the door shut behind them.

"What was that all about?" asked Crystal. "Aren't you the least bit worried the man you love is having dinner with the mother of his child?"

"I'm very worried. But I won't stand in his way. That's Grey's family."

Eighty-Eight

Since their initial meeting, Elizabeth and Cece had driven from Virginia on four consecutive weekends under the premise that Grey and his daughter should get to know each other. Although Lyle felt they would agree it was completely unintentional, it was obvious that the visits were rekindling her parent's relationship as well.

Cece now ran ahead as they all strolled along the beach. It was too cold to get in the water, but the sky was clear and the breeze gentle. Lyle, holding her shoes, was searching for shells near the coastline.

Cece chased after something in the sand. Grey lifted his camera and took several shots.

"She's asking a lot of questions," Elizabeth said. "She's wondering where you've been and why we just now found you. I don't think I ever fully understood the void she's felt being raised without a father."

"What've you told her?" he asked.

"A half-truth. Before my dad passed away, the two of them were very close. I won't tell her it was her own grandfather who drove you away."

"Look what I found, Grey!" Cece held a hermit crab in her palm.

He squatted and aimed the camera at his daughter. She smiled and tilted her head toward the crab, claws flailing, as the shutter whirled.

"I'm going to name him Herman." She petted the hard shell and the animal tucked inside.

"It's never a good idea to name a creature that lives in the wild," he said, straightening up.

"But I'm going to take him home with us."

"And keep poor Herman in a shoe box? That's no life for such a grand crab. His place is here, on Pearl Beach."

She released her captive on the sand then looked up at Grey, squinting. "You think he's grand?" She looked questioningly at the comical crab who was digging frantically.

"If we keep him from living his natural life, we'll never know."

Eighty-Nine

When Lyle walked into the shop on this day, the air felt different. She had brought with her a nervous energy that filled the space. She wasn't visiting Grey or sitting and gossiping with Crystal. Today, she was the client.

Several nights ago, they had lain in his king-size bed. The temperature outside was dropping. He spooned her, keeping her toasty and she began to doze.

"You awake?" he asked quietly.

She rolled onto her back. "Just barely. What's on your mind?"

"I'm ready to finish your ink," he said. "I've been thinking a lot about it. I've come up with three gremlins."

Completing her tattoo had been the catalyst from the beginning. It was what brought Lyle back to Pearl, and back to Grey. At the time, she had imagined a quick process: design, approve, tattoo, home in Raleigh for dinner. But Grey insisted the additions be more than just images filling empty spaces. Like the artist himself, they would be significant and profound. An expression of life, not simply representing all lives, but a meaningful manifestation of *her* life.

Having waited patiently, and sometimes impatiently, for him to realize his vision, she expected to be jubilant over the news that the time had finally come. Snuggling next to him in his bed, she now found herself filled with melancholy. Something more was coming to an end than just her tattoo.

So here she lay, topless on Grey's massage table. She'd worn a wool blanket skirt to help keep her comfortable. He gave her a pillow for her head and cranked up the heat. He placed his hand on her shoulder then moved it down over her tattoo. "This is where it all began for us," he said. "And here we are again. We've come full circle."

"It's been quite a ride. So much has happened. I'm a new, happy person, thanks to you."

Although they wouldn't speak the words aloud, they both recognized that this was the beginning of their end. They'd traveled a long way together, each experiencing positive changes in their lives. But the result left them different people, and the choices they'd made early on were not necessarily the same decisions they would make now.

Crystal came in to help organize inks and to move two free-standing lights into place. Lyle knew it was all a ruse to take a peek at the designs Grey had held close to his vest. She fluttered about the room until he ran her off.

Kissing Lyle's neck, his hair brushing over her back, she knew this was the last pleasant thing she would feel for a while. Once the needle started, it was game on. She took solace in the fact that the three gremlins were small. He estimated he would complete them in about four hours. A walk in the park compared to the endless session she had endured for the initial image.

"Are you sure you don't want to show me the gremlins before you get started?" she teased. "I may have some valuable insight."

"Don't you trust me, Crocodile?"

"With my life."

"Then let's get started."

"I got you," they said in unison.

He studied the massive tattoo on her back and remembered purposefully leaving the voids. He had planned to create gremlins that would live within the spine once he better understood her past. Originally, they were supposed to represent people from her childhood. At the time, he thought Dottie and perhaps Lyle's mother and a third person he had yet to discover. But time changes things, and time had changed Lyle. And so, they would represent the individuals who helped transform her. The ones who loved Lyle enough to help her heal.

He was slow to begin, taking time to reexamine her current tattoo. He then reviewed his new designs and made some corrections. After a few false starts, he began. Lyle got the impression the master artist was nervous. She certainly wasn't—she had total faith in him.

His concentration was unwavering. He held the pen to her back, tattooed a small area, wiped it with a disinfectant cloth and repeated. He finished the first gremlin and asked her if she needed a break. She smiled, remembering their first time together, when she was too stubborn to even ask for a drink of water.

The second gremlin's placement was directly over her vertebrae. The area lacked any fatty cushioning, and it stung as he worked. She took some deep breaths, and with his soothing words, powered through it.

Soon after starting the third gremlin, he stopped to search through his things for additional tinted inks. He studied the colors he found but wasn't satisfied and began mixing his own. He took over an hour to create the exact shades he wanted before continuing.

Crystal returned and stood silently watching over his shoulder. Lyle found this odd for the usually loquacious woman. She suspected Crystal was under strict orders from Grey. Eventually, she touched him on his shoulder and left the room without ever saying a word.

The sun sat low in the sky when she heard him disassemble his tools. He removed the needle from the ink gun, disposed of it, then wiped the instrument down with a sterilizing solution that crinkled her nose. He gathered the small bottles and placed them in a leather case. He closed the box and sat back, resting his hand on it. The tattoo he had begun so long ago was finally done.

She pushed herself up onto her elbows ready to get off the table.

"Stay there. I'm not quite finished yet," he said.

He stood, removed his belt and undid his jeans. Two strong hands slid up her legs, pushing her skirt to her hips then sliding her panties down. She turned to face him and hardly noticed the sting of the new tattoos as she laid back on the table.

"We're all done," he said gazing at her. But the way he said it, she knew he meant *goodbye*.

Through the wide-open door, they could hear voices down the hall. Lyle worried they'd be caught. But as he made love to her, she no longer cared.

Ninety

Grey covered the new tattoos with clear adhesive bandages. He insisted they have time to heal before he would show them to her. As the gremlins settled, they simultaneously itched and burned. On more than one occasion, she was tempted to pick up an old-fashioned back scratcher and let the little monsters have it.

Once sufficient time had passed, he took several photos and downloaded them so they could look together. They sat at his kitchen table as he opened his laptop. He typed and clicked until a file named *Lyle Cooper tattoo* appeared on-screen.

"Ready?" he asked. She nodded and he began to explain: "Here's the tattoo before I added the gremlins." He clicked on a thumbnail image and it expanded to fill the screen.

Although she had been carrying this tattoo for some time now, she rarely saw it. She was again struck by the creation he had drawn for her long before they ever met.

She studied the image. It started at the base of her neck and ended at her tailbone. The spine looked like a hybrid of actual bones and worn metal pipes. The expert shading produced a three-dimensional illusion. It looked as if the bones could be picked up right off her skin. She originally wanted the tattoo in order for it to carry her burdens, to give her strength and help her to find peace in her life. Looking back over the time since the image had been placed on her back, Lyle knew that it had done exactly that.

"Our gremlins aren't monsters at all," he said. "I thought they should represent people who love you. Individuals who will always stand by you. You know now that the tattoo itself isn't going to help you through life, but the people who care about you are. That's where your real strength comes from."

He clicked the mouse again, the spine vanishing and a new image appearing. It was a heart, or rather, two halves of a heart being tacked together—but the halves didn't quite match up. One side was rough with jagged edges and had shining bits of gold dust scattered across it. The other side was marbled in subtle shades of blue and green. It shimmered like water at the top then morphed into scales toward the bottom. A needle and strong cord worked to fit the two pieces together. The base of the heart was joined, the rest not yet united.

"This symbol of coming together represents you and Michael. Two very different halves, but as you can see, they are in the process of being linked. Once completed, the two will beat as one."

"It's perfect," she said.

The image clearly embodied her and Michael. As she thought of him, she was bathed in a certainty that filled her soul. And just as plainly as she saw the image before her, she saw her future. She'd been in love with one man all along. Only she had to suppress that love in order to allow the other one in her life to help her heal.

Months ago, Danesha Clark had asked her to imagine her life without Dottie. If Dottie was no longer available, who would she turn to in times of struggle? There was no doubt that person was Grey. She loved Michael, but the need for Grey during her time of recovery overpowered that love. She knew all along that Grey was the one that could help her through her fight. The only way to have him was to suppress her love for Michael.

"I love him," she said. "I love Michael." A feeling of pure enlightenment filled her and she straightened with her conviction. "You're right, our relationship isn't ideal. It's going to take work for us to become one, but we're willing to commit to each other." She looked at the image now permanently etched on her back. Two hearts so different and yet they would eventually work as one. "I need to tell him. I'm sorry, but my heart lies with Michael. I can't go on being with you when it's so clear to me now."

"He knows," said Grey. "We've both known. We've been waiting for you to realize. We wanted to be sure it was you who made the choice, not one of us pestering you to choose. Michael thought it was best to leave us alone for a while. He wanted to give you some space to discover what's in your heart."

"You've helped me through such a difficult time. I'm not sure anyone else could've done that for me, not even Michael. I'm forever indebted to you for that. I will always hold you near in my heart."

All this time loving two men had eaten at her. She'd felt ashamed and selfish and torn as to what to do. She wiped a tear escaping down her cheek. It wasn't an expression of sadness, but of joy, and relief, from finally becoming aware of how she truly felt. She would be free now to move forward and create a life, not dependent on an imaginary friend, but determined to make her own way.

"And Grey, you should be with your family," she said. "Elizabeth needs you. You're in love with each other." He tried to interrupt, but she continued. "Do you remember what you told me on Bonaire? You said that when I decide, to be sure it's the best thing for all involved. I think this is the best thing for you too." Her tone turned solemn. "As it stands now, your love story is tragic. Don't let it stay that way. There's plenty of time for the two of you to change your ending."

"Thank you," he said sweetly. "I'd spend forever with you if you'd chosen me."

"Loyal to the end—you once said that of me. It can be a good thing, with the right person."

"I think I see my path in life," he said, sitting up taller. "It's being a husband and a father. It's something I've been dreaming of for over twelve years now. I never dared imagine it could come true. I have you to thank for that. You saw the void in my life and encouraged me to reach out and find my daughter. I never thought I'd rediscover Elizabeth too."

They held each other and their new certainties in life comforted them.

"Do you think I'll be okay?" she asked. "With Michael?"

"Do you know the one thing that's more important than loving someone? Having that person love you back. Michael loves you. I can see it." He released her and kissed her forehead. "I've always known that you were in love with him. That was never a secret. I think all this time you've been seeking my approval. You know I'd never let you hurt yourself. If you had asked me this on Bonaire, I would've told you to run. I think I actually did tell you to leave him." They giggled. "But now that he's been cleared of all charges, and is what I believe to be, innocent, I think he's a fine match for you. I'd be the first one to tell you if Michael was a bad choice. Yes, Lyle, I believe you'll have a good life with him."

"Thank you. It means a lot to me knowing you feel that way."

They turned their attention back to his laptop. An image of a soaring eagle jumped to life on the screen. It held a bone in its talons. Not just any bone. The one it carried was worn. It was somewhere between fantastical and realistic. Holes rusted straight through.

"When you're too weak to carry yourself," he said, "I will carry you, always."

Lyle found herself speechless. This man, who had given so much of himself, gone out on a limb simply by loving her, was giving her one last gift. The promise of a future. Maybe life wouldn't be smooth sailing forever, but if she ever fell, he would be there to pick her up. With this reassurance, she knew that she could put all the troubles of her past away and look toward the future.

"It's perfect, thank you. So majestic, just like you."

"One more. This last one is my favorite." He clicked and a lifelike crocodile crawled out from behind the spine. Its jaws were opened wide and its eyes fierce. "You have the heart and strength of this reptile. I imagine you always have. It got clouded by other things in your life, but it was always in you, waiting to be set free."

Ninety-One

A knock sounded at the door and Grey closed the laptop. "They're here," he said smiling.

Elizabeth held a brown paper grocery bag in each arm and Cece cradled a bottle of wine almost as big as she was.

"As promised," Elizabeth said with her brilliant smile. "Dinner's here. The ingredients at least. I'll need to make a little magic happen."

The heavy bottle wobbled as Cece held it up. "I got some wine."

"Thank you, Cece." He saved the bottle from falling. "I can carry it from here."

"Let me show you the kitchen," Lyle said, while taking a sack from Elizabeth. "I'd be glad to help."

While Lyle and Elizabeth prepped in the kitchen, Grey and Cece sat on the floor in front of the sofa and started a no-holds-barred match of *Dancing Dragons*. He had done a little research and discovered the video game was a big hit with kids his daughter's age. Staring at the TV, they each held a death grip on their controller as dragons fought to outdance each other in surround sound. He gave her a quick lesson in trash talk. She mastered the skill easily.

Lyle peeled carrots at the sink. Elizabeth kneaded dough on the floured countertop. They could hear snickering and teasing coming from the front room.

"Thanks for taking care of those vegetables," said Elizabeth. "I thought some good old-fashioned comfort food would be nice." She pounded the ball of dough flat and began rolling it into a circle. "I love homecooked meals on these cold nights."

"I'm glad to help. I'm not much of a cook. I can follow a recipe if it doesn't require too many kitchen gadgets. It's hard to be motivated when it's always been just me at home. I know Grey will appreciate this." The giggling in the front room continued. "Sounds like he and Cece are hitting it off."

"Yes, it's going really well. She's smitten with him." She hesitated. "I know you and Grey are together, at least it sure seems that way to me." She paused again. "I was wondering if you'd explain something to me."

"Sure, I'd be glad to."

"I don't mean to sound nosy or judgmental. Grey mentioned that you have a boyfriend out West. I could've misunderstood him, but that's what I thought he said. It's a little unclear, given the two of you…"

"It does sound strange, doesn't it? I can understand your confusion." She spoke to herself, "Even I didn't understand it and I was knee deep."

She stopped peeling, turned around, and leaned back against the sink. "Grey came into my life at a time when I needed a savior. He didn't have to, but he stepped up and helped me through a very dark period. I'll always love him for that. I've been in a sort of long-distance relationship with another man and have been open and honest with Grey about it. He chose to stay with me, and with his support, I've come out the other side a new person."

"That all sounds like Grey."

"I owe him my life for all he's done for me." She paused. "And now, I'll give him the gift of walking away. I won't be a hitch in the growth of his family." Elizabeth dropped the rolling pin on the counter and turned to Lyle. "He's committed to me, but he loves you and Cece. I'd never get in the way of his happiness."

She lunged at Lyle, covering her back with flour handprints, and held her in a bear hug. "Thank you. Thank you so much." She released her, and dabbed tears with her sleeve. "All these years, I thought he wasn't interested in us. When his lawyer contacted me and said he was demanding visitation with Cece, and that he was prepared to take me to court"—she laughed through happy tears—"I told him yes, that visitation was a great idea. I was so nervous coming to Pearl. I didn't know if he wanted to see me along with Cece or not. When I saw him at the park that day, my heart actually started pounding. I thought certain you all could hear it." They snickered and she continued: "We were so in love back then. Just one look and all the memories of our time together came flooding back." She looked at her flour-covered hands. "Along with my feelings for him."

"Thank you for sharing that with me," said Lyle. "I couldn't understand why the two of you never reconnected. But with the falsehoods your father told you, and the lies he told Grey, it's no wonder." She turned her attention back to the carrots. "We better get this dinner in the oven or we're going to have a very—"

"Hangry man on our hands." Elizabeth finished, laughing.

She pressed the dough into a pie pan, nudging it into place with her fingertips. She diced two chicken breasts and put them in a hot pan on the stove. Lyle chopped the carrots and some potatoes while Elizabeth rinsed green peas then opened a can of chicken broth and poured it in a bowl.

"I wonder if he has a whisk, I don't want lumps in the broth." Elizabeth said, opening and closing drawers.

"Of course, I have a whisk. Do I look like a Neanderthal?" said Grey, walking in the kitchen. "You just need to know where to look."

Once the gravy was bubbling hot and had thickened sufficiently, Elizabeth pushed the chopped ingredients off the cutting board and into the sauce pan. She touched the handles of the heavy pot. "Ouch! I didn't realize that was so hot."

"I got you." Grey held the pot with oven mitts while Elizabeth spooned the mixture into the pie plate.

"I just need to cover it up and throw it in the oven." She lifted the second pie crust and placed the delicate dough over the hearty mixture then pinched the crusts together creating a pretty scalloped edge.

"Let me help you." He slid the chicken pot pie onto the middle shelf. "How much time should I set?"

"Fifty minutes should do it."

"That's just enough time for me to beat our daughter at this video game."

Lyle leaned in the kitchen doorway and watched Grey rejoin Cece on the floor. A fire danced in the hearth. Elizabeth handed her a glass of wine, she then went and sat on the sofa behind the competitors.

Lyle watched as Elizabeth touched Grey on the shoulder and they exchanged a quiet sentiment. The dream of the people she cared about was there, directly in front of her. A warm home, a loving family, and a homecooked meal in the oven. Grey loved Elizabeth. It was obvious he'd never stopped. And Elizabeth loved Grey, as she always would.

And Lyle was madly in love with Michael Miller. It was all so clear to her now. For all that Grey had given her, she in return, would quietly give him this, his dream.

She placed her wine glass on the counter and left out the back door without saying goodbye. He would understand.

Ninety-Two

Lyle sat in her car and watched the cozy home, its windows filled with firelight. Inside, a newly created family was getting to know each other. Grey and Elizabeth were rekindling their long-lost relationship, and Cece was learning that Grey was a man she one day would love. She would grow to know that her father never left her, but rather, she was taken from him. He'd loved her for twelve years, and over that time, had dreamed of one day being her dad.

It was late in North Carolina but still reasonably early on the West Coast. Lyle slipped the phone out of her pocket and brought it to life.

"Hey, baby," Michael answered, sounding sleepy. "I'm glad you called. How are things in Pearl?"

"I love you, Michael. I always have. I'm so sorry you had to wait for me to realize it."

"I knew you'd choose me," he said. "It just took you some time to find me again."

Shadows moved about in the house. Grey stood, then sat next to Elizabeth on the sofa.

"Do we get the happily ever after now?" she asked.

"I'll make sure you get your fairytale ending. Let me start by getting you a home on Bonaire. You and the Hilma Hooker, together forever."

"That would be a dream come true," she said, grinning. "My home, my Bonaire."

"Let's do it, you and me. Let's go back to Bonaire."

Epilogue

They sat huddled in a car parked across the street from an old house in Pearl. Now shivering from the cold, they didn't dare run the engine for fear of being spotted, so they went without heat. They asked themselves *what have I done to end up here*? But the answer was clear. A long list of poor decisions and bad choices had led them to this. But it wasn't all their fault. Unreliable contacts and shady business partners were to blame. It always came down to the same thing, money. They needed cash and were willing to work for it, but something told them this Lyle Cooper chick was getting in the way.

Never did they think they would be hiding in the dark on their very own surveillance watch. It was the first step in working out a plan. They had heard this Lyle Cooper was in love with the wealthy Michael Miller. Probably a gold digger. Who wouldn't want his fortune? They certainly did. But what business did Lyle Cooper have at the little home in Pearl? It belonged to Greyson Locklear, a blue-collar worker. What was she doing with him when she had already hooked Michael Miller? That man was loaded with money.

As they sat bundled in a flimsy jacket, better suited for sunny shores of California than the icy air in North Carolina, they rubbed their hands over their arms in an attempt to warm themselves. They stopped when someone walked from the side of the house. She climbed in the car that had been parked in the driveway most of the day. It was her, Lyle Cooper. They watched as she sat and observed the house. Through the car window, they saw the glow of her cell phone. She opened it and held it to her ear.

"Lyle Cooper, you have worked yourself between me and my money. I can't have that now, can I?"

Interested in baking the pecan pie that Lyle
and Grey enjoyed at the resort?

Would you like to make the clams casino
Lyle recommended to Elizabeth?

Join my mailing list at the link below and I'll
gladly send those recipes to you.

I'll also let you know when book 3,
My Bonaire
A Lyle Cooper Story
becomes available to pre-order. (2024)

https://www.annebennettauthor.com

Acknowledgments

Dr. Tonya Holy Elk, (Lumbee Oglala Lakota). Writer and Poet. Thank you for your time and helpful insight pertaining to the creation of Mr. Locklear and the memory of his grandfather.

Crystal and Julie: I am forever humbled by the determination shown by the very early readers. The typos, the highlighting, the author's notes-to-self and the out of order plots, they were all handed to you in the initial draft. You plowed through, and remarkably, gave meticulous feedback in spite of it.

David Kidd: Photographer and Writer at Governing. Thank you for sharing your expertise and providing me with detailed explanations regarding current photographic trends.

Bobby, you are this close to getting your kitchen table back. Thanks for your support and patience and ordering a lot of carry out.

Thank you, reader, for taking time to read and for your interest in following Lyle as her story continues.

A tip of the hat to the Hilma Hooker, and to my inspiration: the people who live on, love, and care for, the island of Bonaire.

Made in the USA
Middletown, DE
12 August 2023

36585079R00170